L T Shearer has had a lifelong love of canal boats and calico cats, and both are combined in *The Cat Who Caught a Killer*, a one-of-a-kind debut crime novel.

L T SHEARER

PAN BOOKS

First published 2022 by Macmillan

This paperback edition first published 2023 by Pan Books
an imprint of Pan Macmillan
The Smithson, 6 Briset Street, London EC1M 5NR
EU representative: Macmillan Publishers Ireland Ltd, 1st Floor,
The Liffey Trust Centre, 117–126 Sheriff Street Upper,
Dublin 1, D01 YC43
Associated companies throughout the world
www.panmacmillan.com

ISBN 978-1-5290-9801-3

3 5 7 9 8 6 4 2

A CIP catalogue record for this book is available from the British Library.

Typeset by Palimpsest Book Production Limited, Falkirk, Stirlingshire
Printed and bound by CPI Group (UK) Ltd, Croydon, CR0 4YY

Visit **www.panmacmillan.com** to read more about all our books
and to buy them. You will also find features, author interviews and
news of any author events, and you can sign up for e-newsletters
so that you're always first to hear about our new releases.

1

It was a gorgeous summer's day when Conrad walked into the life of Lulu Lewis. The sky was a cloudless blue, birds were singing in the distance and the water of the canal was just starting to turn green from the warm-weather algal bloom.

Lulu was about to go out and cut some fresh mint from the small strip of land on the other side of the towpath. The mooring was hers, courtesy of the Canal and River Trust, but she had squatter's rights on the narrow piece of land between the towpath and the hedge, where she grew a selection of herbs including mint, rosemary, chives and thyme. She had just started experimenting with garlic, but hadn't been having much luck.

As she looked out of the galley window she saw a cat heading her way, walking in the middle of the towpath as if he owned it. Lulu could tell it was a tom, just from the way he strutted along with his tail in the air, but she knew right away that he was special because he was a calico – a mixture of black, white and orangey brown – and most calicos were female.

The cat stopped in his tracks and began sniffing the air, his ears up. The right side of his head was mainly black with a white patch around the nose and mouth, and the left side was brown and white. His eyes were a vibrant green. He seemed to be looking right at Lulu and she felt a slight shiver run down her spine. He started walking again.

Lulu leaned forward over the double gas hob to get a better view. His front legs and chest were white, his body and tail were thick stripes of black and brown, and his rear legs had white socks. He reached the prow of the boat. *The Lark*. She hadn't named it; the boat had been ten years old when she had taken it on. The previous owner, a retired teacher, had owned it from new and had bought it as a lark, he'd said. Lulu had quite liked the name, and anyway it would have been bad luck to change it. It was a traditional narrowboat, painted dark green with black trim and with *THE LARK* in gold capital letters over a painting of the bird.

The cat walked slowly along the towpath. Past the double cabin, past the toilet, and then he drew level with the galley. He stopped and looked up at her, moving his head slightly and sniffing. His tail was upright like an antenna.

'Well, good morning,' whispered Lulu. 'What a handsome boy you are.'

The cat's ears flicked forward as if he had heard her, and he made a soft mewing sound. He wasn't wearing a collar but he looked too well fed and clean to be a stray. He started walking once more and reached the rear of the boat. He stopped again, then jumped smoothly onto the back deck.

Lulu turned away from the window. The cat appeared at the doorway and sat down.

'Welcome aboard,' said Lulu. The cat stared at her for several seconds and then mewed. 'You're welcome to come in,' said Lulu. 'You'll be my first visitor.'

The cat stayed where he was at the top of the four wooden steps that led down into the cabin.

'Well now, Mr Calico Cat, I'll get you something to drink

– let's see if that tempts you to come in.' Lulu bent down and opened the small fridge that was barely big enough to hold a carton of milk and half a dozen bottles of wine and water. She took out the milk and picked up a white saucer from the tiny draining board.

She was just about to pour milk into it when the cat coughed politely. 'Actually, I'm not much of a milk drinker.'

Lulu gaped at the cat in astonishment. 'What?'

'Most cats are lactose intolerant. They don't have the enzyme that digests the lactose in milk. No enzyme, so no digestion, so the lactose just passes through our system. It can be messy. So best avoided.'

'What?' repeated Lulu.

'So maybe pour me a nice, crisp Chardonnay instead.'

'What?'

The saucer slipped between her fingers and seemed to fall in slow motion to the floor, where it shattered. She stared at the cat, her mind whirling as she tried to come to terms with what had just happened.

'Well, that wasn't the reaction I expected,' said the cat.

'What?'

The cat put his head on one side. There was an amused look in his piercing green eyes. 'You do speak English, don't you? You can say something other than "what", or am I wasting my time?'

'What? Yes. Of course. English. What?'

'I think you should pick up the bits of the saucer before someone gets hurt,' said the cat.

'What? Right. Yes. Okay.' Lulu shook her head in bewilderment. She put the milk carton back in the fridge and then went slowly down on one knee and carefully picked up the pieces, placing them in a pedal bin to the side of the fridge. Her knee cracked as she stood up again. 'How did you know I had Chardonnay?' she asked.

'I won't lie, that was a guess. I did see the wine bottles, but it could have just as easily been Pinot Grigio. I didn't really want wine to drink, obviously. It was just a joke, I didn't think you'd go all Greek on me.'

'Greek? What?'

'They smash plates, right? The Greeks. It's what they do.'

'Right, yes, okay. I'm sorry, I'm a bit confused here.'

'I can see that. Could I have some water?'

'Water?'

'Water. H_2O. Tap water is okay. Do these boats have tap water or do they have tanks?'

'I have a mains water supply,' said Lulu. 'It's a residential mooring. Electricity, too.'

'Excellent,' said the cat. He looked expectantly at Lulu.

'So, water?' Lulu said.

'Perfect.'

'I have Evian.'

'Well, that will be a treat,' said the cat.

Lulu opened the fridge again and took out a bottle of Evian. She opened an eye-level cupboard, took out a Wedgwood saucer and poured water into it. She put the saucer at the bottom of the steps, then replaced the bottle of water in the fridge. She went and sat on the sofa as the cat padded down the steps. He sniffed the water cautiously and then began to lap.

Lulu watched as the cat drank, then she sighed. 'This is a dream, right?'

The cat looked up from the saucer. 'Are you asking me, or telling me?'

Lulu pinched her own arm, so hard that she winced.

'What are you doing?' asked the cat.

Lulu shook her head. 'If it's a dream, why can't I wake up?'

The cat finished drinking and jumped gracefully up onto the sofa and sat looking up at her. 'You need to relax.'

'What?'

'Let's not start that whole "what" thing again.' He rubbed his head against her arm. 'I'm real. This isn't a dream. Deal with it.'

'But cats can't talk,' sighed Lulu.

'Says the lady who is talking to one.' He gently headbutted her. 'You can hear the lack of logic in your statement, right? If cats can't talk, then we couldn't be having this conversation, could we?'

'Maybe I'm going crazy.'

'Well, that's a whole different conversation, isn't it?'

'If you can talk – and I'm not discounting that this is all a figment of my imagination – but if I'm not crazy and you are talking to me, then why?'

'Why? I suppose that's a step up from what.'

'I mean, why me? Why are you talking to me?'

'You mean of all the canal boats in Little Venice, why did I jump onto yours?'

'If you like. Yes.'

The cat shrugged. 'You seemed like a nice person. And you have a good aura. Lots of bright yellow and indigo.'

'That's good, is it?'

'It's perfect.' The cat chuckled. 'I suppose I should say purr-fect.'

'So I suppose black is bad? For auras.'

The cat nodded. 'It can mean there is anger that's being held inside. Or it could be that the person is sick. Of course, sometimes it's the anger that causes the sickness. Or the other way around. Dark blood red also points to a lot of anger. We tend to keep away from blood-red auras but with black auras we can sometimes help.'

'We? Who's we?'

'Cats. We see auras. Cat auras and human auras. The auras of all living things, actually.'

'I didn't know that.'

The cat snorted softly. 'Why would you? You're a human.'

Lulu frowned. 'You said you could help people whose auras are black.'

'We can make it easier for them, when they pass.'

'When they die, you mean?'

The cat gave the slightest twitch of its whiskers. 'We prefer to say pass. But, yes, if we see someone with a black aura, we can sit with them and help calm them.'

'That I have heard of,' said Lulu. 'There used to be a cat at a nursing home I visit. She was friendly enough but never got onto anyone's bed. Unless they were dying. Then she would jump up and lie next to them.' Her eyes widened and her hand flew up to cover her mouth. 'Oh, my. Oh no. Is that why you're here?'

The cat's eyes narrowed. 'What? No. Of course not. I told you already, your aura is fine. Better than fine.' The cat purred. 'What do I call you?'

'My name? It's Lulu. And you?'

'Conrad.'

'Conrad? Conrad the Cat? Conrad the Calico Cat?'

'That's my name, don't wear it out.'

'It's unusual.'

Conrad snorted softly. 'Says the lady called Lulu.'

Lulu chuckled. 'My dad gave me the name Lulu. There was a singer, a little Scottish girl, who had the number one song when I was born – "Shout" – and Dad said I was shouting all the time from the moment I was born. Who gave you your name?'

'I chose it myself.'

'Good choice.'

'That's what I thought. It means brave counsel. It's German. Originally.'

'And are you brave?'

'Fearless.'

'And you give good advice?'

'I try.'

Lulu turned to look at him. 'Is that why you're here? To give me advice?'

Conrad squinted at her quizzically. 'You keep looking for a reason as to why I'm here,' he said.

'Because it's strange. It's not every day I get approached by a talking cat.'

'Don't overthink it, Lulu. Sometimes paths just cross, that's all there is to it.'

'But why me, Conrad? Why talk to me?'

'You seem like a nice person.'

Lulu couldn't help but smile. 'Well, thank you,' she said. 'You seem like a nice cat, too.' She sighed. 'I need a drink.'

'A nice crisp Chardonnay?'

Lulu chuckled. 'I was about to make myself a glass of fresh mint tea.'

'That does sound rather good.'

'I think that's what I'm going to do,' she said. She stood up, filled the kettle at the sink and then used a match to light one of the hobs. She put the kettle on the flames and went up the steps to the back deck. Conrad followed her. Lulu stepped carefully off the boat and onto the towpath. She heard a whirring sound off to her right and turned to see a young man in a grey hoodie and tight jeans hurtling towards them on an electric scooter. She stood back, as the man clearly had no intention of slowing. 'Idiot,' she muttered under her breath as the man whizzed by. An increasing number of people were using electric scooters along the towpath and several people had been injured. The main problem was that they were practically silent so you couldn't hear them coming. Lulu smiled. Actually the main problem was that they were driven by morons who cared nothing for their fellow man – or cats.

'Aren't you just so tempted to push them into the canal?' said Conrad from the safety of the deck.

Lulu laughed. 'Definitely,' she said. She looked right and left again and walked over to her tiny vegetable plot. Conrad jumped off the boat and joined her. He sniffed the plants, one by one.

'How long have you lived on the boat?' he asked.

'Just two months.'

'I thought you'd been here for years, you seem so comfortable on her.'

'I am, I love it.' She pointed across the road. 'I used to live down there, on Warrington Crescent.'

Conrad nodded. 'Warrington Crescent is nice.'

'It's lovely, but . . .' She shrugged. 'It doesn't matter.' She

8

bent down and ran her hand through the mint plants, then sniffed her fingers. The aroma took her back to her childhood, when she would pick fresh mint from the garden whenever her mother cooked roast lamb. Half a century vanished in a flash and she was a child again.

'Smells always take you back, don't they?' said Conrad. 'More than any of the other senses. Smell just goes straight to the olfactory cortex in the temporal lobe and triggers memories that you never thought you had.'

Lulu looked across at him. 'Did you just read my mind?'

Conrad chuckled. 'Mind-reading isn't in my skill set,' he said. 'You smelt the mint and then you had a faraway look in your eyes as if you were remembering something.' He tilted his head to one side and blinked. 'Elementary, dear Lulu.'

Lulu picked four stems, one from each mint plant. She took them back to the boat. This time Conrad ran ahead of her and jumped onto the deck first. There was a grace to his movements that reminded her of a cheetah she'd once seen on safari in Botswana, many years ago. He turned to watch her walk to the boat. 'Do you ever take her out, along the canal?' he asked.

'Not yet, but I will do,' she said. She stepped onto the deck. 'The engine has been serviced and there's fuel on board. But so far I'm just enjoying living on her. But one day, I plan to go travelling.' She went down the steps. The kettle was already boiling and Lulu turned off the gas. She washed the mint under the tap, placed it into a glass and poured on the hot water. The minty aroma filled the galley. Lulu took the glass over to the sofa and sat down. Conrad gracefully jumped up and sat next to her. She sniffed at the glass, then held it out for Conrad to smell. He nodded his appreciation. 'Nice,' he said. 'But I prefer catnip.'

'What is it about cats and catnip?' asked Lulu.

'We love it,' said Conrad. 'You know how you like Chardonnay? I guess it's the same. The leaves contain an oil called nepetalactone and it stimulates the pheromone receptors.'

'So you get high?'

'We feel euphoric, yes. Happy.'

'So probably more like cannabis than alcohol.'

'Do you smoke cannabis?'

Lulu shook her head. 'No.'

'I didn't think so. I would have smelt it.'

Lulu sipped her tea and looked at the cat over the top of her glass. A talking cat? It had to be a dream. There was no other explanation. Cats didn't talk. End of. But she was clearly hearing this one speak and the only way that made any sense was if she was asleep. At some point she would wake up and everything would be back to normal. She had been having some strange dreams recently. They were often about her husband and, under the circumstances, that was to be expected, she knew. But the chances of her ever having a conversation with Simon again were on a par with her meeting a talking cat. Dreams were dreams, and that was the end of it.

'Penny for your thoughts?' asked Conrad.

Lulu just laughed and shook her head.

2

Lulu finished her mint tea and washed the glass. Conrad sat on the sofa, grooming himself. She turned to look at him, wondering when exactly the dream would end and she would wake up. It was a detailed dream, no doubt about that – probably the most realistic she had ever had – but there was no way any of this could be real. Cats did not talk. They simply didn't.

Conrad stopped grooming and sat up. 'You look as if you want to say something,' he said.

Lulu looked at her watch. It was a gold Rolex. Simon had bought it for her on their tenth wedding anniversary and she had worn it every day since he'd died. 'I should be going.' She wondered if now was the time for her to wake up.

'I'll come with you,' said Conrad. 'Is that okay?'

'Yes, sure, I guess. But there are quite a few roads to cross. Are you okay with roads?'

'I can ride on your shoulders.'

'What?'

'And we're back to "what" already,' said Conrad. 'I thought we'd moved past that.'

Lulu laughed. 'I'm sorry, it's just that I've never heard of that before.'

'It's quite common,' he said.

'I've heard of parrots on shoulders. Long John Silver and all.'

'Same principle,' said Conrad. 'Sit down. I'll show you.'

Lulu walked over to the sofa and sat down. Conrad arched his back and stretched his legs, then smoothly jumped up onto her shoulders. He wrapped his tail around her neck and sat on her left shoulder. 'This is the side position,' he said. 'It's fairly comfortable but it's slightly less secure. He moved slowly, until he had wrapped himself around the back of her neck, his head on her right shoulder, his back legs on her left. 'I call this the scarf position,' he said.

'I can see why,' said Lulu. She was surprised at how little he weighed; it was almost identical to wearing a fur scarf. Not that she would wear anything made of fur, of course. Not these days.

'Try standing up,' said Conrad.

She did. He was perfectly balanced and within seconds it felt completely natural. 'I love this,' she said.

'Walk up and down.'

She walked past the shower to the main cabin door, then slowly turned. 'This is amazing,' she said. She walked back through the galley and did a twirl. 'You're so light.'

'Why, thank you.'

'And you feel so warm against my neck. Seriously, we can walk around like this? You won't fall off?'

'Not unless you decide to spin around suddenly,' said Conrad. 'So, where exactly are we going?'

'To see my mother-in-law. She's in a nursing home.'

'Is she sick?'

'Actually she's quite strong. But she has a few issues with her memory, so she has to be in a place where she can be looked after.' She picked up her handbag and walked carefully up the steps, then onto the towpath.

The nursing home was close to Lord's Cricket Ground, just over a mile from the canal. There were two ways to get there: along Warrington Crescent or down Clifton Road. Warrington Crescent was slightly shorter but Lulu tended to go the longer way.

Walking with a cat on her shoulders was a novel experience. She walked slightly slower than normal, but there was never any sense that Conrad was uncomfortable or about to fall off. Most of the time he purred softly in her ear.

She got a lot of smiles from passers-by as she walked, especially from children. She headed down Clifton Road, past Tesco and the Venice Patisserie, and walked by Raoul's Deli, a Maida Vale institution that had long been one of Lulu's favourite food shops. Their duck eggs were out of this world. She smiled to herself. Talking cats were also out of this world.

She stopped at the traffic lights at the top of Clifton Road. A postman pushing a cart of letters and parcels stopped and grinned at the cat. 'Did it take a lot of training to do that?' he asked.

'No, he taught me in a couple of minutes,' said Lulu.

The postman frowned, then opened his mouth to reply, but then the lights changed and Lulu walked across the road, chuckling to herself.

'That was funny,' said Conrad.

'Yes, I thought so,' said Lulu. Their route took them from Maida Vale into St John's Wood. St John's Wood was usually regarded as being slightly more posh than Maida Vale, with its high street chock-a-block with trendy cafes and overpriced delis, and its whitewashed villas with Bentleys and BMWs parked outside. It was where The Beatles had made many of their albums in the Abbey Road recording studio, and where Sir Paul McCartney still lived.

Lulu had always preferred the edgier Maida Vale, where three-quarters of the homes were mansion block flats and houses were owned by the likes of Paul Weller and Ronnie Wood. Earl Spencer used to live there, but he had moved.

It took another five minutes to reach the nursing home, a four-storey block built around a central courtyard with a small lawn and shrubs and rockeries, with benches for the residents to sit on and paved areas where wheelchairs could be parked.

The main reception area was small but functional, with two low sofas and an armchair around a glass coffee table. There were two employees behind a teak counter, a young man in his twenties with blue-framed spectacles and curly hair whom Lulu knew only as Gary, and an older woman in a dark blue suit who was one of the home's duty managers, Mrs Fitzgerald. The area was overseen by two domed CCTV cameras and all visitors had to be signed in and given a stick-on badge.

Mrs Fitzgerald smiled brightly when she saw Lulu, but then her eyes widened in surprise when she saw the cat lying across her shoulders. 'Oh my goodness,' she said. 'Will you look at that?'

Gary peered through his glasses. 'Is it real?'

Lulu laughed. 'Yes, of course it's real. Do you think I'd walk around with a fake cat around my neck?'

Gary's cheeks reddened and he shrugged.

'Is it yours?' asked Mrs Fitzgerald.

'He's sort of adopted me. Is it okay if I take him in to see Emily?'

'Of course. We're animal friendly here. We always have been. Animals have a calming influence. Well, most of them. We had one of our residents who wanted to bring his venomous snake collection with him; we had to draw the line there.'

She handed Lulu a paper badge with the date and LULU LEWIS on it. Lulu stuck it on her jacket. 'Does Conrad need a badge?'

'I think he probably does,' said Mrs Fitzgerald. She wrote CONRAD on another badge and gave it to Lulu, who stuck it onto her shoulder, just below Conrad's head.

There were glass doors to the left and right; Lulu went through the ones on the right. The door slid open electronically and she walked down a corridor and then up a flight of stairs to the first floor. There was a lift but Lulu always preferred to use the stairs.

'These places always smell the same,' said Conrad. 'Pee and disinfectant. I'm told that prisons smell the same.'

'Who told you that?'

'A cat who had been into a prison, obviously,' said Conrad.

They reached the first floor and Lulu walked along another corridor to Emily's room. To the left of the door was a small frame and inside it was a typed card. EMILY LEWIS. The typed card and the frame always worried Lulu. It was nice that everyone would know who was inside, but there was a lack of permanence about it: it would be all too easy to slide out the card and slip in another one.

She knocked quietly on the door and then slowly turned the handle. Emily was sitting in the high-backed armchair next to her bed. Her eyes were closed and they stayed closed as Lulu walked over and stood next to the bed. It was a hospital bed with sides that could be raised. Emily had fallen out of bed four months earlier. Luckily she hadn't broken anything but she had been badly bruised so the home had brought in the special bed for her. The cost – an extra hundred pounds a week – had been added to Emily's monthly bill. That seemed a little steep to Lulu; when she had googled the model she'd found similar beds available online for less than seven hundred pounds.

The staff had dressed Emily, probably after giving her a bath or at least a good wash, and brushed her hair. They usually took her down to the restaurant on the ground floor for breakfast. After breakfast she either returned to her room or went to sit out in the garden. Then she'd have lunch.

'Is she okay?' asked Conrad.

'She's sleeping. She often has a nap after lunch.'

Conrad jumped off Lulu's shoulders and landed on the bed. He sat there looking at Emily.

The room was pleasant enough, with a window over-looking a strip of grass and the car park. There was a beech tree in the distance. Other than the bed and the chair, there was a modern teak wardrobe, a matching dressing table and mirror, and a chest of drawers. On top of the chest were a dozen framed photographs of a younger Emily and her family members. Among the pictures was a wedding photograph of Lulu, standing arm in arm with Simon. They had been one hell of a good-looking couple, no doubt about that. Her hair was long and blonde, her skin flaw-less with high cheekbones and a delicate chin. The once-blonde hair had turned a steely grey, but she was proud of the way her skin had remained pretty much flawless. And her eyes had stayed a brilliant green. Simon looked dashing in the photograph. Like Timothy Dalton when he had played James Bond. Simon had the actor's hair and his smile.

Other than the bed, there was no medical equipment in the room. Physically, Emily was in good shape. Her blood pressure was slightly high and she had arthritis in her knees, but the doctors always said she could easily live to be a hundred.

Emily's eyes fluttered open, then she frowned as she saw Lulu. 'Who are you?' she asked.

'You know who I am,' said Lulu, smiling. 'It's Lulu.' She walked over and stood in front of her.

Emily frowned. 'Lulu?' she repeated. 'Are you a doctor?'

'I'm Lulu. Your daughter-in-law.'

Emily smiled. 'Oh, that's nice.'

Lulu picked up the wedding photograph and showed it to her. 'That's me. With Simon. On our wedding day.'

'Simon?' she repeated, as if hearing the name for the first time.

'Yes, Simon. Your son.'

Emily peered at the door. 'Is Simon with you?'

Lulu forced a smile. Emily had been told more than a dozen times that her youngest son was dead, but she never remembered. Each time she learned of his death she broke down in hysterics, so the home's doctor had suggested that they simply stopped telling her. 'He's busy at the office,' said Lulu.

'Oh, that's nice,' she said again. She looked over at the

bed and her eyes widened when she saw Conrad. 'Oh. Is that a cat?'

'Yes it is. That's Conrad.'

'Is he my cat?'

'No. He's just come to visit you.'

'He's lovely.'

'Do you want to hold him?'

'Oh, yes.'

Lulu smiled at Conrad. 'Would that be okay, Conrad?'

Conrad meowed and stood up. Lulu went over and picked him up. She took him over to Emily and gently placed him in her lap. Conrad began to purr loudly as Emily stroked his back.

'Conrad is a very special cat,' said Lulu.

'I can see that. His colour is very unusual.'

'No, it's something else. Conrad is super special. He can talk.'

Emily frowned. 'A talking cat?'

'Yes.'

Emily nodded. 'Now that is special.' Conrad continued to purr as Emily stroked him.

There was a bowl of fruit on the bedside table, a box of chocolates and a John Grisham novel. Lulu picked up the book. 'Is this good?'

Emily looked over at it and frowned. 'I think so,' she said.

'Have you read it?'

'I think I have, but every time I pick it up I don't remember any of it so I start from the beginning. But yes, he's a good storyteller, isn't he? Like that Jeffrey Archer. He's a wonderful writer, Jeffrey. Frank and I met him once. We went to one of his parties. Champagne and shepherd's pie. John Major was there and so was that Edwina Currie. They were having an affair, you know?'

'Yes, Emily, I know.' Emily told the Jeffrey Archer story at least once every three visits. It was one of a dozen anecdotes that she would repeat word for word whenever it occurred to her.

As Lulu put the book back on the table, the door opened. It was one of the home's nurses, a young Hungarian girl called Ildi. 'Oh good, you've got a visitor,' she said. She grinned when she saw the cat in Emily's lap. 'That's a beautiful cat. What do they call that pattern?'

'Calico,' said Lulu.

'A calico cat.' She knelt down and stroked him. 'So smooth.'

'His name is Conrad and he's very special,' said Emily. 'He's a talking cat.'

'Is he now?' Ildi tickled Conrad behind the ears and he purred with pleasure. 'That is very special indeed. There aren't many talking cats, that's for sure.'

'Go on, Conrad,' said Emily. 'Say something.'

Conrad looked up at Ildi and put his head on one side. 'Meow,' he said.

Ildi laughed. 'He is talkative, isn't he?'

'Meow,' Conrad repeated.

'He's adorable,' said Ildi. She smiled at Emily and pointed at the box of chocolates. 'Is it okay if I have another, Emily? They are the best chocolates I've ever tasted.'

'Of course you can,' said Emily, still stroking Conrad.

Ildi picked up the box, opened it and selected a chocolate, which she ate slowly. She offered the box to Lulu. 'They do look lovely,' said Lulu.

'They're handmade. They melt in your mouth. Can Lulu have one, Emily?'

'Of course. When is she coming?'

Lulu smiled and shook her head. 'Emily, I'm Lulu. Remember?'

'Of course I do. I'm not senile.'

Lulu looked down at the chocolates. It was a large box with two layers of six chocolates – a mixture of plain and milk. There were only two left on the top layer; she took one and popped it into her mouth. The chocolate melted almost immediately and a warm caramel flavour filled her mouth.

'Good, right?' said Ildi, putting the box back on the bedside table.

Lulu nodded. It was amazing. She swallowed and licked her lips. 'Who gave you the chocolates, Emily? They're delicious.'

Emily looked up from stroking Conrad. 'Simon, of course.'

'Simon?'

'Yes. Simon.'

'Are you sure?'

'I'm not senile, dear.'

Ildi looked across at Lulu. 'Who is Simon?'

'My husband,' she said. 'Emily's son.' She lowered her voice to a whisper. 'He passed away three months ago.'

'Oh, I'm sorry to hear that.' Ildi gestured at Emily. 'And Emily . . . ?'

Lulu nodded. 'Yes. She forgets. Dr Khan said it's best not to correct her.'

'I understand,' Ildi said. She smiled at Emily. 'So, do you want a chocolate, Emily?'

'Oh, no,' replied Emily. 'I don't want to spoil my appetite. I have just one, before I go to sleep.'

'Why don't I take a photograph of you with Conrad and Lulu?' suggested Ildi.

Emily looked around. 'Is Lulu coming?'

'I'm Lulu, Emily,' said Lulu, putting her hand on her mother-in-law's shoulder. She looked at Ildi. 'You want to take a photograph?'

'It's something we've started doing with our more forgetful guests,' said Ildi. 'We take pictures of visitors and we print them out and put them on the wall. We've only just started the programme, and it makes sense. It means that when you're not here they've got something to look at to remind them.' She took out her phone and motioned for Lulu to stand next to Emily's chair. Emily and Lulu smiled and Conrad lifted his head and looked directly at the phone, as if he was posing.

Ildi showed the screen to Lulu. 'Oh, that is a lovely picture,' Lulu said.

'I'll get it printed in the office and give it to Emily later. I have some others I can give you, too.'

Lulu took out her phone. 'Would you send them to me? I'd love copies.'

'Of course,' said the nurse.

Lulu gave her the number and Ildi sent it through to her phone. Ildi left the room and Lulu knelt down next to Emily's chair. Conrad was rubbing his head against Emily's hand and purring loudly. 'He likes you,' said Lulu.

'I like him,' said Emily. 'What was his name again?'

'Conrad,' said Lulu. 'It means brave counsel.'

'Oh that's nice,' said Emily. She smiled as she continued

to stroke him, from the top of his head to the base of his tail. He was pushing up against her hand with every stroke and was clearly enjoying it. 'He's such a lovely boy.' She looked at Lulu and blinked her eyes. 'What did you say your name was again, dear?'

3

Lulu walked out of the nursing home and stood for a few seconds to gather her thoughts. It was always stressful spending time with Emily because her fading memory made conversations difficult at best. At times she clearly knew who Lulu was and would chat away as if she didn't have a care in the world. Lulu would bring her up to date on what was happening in Maida Vale and Emily would tell her about the visitors she'd had. Emily had a lot of friends and every day at least two or three would pop in to say hello and keep her company. But at other times, Emily appeared to have no idea who Lulu was, or why she was in the home. Those were the worst times, when she cried and begged to be allowed to go home. It was the unpredictability that made it so stressful. One moment she might be in full flow, telling Lulu in great detail about something that happened during the war, the next she would be screwing up her face and asking who Lulu was.

'So what's wrong with your mother-in-law?' asked Conrad, who was on her shoulders and wrapped around her neck.

'It's Alzheimer's and probably a bit of senility thrown in,' said Lulu.

'Will she get better?'

Lulu shook her head. 'No. She's been in the home for six months or so and she won't be leaving.'

23

'She has a good aura. She's a nice person.'

'Yes. Yes, she is. What else can you tell from her aura?'

'About her illness, you mean?'

Lulu nodded.

'She's healthy and she's strong. You can see the confusion in her aura, but she's in no pain and she is at peace with herself. She doesn't have the aura of a sick person. There are a lot of pinks in her aura, which shows that she is happy and in harmony with the people around her. But there are traces of lemony yellow, which is fear of loss. I think she's a little bit scared of what's happening to her but she doesn't want to show it. There's plenty of deep red, which is the sign of a warrior spirit. People with deep red in their auras can survive anything. They're tough. They're fighters. You have a lot of deep red in your aura.'

'Thank you for that,' said Lulu.

'I'm not flattering you, I'm telling you what I see.'

'And I appreciate that,' said Lulu. 'So, why did you suddenly stop talking when you were in the home?'

'Seriously? If I talk to everyone, then my life changes for ever.'

'You'd be famous,' said Lulu. 'You'd be on the breakfast TV sofa. Or more likely the evening news.'

'It would end badly,' said Conrad. 'Very badly. Believe me.'

'So you'll only ever talk to me?'

'I'm not saying that. But I am very selective. It's a matter of trust.'

'And you trust me?'

'Of course.'

'Thank you.'

'You're welcome.'

Lulu began to walk back to Maida Vale. 'Where did Emily used to live?' Conrad asked her.

'Warrington Crescent.'

'That's near here. On the way back to the boat.'

'That's right.'

'Can we walk that way? I'd like to see where she lived.'

Lulu sighed. She usually tried to avoid the house, unless she had to go round and collect mail or do a meter reading. But she didn't want to explain to a cat why she preferred to avoid the place, so she just nodded. 'Sure, why not?'

She walked to Hall Road, and followed it to Maida Vale, passing the Everyman Cinema on the left. She and Simon had been regulars there, drinking red wine and eating pizza as they sat on a sofa watching the latest Hollywood movie. She doubted that she would ever go back, now she was alone.

'Do you like movies?' asked Conrad.

Lulu stopped. 'You can read my mind, can't you?'

Conrad laughed. 'You slowed down and you were staring at the Everyman. I put two and two together, that's all.'

'It's very disconcerting, the way you're able to tell what I'm thinking.'

'Cats are good at body language. They have to be. That and auras tell us pretty much everything we need to know about a person.'

'What do you do if you see a bad person? Someone with a bad aura?'

'Just move away, that's all you can do,' he said.

Lulu started walking again. They went by the Warrington, a white-painted Victorian boutique hotel with an opulent bar that Simon had loved. The hotel had opened in 1857 and it had kept almost all of its original features, including mosaic floors, pillared porticos and a huge marble fireplace. At one point there had been a Gordon Ramsay restaurant on the first floor but the food had always been mediocre and the great man had never been seen in person. Before that, the first floor had been home to a Thai restaurant that Emily had loved, and she had never forgiven Ramsay for replacing it with what she saw as overpriced pub food.

Warrington Crescent was one of the prettiest thoroughfares in Maida Vale, a wide road that curved from the Warrington in the north to Warwick Avenue Tube station in the south. The terraced house where Lulu had lived – Emily's house – was halfway down the crescent on the left-hand side. Like most of the houses in the road, it was five storeys tall, with a basement with its own entrance and a low-ceilinged top floor in the eaves. Most of the houses had been split up into individual flats and duplexes; only a handful remained in their original state. She stopped outside Emily's house. Conrad craned his neck to look up at the building. 'It's huge,' he said.

'Yes. You're always going up and down stairs.'

'Did you live there?'

Lulu nodded. Conrad jumped off her shoulders and landed on the pavement with a soft thud. He walked over to the white balustrades and peered down at the basement entrance. 'Why did you move out?'

'It's not important.'

'I was just asking. Something happened, right?' He looked over his shoulder at her, waiting for an answer.

Lulu snorted softly. 'Yes, Conrad. Something happened.'

He sat down and looked up at her. 'Is it to do with your late husband? Tell me. Please.'

Lulu bit down on her lower lip as she stared down at him. 'I had to move out,' she said. 'I couldn't stay there any longer.'

'Why not?'

Lulu sighed. 'Because after Simon passed away I just couldn't bear living here.'

'Oh, Lulu, I'm sorry.' Conrad padded over and rubbed himself against her legs. 'So you and your husband stayed here with Emily, right?'

Lulu nodded. 'Simon and I used to live in Islington and Emily lived here alone. But when she started to have problems, we sold our house and moved in. She lived in the basement, which has a door out to the garden, and we lived in the upper floors. That way she had her independence but we were close by if she needed anything.' She forced a smile. 'Then she got so bad that she had to move into the home and Simon . . .' She couldn't bring herself to finish the sentence and just forced a smile. 'It's a lovely house, it really is. But at the moment I can't live there, I just can't.' She shrugged. 'I'm just taking it one step at a time.'

'What happened to Simon? Is it okay to ask?'

'Yes, it's okay. He was run over. A hit and run. A stupid accident. He had just left a pub. He was coming home and he crossed a road and a car hit him. They never even stopped. Just kept on going. He died in the street. His blood was there for almost a week.' She shuddered.

'I can't tell you how often that's happened to friends of mine,' said Conrad. 'If it was up to me, no one would drive cars.'

'The world would be a safer place, that's true.'

'Canals are the answer,' said Conrad. 'No one ever got run over by a barge.'

'Now, that is most certainly true,' said Lulu.

'Do you think you'll sell the house?' he asked.

'It's not actually mine to sell,' said Lulu. 'It belongs to Emily.' Lulu bent down, scooped him up and held him tightly. She buried her face in his fur as she fought to keep from crying. She held him for almost a minute, then took a deep breath to calm herself. 'I tried staying there on my own, but I couldn't. It was too painful. Every time I woke up it was as if I'd lost him again. I'd be in the kitchen and I'd call to his study to see if he wanted a cup of tea. If I was making tea I'd put out two cups without thinking about it.'

'Three months isn't long.'

'I know,' she said. 'But I couldn't stay there. I was walking on the towpath and there was a "For Sale" sign on *The Lark*. The owner was sitting there on a deckchair and we got to talking and he showed me around and I put the money in his bank that afternoon. He moved out the next morning and I moved in.'

'And did it work? Do you feel better now?'

Lulu nodded. 'I feel a bit better. But only a bit.' She forced a smile. 'At least now, when I open my eyes in the morning I don't expect Simon to be lying next to me. So that's progress, I suppose.' She frowned. 'I know this is going to sound crazy, but you're not channelling Simon, are you?'

Conrad opened his eyes very wide. 'Say what now?'

'Well, Simon is on my mind all the time, obviously. Are you his way of contacting me?'

The cat stared at her and wrinkled his nose. 'You're right,' he said eventually.

'I am?'

'Yes. It does sound crazy.'

Lulu's jaw dropped and, despite herself, she burst into laughter. 'But no crazier than talking to a cat in the street, right?' She ran her hands through her hair. 'When am I going to wake up?'

'Think about this logically, Lulu,' said Conrad. 'If I was Simon, I'd tell you I was Simon – there'd be no point in pretending to be someone else, would there?'

'I suppose not.' She bent down and placed him on the ground.

'And then there's the timing. Simon passed three months ago and you can see I'm not a kitten.'

'I thought maybe his soul might have moved into your body.'

'Does that happen?'

'I don't know.'

'It sounds unlikely.'

Lulu chuckled. 'I can't believe I'm having a conversation about logic with a cat.'

'Well, I can't believe I'm having a conversation with a lady who thinks her husband might have parked his soul in my body.'

'Maybe I am crazy, after all.' She started walking again.

'I think you're under a lot of pressure,' said Conrad, as he strolled next to her. 'Maybe I can help.'

'They do say that cats are great stress-relievers,' said Lulu.

'Because it's true.'

Lulu took a deep breath and exhaled slowly. 'I need a drink.'

'A nice crisp Chardonnay?'

Lulu laughed. 'You are definitely a mind-reader,' she said. She held out her arm. 'Do you want a shoulder ride?'

'I'm happy to walk,' said Conrad.

'Maybe I should get you a lead,' she said.

'And maybe you shouldn't.'

'You're not one for leads?'

'No, Lulu. I'm not.'

They headed back to the canal, then turned right along Blomfield Road. At the far end, where the road turned a sharp right and became Formosa Street, there was a modern brick pub with a terrace overlooking the canal. The Waterway had always been one of Simon's favourite places. He probably preferred it to the Warrington. Many an evening they would sit and share a bottle of wine and watch the narrowboats go by. He'd always talked about buying one and taking time off to explore the canal system with Lulu. It had never happened; he'd always had too much work to be able to take more than a couple of weeks off.

'Penny for them?' asked Conrad, as they walked onto the terrace.

'I thought you were a mind-reader.'

'That's what you keep saying. I just read body language and you had that faraway look in your eyes again.'

'Sorry. I was thinking about Simon. You'll have to get used to that, it probably happens a thousand times a day.'

'I think that's likely to be an exaggeration,' he said. 'Assuming you sleep for eight hours a night, that'd mean thinking about him once every minute throughout the day.'

'That sounds about right, actually,' said Lulu.

A young blonde waitress came out with two menus. She grinned at the cat and smiled at Lulu. 'Table for two?'

'Perfect,' said Lulu. She pointed at a table next to the

towpath. It was the one that she and Simon always chose. 'Can we sit there?'

'Of course you can.' She bent down and stroked Conrad. 'What a lovely cat. Does he go everywhere with you?'

'It certainly seems that way,' said Lulu.

'You're so lucky.'

'Yes, I rather think I am.'

The waitress led them across the terrace to the table. Lulu sat down and Conrad jumped up onto the chair facing her. 'Oh, my God,' said the waitress. 'How cute is that? It's like he's on a date.'

'Thank the young lady, Conrad,' said Lulu.

Conrad looked at the waitress and nodded. 'Meow,' he said.

'That is adorable. Would he like a drink?'

'Meow,' said Conrad.

'He does like Evian, so a bottle of that and a saucer would be wonderful. And a glass of Chardonnay for me. A large one.'

'I could bring you the bottle. Any you don't finish you can take with you.'

Lulu smiled. 'You've talked me into it.'

4

The Lark began to rock from side to side and Lulu opened her eyes. A narrowboat was passing at faster than the approved speed on the canal; probably tourists in a rental. She sighed and squinted at her wristwatch. It was just after eight. She sat up and ran a hand through her hair. She'd finished off most of the bottle of wine that she'd brought back with her, sitting at the back of the boat, watching the sun go down with Conrad. She frowned at the thought of the talking cat. It had to have been a dream, surely? And yet the memory of taking him to see Emily was clear enough. And she could still picture him lapping his water on the terrace of the Waterway. A beautiful afternoon had turned into a wonderful evening and Lulu had ended up ordering a grilled tuna steak which she had shared with Conrad. Had she imagined all that? She shook her head to clear her mind. Cats didn't talk, but the dream had been so vivid.

She sat up. The cabin door was open so she could see the full length of the boat. There was no sign of a calico cat. She rolled out of bed and padded along to the galley to put the kettle on to boil, then went back to clean her teeth. She pulled on a pair of jeans and a baggy sweater. The kettle had boiled by the time she had dressed and she made herself a cup of instant coffee and added a splash of milk.

She bent down and opened the door of the cast-iron stove. The embers were still glowing. She didn't need the stove burning during the day, but at night the temperature dropped so she usually lit the fire each evening and let it burn through the night.

She closed the stove door, walked slowly up the steps and opened the twin doors.

'Good morning,' said Conrad. He was stretched out on the back deck, basking in the morning sun.

'Oh, good Lord,' said Lulu. 'I thought I dreamed you.'

Conrad lifted his head to look at her. 'You mean you had a dream about me? That's sweet.'

'No, I mean I thought that I had imagined you.'

Conrad sighed. 'Oh no, we're not starting that again, are we? Any moment now you'll be back on that whole "what?" thing.'

'What?'

Conrad sighed theatrically. 'And so it begins.' He sat up and scratched behind his ear with his hind leg. 'I'm real, Lulu. As real as this boat and as real as that mug of coffee you're holding.'

Lulu climbed out onto the deck and sat down. 'But cats can't talk.'

'I'm getting an awful feeling of déjà vu here, Lulu,' he said. He walked over and rubbed himself against her legs. She reached down to stroke his soft fur and he purred loudly.

'So, have you adopted me, is that it?' she said.

'Exactly.'

'But you'll come and go, right? I'm guessing you have a girl in every port.'

'At the moment I'm very happy here,' he said. 'There's not many places that have Evian water on tap.'

'Would you like a drink?'

'It's uncanny how you seem to be able to read my mind,' he said. He jumped up onto the seat as Lulu went down into the galley to fetch a saucer and the Evian. She poured water into the saucer and carried it up the steps. She placed it on the seat next to him and he started lapping. Lulu sat down and sipped her coffee as she watched him drink. Was she still sleeping? She had to fight the urge to pinch herself.

Eventually Conrad finished drinking. He sat down and looked up at her. 'So what's your plan today?'

Lulu looked at her watch. 'I'm going to see Emily this morning. She has a doctor's visit this afternoon and there's a lady coming in to do her hair after that. So I'll pop in, say hello and then go for breakfast. And after that I'll probably wash down the boat. And what about you?'

'No plans,' said Conrad. 'Would you like some company?'

'Actually, I would,' she said. She finished her coffee, washed the mug and then stepped off the boat onto the towpath. She bent down so that Conrad could jump onto her shoulders, and the pair headed towards St John's Wood. It was a warm day and the sky was pretty much cloudless. She kept receiving smiles from passers-by when they saw Conrad around her neck, and the occasional car would slow so that the driver could get a better look.

She reached the nursing home and pushed open the door to the reception area. There was no one behind the counter. There was an old-fashioned chrome service bell next to the signing-in ledger but Lulu had always resisted using it. It smacked of a Victorian lady of the house summoning a maid, so she just stood and waited. Conrad dropped down off Lulu's shoulders and landed on the counter. He sniffed at the bell. Lulu picked up a pen and wrote down her name, the date and time, and scrawled her signature.

Eventually Gary appeared from the side office, carrying a manila file and a mug of tea. He squinted at her. 'Ah. Hello. Good morning.'

He seemed confused at seeing her there, so Lulu smiled brightly. 'Hello, I'm here to see my mother-in-law. Can you give me a badge?'

Gary grimaced. 'She's not here. They took her away.'

'They what?'

'They took Mrs Lewis away earlier this morning.' He was looking at the floor, unwilling to look her in the eyes.

'Who did?'

'The funeral director.'

'What?'

'Your mother-in-law passed away, in the night.' His voice had dropped to a low mumble.

'No, that's not possible,' said Lulu. 'I was here yesterday. She was fine.'

'Mrs Lewis was almost ninety,' said Gary. 'She had a good innings.'

'What?'

Gary shrugged. 'She was a good age. It happens. People die.'

Lulu opened her mouth but realized that she was only going to say 'what?' again, so she closed it.

'I'm so sorry for your loss,' said Gary, but there was no sincerity in his voice and he was still staring at the floor.

Mrs Fitzgerald appeared from the office and a look of concern flashed across her face when she saw Lulu. 'Oh, my goodness, Lulu, I'm so sorry,' she said. She came out from behind the counter and hugged her. 'I'm so, so sorry. Emily was a truly lovely person. She brought joy to everyone who met her.'

'Thank you,' said Lulu. 'But what happened? She was fine yesterday.'

Mrs Fitzgerald released her grip on her. 'I know. And she was fine at dinner. We took her back to her room and helped her to bed and she was as right as rain when we checked on her at nine o'clock. No alarms sounded during the night, but when Ildi went in this morning to help her get up, Mrs Lewis had passed away.'

Lulu frowned. 'This morning? Why did nobody call me?'

'I assumed they had. You're listed as next of kin, aren't you?'

'Of course.'

'Then you should have been called.' She looked over at Gary. 'Gary, did you call Mrs Lewis?'

Gary frowned at her. 'Mrs Lewis, the lady who died?'

Mrs Fitzgerald shook her head in annoyance. 'This Mrs Lewis. Her daughter.'

'Daughter-in-law,' said Lulu.

'I called the next of kin number and spoke to a lady. I told her what had happened.' He squinted at Lulu through his glasses. 'That wasn't you?'

'No,' said Lulu. 'It wasn't me.' Her head was swimming. Emily couldn't possibly be dead. She had been fine the previous day. There had to have been some mistake.

'Let me find out what's going on,' said Mrs Fitzgerald. She walked back behind the counter and sat down at the computer terminal. Lulu looked over at Conrad. He had jumped off the counter and was sitting on one of the chairs, watching everything. 'Meow,' he said.

Lulu forced a smile but she could feel tears pricking her eyes.

Mrs Fitzgerald tapped away on her keyboard, then peered at the screen. 'Ah, I see what happened,' she said. 'The next of kin details were changed.'

'Changed?' said Lulu. 'When?'

'Just over two months ago. Yes, her son Richard was made next of kin.'

'By whom?'

'I suppose by him. Next of kin generally means a blood relative, and . . .' She left the sentence unfinished.

'And I'm not?' said Lulu.

'Well, yes, strictly speaking you're not. I know how much you cared for Emily and that you were here every day for her, but in terms of next of kin her son would take priority.'

'But Gary didn't talk to Richard.' Lulu looked over at him. 'Did you?'

He looked away and mumbled at the floor, 'It was a woman I spoke to.'

Lulu went over to the counter. 'What number do you have?' she asked Mrs Fitzgerald.

'I'm sorry, I can't tell you, it's covered by data protection, I'm afraid.'

Lulu took out her mobile phone, went through to her address book and brought up Richard's number. 'Is this the number?' she asked, and read out the digits.

Mrs Fitzgerald shook her head. 'No, it isn't.'

'Well, that's Richard's number.'

Mrs Fitzgerald looked at the screen again. 'It's definitely him. Richard Lewis. There's an address in Beckenham.'

That was where Richard and Maria lived. 'I suppose it

might be Maria's number, but she's no more next of kin than I am.'

'Well, yes, she might have answered, but it's Mrs Lewis's son who is down as her next of kin, which he is.'

'But prior to that, I was the next of kin, right?'

'Well, strictly speaking, it was your husband who was down as next of kin, but I take your point.'

'And who requested the change?'

'I really couldn't say,' said Mrs Fitzgerald. 'I assume Mr Lewis would have done that.'

'Richard's never here,' said Lulu. 'He never visits.' She flinched and corrected herself. 'Visited.'

'No, he was here on Friday. And the previous week. And a month or so ago. He came with his wife.'

'Emily never mentioned it,' said Lulu.

'Well, her mind has been wandering of late. But I can assure you, they were here.'

Lulu walked away from the counter, her mind in a whirl. It was understandable that Emily hadn't mentioned the visits, but why hadn't Richard? If he'd come in to London from Beckenham, the least he could have done would have been to have phoned her. Lulu ran her hands through her hair. Emily dying was the last thing she'd expected. It made no sense. She'd been fine the previous afternoon. A little confused, as always, but it had been one of her better days, and there hadn't been any physical problems that Lulu had seen. She sat down next to Conrad and stroked the back of his head. He purred and pushed against her. She was having trouble believing that Emily had died. Maybe it was a dream. Maybe it was all a dream and Emily was alive and cats didn't talk.

Mrs Fitzgerald came to stand in front of her. 'I'm so sorry for your loss, I really am,' she said. 'Everyone loved Emily. She'll be missed.'

'Thank you,' said Lulu.

'And I apologize for the fact that you weren't notified immediately. I can't imagine how upsetting it must be to find out like this.'

Lulu nodded. 'It was a shock, yes.'

Mrs Fitzgerald patted her on the shoulder. 'It must have been. Can I get you a cup of tea or a glass of water?'

'No, thank you.' She took a deep breath. 'Could I have a word with Dr Khan?'

'Can I ask why?'

'Presumably he signed the death certificate? He's the resident doctor.'

'He is, yes. And you're quite right, he signed the death certificate. But I don't see that you need to bother him.'

'I won't bother him, I promise. I'd just like to know what happened.'

Mrs Fitzgerald patted Lulu's shoulder again. 'I understand, of course I do. But your mother-in-law was an old lady. Coming up to ninety. That's a good age.'

'But she didn't die because she was old, did she? She was fine yesterday. Something must have happened.'

Mrs Fitzgerald opened her mouth to argue, but had a change of heart. She patted Lulu's shoulder a final time and then went into her office. Lulu heard her on the phone and a minute or so later she returned. 'Dr Khan is in his office and he'll be happy to see you.'

Lulu thanked her and stood up. 'Do I need a badge?' she asked.

Mrs Fitzgerald smiled. 'No, you go ahead. You know where his office is.' Lulu pushed open the door to the left. Conrad immediately jumped down from the chair and slipped through the doorway. 'I'm sorry,' said Lulu, gesturing at the cat.

Mrs Fitzgerald laughed. 'It's fine, I'm sure Dr Khan won't mind.'

Lulu closed the door behind her. 'I'm sorry about Emily,' said Conrad. 'That's just awful.'

'It's a shock,' she said. 'I still can't believe it.'

'She didn't seem sick yesterday, did she?'

'No,' said Lulu. 'She didn't.'

They walked down the corridor to a door marked MEDICAL STAFF and Lulu knocked.

'Come in, come in,' said Dr Khan. When Lulu opened the door he was already up out of his chair and walking around his desk. He was in his mid- to late thirties, dark-skinned with square glasses and wearing a rumpled grey suit and a red and blue striped tie. 'Mrs Lewis, my most sincere condolences,' he said. 'I am so sorry for your loss.' His eyes flicked to the floor and he frowned when he saw Conrad. 'Oh, a cat.'

'Yes, sorry, Dr Khan, he's with me.'

'No, it's fine. I'm not one for pets myself but I can see the attraction. Please, sit down.' He waved at a wooden chair and went back to sit in his high-backed executive-style seat. He steepled his fingers under his chin. 'I realize that Mrs Lewis's death must have come as a shock, but I can absolutely assure you that it was painless and there was no distress.' He flashed her what was obviously meant to be his most professional, reassuring smile, but Lulu wasn't in the least bit reassured.

'Were you there when she died, Dr Khan?'

He picked up a pen and began fiddling with it. 'No. No, I wasn't.'

'She was dead when you got there?'

'Well, yes.'

'In fact, Mrs Fitzgerald said that she was already dead when Ildi found her this morning.'

Dr Khan shifted uncomfortably in his chair. Conrad was sitting by the door, staring at the doctor with his unblinking green eyes. 'Yes, that's what happened. Ildi discovered that Mrs Lewis had passed away and I was contacted and came in early.'

'Well, no offence, but you're not really in a position to say that her passing was painless. She died alone. You really don't know if she was in pain or not.'

Dr Khan held up his hands. 'No, that's not the case. Mrs Lewis looked relaxed in death, as if she had just passed away in her sleep.'

'Do you know when she died?'

'Sometime during the night, obviously. She was last seen at nine p.m., I understand. And Ildi went into the room at eight o'clock in the morning. So somewhere between nine p.m. and eight a.m.'

'You can't be more specific than that?'

'Well, the body was cold when I saw her, so it would have been at night rather than the morning.'

'There are ways of using the temperature of the liver to determine the time of death.'

He smiled coldly. 'I assume you're a fan of *CSI*?'

'Actually, I was a police officer,' she said. 'For thirty years. Retired now, obviously. But even when I was a serving officer, body temperature could be used to determine time of death.'

'Well, yes, it can be. And that might have been necessary if a crime had been committed. But we can be less exact when someone passes away through natural causes.'

'But there'll be an inquest, won't there? And a post mortem?'

'No, Mrs Lewis. Inquests aren't normally held unless there's something that requires further investigation. In fact, more than half of all deaths aren't even referred to the coroner. If it's just a regular death then a doctor such as myself signs a medical certificate of cause of death, which is the official document that allows a death to be registered. That is what happened in your mother-in-law's case. I signed the certificate and the funeral director took her away. That really is the end of it.'

'So you haven't even told the police?'

Dr Khan frowned. 'There was nothing remotely suspicious about her death, so there was no need to talk to the police. As a former officer you would presumably know that.'

'So no one has officially been told about her death?'

'The cause of death certificate has been signed. That's really all there is to it.' He leaned forward. 'There are certain specific deaths that have to be reported to the coroner. Children, for instance. Any death of a person under eighteen has to be referred. Deaths that occur within twenty-four hours of being admitted to hospital, or that might have been caused by medical treatment. Deaths that are the result of an accident have to be reported, as do cases of suicide or if there are any suspicious circumstances. Then there are certain reportable illnesses, such as tuberculosis or hepatitis. Your mother-in-law did not fulfil any of those criteria so there was no need for the coroner to be informed.'

'And what did you put down as the cause of death?' asked Lulu.

'Alzheimer's, of course.'

Lulu frowned. 'Why on earth would you say that? She didn't die of Alzheimer's. She was forgetful, that was all.'

'She had late-stage Alzheimer's. You know that. That was why she was admitted to the home in the first place.'

'Yes, but it couldn't have killed her. Not overnight.'

'Mrs Lewis, in 2015 dementia overtook heart disease and stroke as the biggest cause of death in the United Kingdom. It's very common. Your mother-in-law was a very sick woman.'

'Well, on that we disagree, Dr Khan. I was with her yesterday afternoon. Yes, she was a bit confused, but she was happy enough. She loved meeting Conrad.'

'Conrad?'

'My cat.' She gestured at Conrad, who was now sitting next to her chair, still staring up at the doctor. 'Emily was stroking him and talking to him. She was reminiscing about a party she went to with her husband, years ago. She was fine. Really.'

'But she wasn't fine, Mrs Lewis. She was almost ninety and she had late-stage Alzheimer's, for which there is no treatment and no cure.'

Lulu sighed. 'She wasn't frail. She wasn't slipping away. She was sitting in her chair and she was fine. Look, Dr Khan, I nursed my father through his final days and I know what death from old age looks like. I saw him gradually become less mobile and then I saw him confined to bed and eventually I was with him when he died. My mother-in-law wasn't like that. As I keep saying, yesterday she was fine.'

Dr Khan folded his arms and looked at her over the top of his glasses. 'I am starting to feel that you are accusing me of acting less than professionally,' he said. 'But I can assure you that I did my job properly.'

'You know my mother-in-law was allergic to sesame seeds and that she always had at least one epinephrine pen in her room?'

'Yes, of course I know that.'

'So maybe she had an allergic reaction?'

'The kitchen staff are aware of all the allergies the patients have. They take great care in the preparation of the food here.'

'But people make mistakes.'

The doctor tilted his head to one side and narrowed his eyes. 'And now I'm starting to think you're looking to blame someone.'

Lulu shook her head. 'That's not it at all. I'm not looking to blame anyone, Dr Khan. I just want the truth.'

'So now you think I'm not telling you the truth? You think I'm a liar?'

'No, but I do wonder if you might have overlooked something.'

'Like an anaphylactic reaction?'

'Well, yes.'

'I gave your mother-in-law a complete examination and saw nothing that suggested she had an anaphylactic attack.' He saw she was about to speak and held up a hand to silence her. 'Now, the problem there is that she had been dead for several hours before I got there so it is possible that if there had been a rash it had subsided, and any swelling in her throat and airways could have gone. But I didn't see any signs of an attack. And then, of course, there's the timing.'

'The timing?'

'Your mother-in-law ate dinner at six-thirty. She was seen by a nurse at nine o'clock that evening and she was perfectly fine then. If she had suffered an allergic reaction she would have felt something within minutes of consuming any sesame seeds. She'd had attacks before?'

'Yes. Her sons, too. They were also allergic. They all had very bad reactions to sesame seeds.'

'Well, then you'll know what happens. The lips tingle and go numb and then the throat closes. That all happens quite quickly. It would certainly have happened before nine p.m.'

Lulu gazed down at the floor, not sure what to say.

'There were no signs of anything untoward, nothing to suggest that anyone had harmed her. She was a ninety-year-old lady with a terminal illness and she died of natural causes.'

Lulu looked up. 'What if I wanted a post mortem, to know for sure?' she said. 'How would I go about that?'

'You would need to persuade a coroner to order one, and under the circumstances I've outlined, it's doubtful that would happen. You could, I suppose, commission a private post mortem, but would you want to go to all that trouble?'

'If it means finding out the truth, yes. Absolutely, I would.'

Dr Khan sighed. 'But what is the truth? Your mother-in-law had terminal Alzheimer's. Now, it's possible that last night she might have had a massive heart attack, or a stroke, but because she was in late-stage Alzheimer's, that generally would be put down as the cause of death. In the same way that heart attacks and pneumonia were written up as Covid deaths during the pandemic. Now, you might well decide to get a private post mortem carried out, but do you realize what that entails? They will cut your mother-in-law's chest open.' He made the shape of a large Y on his chest. 'Then they will remove and examine all her organs. Then they will use a saw to take off the top of her head and remove her brain. And when they've finished, you'll be burying her in pieces. Is that what you want? As your last memory of her?'

Lulu sighed. 'I don't know.'

'Look, you've had a shock, I understand that. Why don't you sleep on it? Try to relax and maybe you'll think differently tomorrow. If you like, I can prescribe something to help you sleep.'

Lulu shook her head. 'No, I'll be fine, thank you.' She stood up. 'You're right, I suppose. I need to clear my thoughts.'

'Again, I am very sorry for your loss,' said Dr Khan. 'Mrs Lewis was a wonderful lady. I know she had a lot of friends here.'

'Yes, she did,' said Lulu. She opened the door. 'And thank you for your time. I'm sorry if I sounded disrespectful; that's not what I intended. Emily always referred to you as "that nice Dr Khan" so I know she liked you.' She flashed him a tight smile and followed Conrad out of the door.

Mrs Fitzgerald had gone from reception but Gary was still there. He avoided eye contact with Lulu but managed to mumble again that he was sorry for her loss.

5

Lulu stopped at the traffic lights and waited for the green man. Conrad was standing next to her and he looked up at her. 'I know it's not something to laugh about, but when the doctor talked about the post mortem, I really thought he was going to say something about her resting in pieces.'

Lulu's mouth fell open as she stared at the cat, then a smile slowly spread across her face. 'You know, for one crazy moment, so did I.' She chuckled. 'I suppose you've got to laugh, or you'd just burst into tears.'

'It's grief, you deal with it any way you can.'

Lulu nodded. 'Wise words.'

'I'm a wise cat.'

'Yes, you are.'

The green man appeared. Lulu bent down and Conrad jumped up onto her shoulders. She straightened up and crossed the road. 'Am I being stupid, Conrad? Giving Dr Khan a hard time like that?'

'You were asking valid questions.'

'I was, wasn't I?'

'Emily looked fine yesterday.'

'She did, didn't she?'

'And her aura was strong. Very strong. She might have been a little confused, but other than that I'd say she was healthy.'

'Why doesn't Dr Khan understand that?'

'I suppose he's just doing his job. He's probably right – a lot of people do die at the home. That's what it is really, a place where people go to die.'

'It sounds horrible when you say that.' She shrugged. 'But you're right. It is a bit Hotel California, people check in but they don't check out. I just want to know what happened. I want to know why Emily died.'

'Is it because you want someone to blame? Like the doctor suggested?'

'I don't think so, Conrad. It'd be easier to know that she just passed away in the night. If anything, that's what I want to be told.'

'But isn't that what Dr Khan said to you?'

Lulu nodded. 'It is, but I don't believe him. Conrad, what do you think? Be honest with me.'

'I will always be honest with you, Lulu. You don't have to say that.'

'I mean I don't want you to spare my feelings. If you think I'm wrong, I'd rather you told me.'

Conrad looked at her for several seconds. 'I don't think you're wrong,' he said eventually. 'Something isn't right about this.'

'Thank you.' She sighed. 'I need a drink.'

'Chardonnay?'

'I think a double malt would hit the spot, but at this time of the day I suppose it ought to be coffee. I tell you what, let's go to the Colonnade Hotel,' she said. 'Emily loved it there.'

'Perfect,' said Conrad.

'Purr-fect.'

'Exactly.'

The Colonnade was at the southern end of Warrington Crescent, a huge white Victorian building with tables on a terrace overlooking the soaring, angular brick-built facade of St Saviour's Church. All the outside tables were empty so Lulu sat down at the one closest to the church. A blond waiter appeared and Lulu ordered a coffee.

'One cup or two?' the waiter asked, giving Conrad a sly glance. He had a Polish accent.

Lulu smiled. 'Oh, I'm sure he'd love some water. Evian, if you have it.'

'We have Evian,' said the waiter.

'You know about this hotel, do you?' asked Lulu, once the waiter had gone back inside.

'Not really,' said Conrad, settling down on the chair opposite her.

'Well, it started life as two Victorian houses which were converted into an all-girls boarding school and then it became a maternity hospital and then finally a hotel. It became the Colonnade in 1944. Emily says she knew the Richards family, who owned it back then. I'm not sure who owns it now, but Emily used to come here for afternoon tea at least once a month.'

The waiter returned with a cup of coffee for Lulu and a bowl of water for Conrad. Conrad jumped off his chair and lapped quietly and Lulu sipped her coffee as the waiter walked away. 'I hope this is all a horrible dream and that I wake up soon,' said Lulu.

Conrad continued to drink his water.

'You know, a year ago, I would have said my life was perfect. Simon was starting to work less and we were spending more time together. We went to St Lucia and

Monaco and we had two weeks driving around New Zealand. Emily was fine most of the time, just a bit forgetful. We knew what was coming, but it was down the line. Life was – well, it was wonderful. And now? Simon dead in a stupid road accident, Emily dead and I don't know why, and I'm talking to a cat.' She put down her cup and wiped away tears with the back of her hand. She reached into her handbag and found a handkerchief. As she began to dab at her eyes, Conrad jumped up onto a chair and then onto the table.

He walked over to her, casually avoiding the coffee cup, and gently butted his head against her chin.

Lulu smiled. 'Thank you,' she whispered.

'For what?'

'For being here. For helping me get through this.'

Conrad nodded. 'You will. One day at a time. And I'll be with you.'

'Thank you.' She wiped her eyes and put the handkerchief back into her bag. 'I know I sound as if I'm crazy, but I just have the feeling that something bad happened to Emily.' She took out her phone. It had been more than a year since she had spoken to Detective Inspector Philip Jackson. He was an old-school officer, one of the few left as most of them had quit in frustration when the Met had become dominated by paperwork and targets instead of catching criminals.

He answered almost immediately. 'Bloody hell, boss, you're a blast from the past.'

It had been more than ten years since they had worked together, but he always called her 'boss'. She took it as a sign of respect. His voice was deep and resonant, the vocal equivalent of treacle, soft and warm, almost cloying. It was the sort of voice that could present a late-night radio show playing easy listening tunes for people preparing to go to sleep.

'Yeah, sorry Phil. I'm lousy at keeping in touch. How are things?'

'Same old, same old. Two more years and I'm out.'

'Where are you these days?'

'Kensington nick, currently overseeing Neighbourhood Policing. They're trying to shove social media offences onto me and I'm resisting.'

'It's valuable work, Phil – we can't have people's feelings being hurt, can we?'

They both laughed. 'How can I help you, boss? I'm guessing you need something.'

'It's a bit of an embarrassing one, Phil. Sorry to dump it on you but I don't have too many friends left at the Met.'

'Rats deserting the sinking ship, tell me about it. Half the guys I work with are straight out of university and most can barely walk down the street, never mind run. I swear that one of them is a midget.'

'I think you're supposed to refer to them as little people these days, Phil.'

'Little? She's tiny.' He laughed, a deep, booming thudding sound that made the phone vibrate against her ear. 'Anyway, I'm a dinosaur and the powers that be have made it clear I'm heading for extinction.'

'Sorry to hear that.'

'No, I'll be fine. I've got options, I just need to decide what to do with my life. So how can I help?'

'It's going to sound silly but I need to get it off my chest. My mother-in-law died last night or early this morning. They haven't been specific about time of death.'

'Oh, boss, sorry to hear that.'

'She was in a nursing home in St John's Wood. She'd been struggling with Alzheimer's and dementia, but she passed away very quickly.'

'Is there going to be an inquest?'

'No, that's the thing. The home's doctor was happy to put it down to natural causes. He put Alzheimer's on the death certificate, though for the life of me I don't see how that killed her. Physically she looked fine yesterday.'

'You think foul play?'

'I don't know. But we all remember Harold Shipman. He went down for fifteen murders but they reckon he killed closer to two hundred and fifty of his patients, and eighty per cent of them were elderly women.'

'You want me to check out the home?'

'If you would. And the doctor. He's Dr Kamran Khan.' She spelled out the name for him.

'I'm at my desk as we speak. Give me the name and address of the home.'

Lulu gave him the details and she heard him tapping on his computer.

'Well, there are no investigations at the home, ongoing or historical,' he said eventually. 'Clean as a whistle. Some of these places are real horror stories, with residents being starved or dying of thirst, with the staff abusing the residents and stealing from them. But this place hasn't had a single complaint of that nature.'

'We did do a lot of research before we put her in there,' said Lulu.

'Well, you clearly made a good choice,' said the inspector. 'Let me run the doc through the system.' There was more tapping, a pause, and then tapping again. 'No, he's clean. Not even a speeding ticket, which is more than I can say for myself. He's an exemplary citizen. I suppose you could check with the BMA but from where I'm sitting there are no red flags.'

'Okay, Phil, thanks for that.'

'I can tell from the sound of your voice that I haven't put your mind at rest, boss.'

'No, you've told me what I wanted to hear. I think I'm just working my way through the stages of grief and got stuck at denial. Thanks for checking for me.'

'It's a pleasure, boss. Any time. And if you ever find yourself out on Earls Court Road, give me a call and we'll go for a drink. We can talk about old times and the way the world is going to hell in a hand basket.'

'I will, Phil. For sure.' She ended the call and put her phone away.

'Everything okay?' asked Conrad.

'I think so, yes.'

'What do you want to do?'

'About what?'

'You've had a nasty shock, Lulu. Is there someone you want to talk to?'

She shook her head. 'I'm fine.' She forced a smile. 'Besides, I can talk to you.'

'Yes, you can.'

Lulu sipped her coffee. 'I need to stay busy,' she said. 'That's really what I need to do right now.'

6

Lulu took a painted tin bucket to the galley, filled it with water and added a squirt of detergent. There was a long-handled brush on the roof and she took it and the bucket to the prow. She began cleaning the roof and sides, working slowly and steadily. After a few minutes Conrad came padding along the roof. He stopped at the midway point, next to one of the mushroom-shaped air vents, and sat and watched her.

'I love to watch humans work,' he said.

Lulu laughed. 'I guess our lives must look a little crazy to you,' she said.

'You do keep yourselves busy, while cats spend their time enjoying the moment.' He began to groom himself, licking his paw and then rubbing it across his face.

She refilled the bucket and Conrad moved to the prow as she cleaned the mid-section, then after refilling a second time she went to work on the stern. It took her the best part of an hour and she was sweating by the time she finished. Focusing on the job in hand meant that she didn't dwell on what had happened to Emily, but images of their last meeting kept flashing through her mind. Emily had been confused and at times had made no sense, so Lulu tried to blot out the memory and thought about happier times instead. But when she recalled the good times, they just brought home the loss and the fact that she would never see Emily again.

Every time her eyes began to fill with tears, she pushed herself to work harder and to focus on what she was doing. Eventually the job was done and the boat was sparkling clean. She washed the bucket and brush and left them on the roof of the boat while she went down and showered and changed into a blue dress and cardigan. Conrad was still grooming himself when she re-emerged from the cabin.

'Are you hungry?' Lulu asked.

'I could eat.'

'I'll take you for lunch, then.'

Conrad's eyes narrowed. 'Are you okay?'

Lulu forced a smile. 'Not really.'

'Do you want to talk about it?'

Lulu blinked away tears. 'No, not really.' She took a deep breath to steady herself. 'I just need time to process what's happened.'

'It was a shock, wasn't it?'

'She was fine yesterday,' said Lulu. 'How can she be dead today?' She took another deep breath and let it out slowly. 'I'll be okay. Let's go and eat. Maybe my blood sugar is low.'

Conrad stared at her, clearly concerned. 'Okay,' he said eventually. She could hear the hesitation in his voice.

She stood up. 'Right, off we go.' She bent down so that Conrad could jump onto her shoulders, then she let herself out of the cabin. She stood on the back deck and looked both ways. When she was sure that the path was clear she stepped off the boat and headed towards Venice Patisserie on Clifton Road, one of her favourite cafes. Lulu ordered a smoked salmon salad with Dijon honey dressing and a glass of iced tea. She shared the salmon with Conrad, who sat next to her chair, saying nothing other than 'meow' because there were three young mothers with pushchairs sitting at an adjacent table. The food at Venice Patisserie was always delicious, but today Lulu chewed the salmon without tasting it. Conrad watched her anxiously and from time to time he meowed as if to reassure her.

Lulu was just putting down her knife and fork when her mobile rang. She looked at the screen. It was the home calling her. For a wild moment she hoped that they were calling to say that they had made a mistake and that Emily was still alive. She put it to her ear. 'Lulu Lewis,' she said, blinking away tears.

'Mrs Lewis, this is Gary at the nursing home.'

'Yes, Gary.' Her heart was pounding as if it wanted to burst free from her chest. Was Emily alive? Had there been a mix-up? Had it all been a terrible mistake?

'I have Mrs Lewis's things for you.'

Lulu frowned. 'Her what?' The mothers at the neighbouring table stood up and started fussing over their strollers. One of the toddlers spotted Conrad and pointed at him excitedly.

'Her personal effects. I have them here.'

'I'm sorry, what? I don't understand.'

'Mrs Lewis's things. You need to come and collect them.'

'Right. But I'm not Emily's next of kin, am I? Doesn't Richard have to get them? He's responsible for everything now, right? I'm just . . .' She sighed. 'I don't know what I am any more.'

'Yes. Right. That's correct, he is the next of kin so he is responsible for collecting her belongings. But I rang his number and he said he was busy and that his wife was out. I asked him what I should do and he said I should call you, that you were local and it wouldn't be a problem for you to come and pick them up.'

'Did he now?' The mothers moved away, walking three abreast down the pavement. An elderly man had to step into the road to walk around them.

'Is it a problem?' Gary asked.

Lulu sighed. 'No, Gary. It's fine. I'll be around shortly.'

'Just ask whoever is on reception to get Mrs Lewis's things.'

'I will do,' said Lulu. She ended the call and sighed.

Conrad looked at her. 'Something wrong?'

'I have to go to the home again,' said Lulu.

'Do you want company?'

'That would be nice, thank you.'

7

Lulu walked into the nursing home's reception area and stood by the counter. There was no sign of Gary or Mrs Fitzgerald. She looked at the service bell but, as always, was reluctant to press it. Mrs Fitzgerald's door was open, so after a couple of minutes she leaned towards it and said 'Hello,' in a hesitant voice. Conrad jumped off her shoulders and landed on the counter with a soft thud.

A woman appeared in the doorway. It was Mrs Reynolds, a Scottish lady with a fondness for tartan skirts who was employed as Mrs Fitzgerald's secretary and who also did basic repairs around the home. She had her red hair in a plaited ponytail and was carrying a stack of manila files.

'Hello, I've come to pick up my mother-in-law's effects,' said Lulu.

'Oh, my gosh, yes,' said Mrs Reynolds. She hurried over to the counter, put down the files and took Lulu's hands in her own. 'I'm so sorry about your loss,' she said. 'Mrs Lewis was a lovely lady, everybody liked her. She was so sweet to everybody. I never heard her say a bad word about anyone, she was truly a good soul.'

'Thank you so much,' said Lulu.

'Please let me know when the funeral is, I would really love to come.'

'Of course,' said Lulu. 'As soon as I know, I'll tell you.'

'I popped in to see her, just before dinner,' said Mrs

Reynolds. 'Her television was playing up so I reset the channels for her. She was telling me about the cat that visited.' She smiled at Conrad. 'This is him, right?'

'Yes, this is Conrad.'

'Ildi had put some photographs on her wall and one of them was of Mrs Lewis with the cat. She was so happy to have met him.' She released her grip on Lulu's hands and began to stroke Conrad. 'She said he could talk.' She bent down and put her face next to his. 'Can you, Conrad? Can you talk?'

Conrad blinked at her. 'Meow,' he said.

She laughed. 'You can talk!' she said. She smiled at Lulu. 'I love him,' she said. 'Does he go everywhere with you?'

'He seems to, at the moment.'

'He's a lovely colour. What do they call that?'

'Calico,' said Lulu.

'Conrad the Calico Cat. I love it.' She straightened up. 'Let me get Mrs Lewis's things,' she said.

'I wonder if, while I'm here, I could have a word with the chef?'

Mrs Reynolds frowned. 'The chef?'

'The cook. The person who prepares the meals.'

Her frown deepened. 'Why would you want to see the cook?'

'Just for a chat about what my mother-in-law had to eat.'

'Visitors aren't allowed to go into the kitchens, I know that,' said Mrs Reynolds. 'Health and safety.'

'Could he maybe come out here, just for a brief chat?'

'It's a she. Kayla.'

'Do you think I could possibly have a quick word with Kayla? Just for a minute or so. I really won't keep her long.'

Mrs Reynolds forced a smile. 'I'll call her from the office, see if she's free.'

'Thank you so much,' said Lulu.

Mrs Reynolds nodded and disappeared into the office. Conrad jumped down off the counter, padded across the carpet and leaped up onto a sofa. 'Why do you want to talk to the cook?' he asked.

'I just want to know what Emily had to eat last night, that's all.'

'But the doctor already said it couldn't have been the food because she was perfectly fine afterwards.'

'Just humour me, Conrad. Please.'

Mrs Reynolds appeared at the counter just as Lulu finished speaking. Lulu put her hand up to her mouth and faked a couple of coughs, but she could see from the look on the secretary's face that she had heard her talking.

'Meow!' said Conrad, loudly.

'What did he say?' asked Mrs Reynolds.

'Oh, he wants to go outside,' said Lulu.

'I do love the way he talks.'

'Yes, so do I,' said Lulu. Mrs Reynolds walked around the counter. She was holding a cardboard box in one hand and a black rubbish bag in the other. 'I didn't realize there would be so much,' said Lulu.

'It's clothes, mainly,' said the secretary, holding up the bag. 'Her personal effects are in the box.'

Lulu took the box from her. 'What do people usually do with the clothes?' she asked.

'Sometimes they take them away, but we can deal with them if you'd prefer.'

'What do you do with them?' asked Lulu.

'The clothes that are in good condition we send to a charity shop, and the rest we . . .'. She shrugged. 'Well, we dispose of them.'

Lulu sighed. She didn't like the idea of throwing away Emily's clothes, but what was the alternative? Take them back home and put them in a drawer with yet more clothes that would never be worn? 'Would you mind?' she asked.

'No, that's fine,' said the secretary. 'And I spoke to Kayla. She has some prep work to finish and then she'll pop out for a chat.'

'Brilliant, thank you,' said Lulu.

Mrs Reynolds looked over at Conrad. 'And it has been a pleasure meeting you, Conrad. You have a great day.'

Conrad's ears twitched. 'Meow,' he said.

'I love it,' said Mrs Reynolds. She took the bag back behind the counter and went into the office.

Lulu went to sit down on the sofa next to Conrad. He sniffed the box, his whiskers twitching. 'What are you going to do with the box?' he asked.

'I'll take it back to the house,' said Lulu. She put the box on the floor by her feet.

The door to their left opened and a black girl in chef's whites walked over, her dreadlocks wrapped in a hairnet.

'Mrs Lewis?' she said. She was in her late twenties and had a friendly smile.

Lulu stood up. 'Yes. Thank you for seeing me, I know how busy you are.'

'Oh, I wanted to meet you anyway, just to tell you how sorry I am about Emily. She was a truly lovely lady.'

'Thank you, so much. That's so nice to hear.'

'She was always asking about my parents, and always said

my food was delicious, which is obviously what every chef wants to hear.'

'She did enjoy her food.'

'If it was something she particularly liked she'd make sure the server went to the kitchen to give her compliments to the chef. You've no idea how happy that made me. A lot of the residents here aren't even aware of what they're eating, and the ones that are only pass on their complaints. Emily was a breath of fresh air.'

'Thank you so much for that.' Lulu smiled awkwardly. 'I know this sounds a little silly, but I just wanted to ask you what she ate yesterday.'

'She had her regular breakfast of omelette with toast and some fruit. Cottage pie and peas for lunch, with peach cobbler for dessert, and baked cod with new potatoes and carrots for dinner.' Her eyes narrowed. 'I assume you're worried about her sesame allergy?'

'Yes, I am. I'm sorry. I don't mean to imply anything . . .'

Kayla put up her hands. 'Absolutely no offence taken,' she said. 'In fact I've already spoken to Dr Khan and Mrs Fitzgerald and I can tell you exactly what I told them – none of our recipes use sesame oil or sesame seeds and there is none in our kitchen.'

'You know all of the allergies that the residents have?'

'Oh gosh, yes. We have a huge chart up on the wall and once a week Dr Khan comes in to check it. Mrs Lewis is . . .' She grimaced as she realized she had inadvertently used the present tense. 'I'm sorry, Mrs Lewis was the only resident with sesame allergy. We currently have three residents with serious nut allergies and two who are allergic to shellfish. We have quite a few who are allergic to dairy or gluten; we regard those as less serious because they tend to cause tummy problems rather than anaphylactic shock, but we don't take any less care with them. Ideally we wouldn't use nuts at all but we have quite a few residents who are vegetarian or vegan and nuts are a useful source of protein for them. But we only prepare dishes with nuts in one part of the kitchen, which is deep cleaned afterwards. In my two years here we've never had anyone have an anaphylactic shock and my understanding is that it has been that way since the home opened.'

'You're clearly very knowledgeable about it.'

'Oh, it's a crucial part of any chef's job, but more so in a place like this. We're here to take care of our residents, not to cause them any distress.'

'I can see how conscientious you are.'

Kayla nodded enthusiastically. 'I am, I really am.'

'But is it possible that somebody brought something into the kitchen from outside, something that might have contained sesame seeds?'

Kayla shook her head. 'We don't allow in any outside food at all. No snacks, no packed lunches. If any of my team get hungry I'll make them something. I can assure you, I can swear on the Bible if necessary, that our food did not hurt Mrs Lewis in any way.'

'Thank you, Kayla. Thank you so much.'

Kayla reached out and touched Lulu gently on the arm. 'And again, I am so, so sorry for your loss.'

Lulu could feel tears welling up in her eyes; she blinked them away. 'Thank you. And thank you again for looking after Emily so well. I can see how much you cared about her.'

'I did. I really did.'

Kayla looked as if she wanted to say more, but she flashed a nervous smile and headed back to the door. Lulu sat down next to Conrad again. 'Are you okay?' he whispered.

Lulu wiped a tear away with the back of her hand. 'I'm fine.'

8

Lulu walked back to Maida Vale, carrying the box and with Conrad sitting on her shoulders. Yet again she was impressed at the way he managed to stay perfectly balanced. The box was surprisingly light, but then Emily hadn't taken much with her when she had moved into the home. She had always insisted that the stay was temporary and that she would be moving back to her own place eventually. Lulu and Simon had never contradicted her, and in a perfect world maybe one day she could have gone back to her own home; but the world wasn't perfect and the Alzheimer's would only ever get worse. 'Life isn't fair,' she muttered under her breath.

'I'm sorry, what?' murmured Conrad.

'Nothing,' said Lulu. 'I was just thinking out loud.' She crossed the road and walked down Warrington Crescent. The sun was shining and there were birds singing and a soft breeze blew from the south, ruffling her hair and Conrad's fur.

She reached the house. The main door was painted black with a doorbell to the left. To the right of the house were the stone steps that led down to the basement entrance. 'Downstairs,' said Lulu. 'The basement.' Conrad jumped off her shoulders onto the white balustrade and then onto the pavement. He headed down the steps, his tail held high. Lulu followed him, holding the box with her right hand and keeping the other on the metal handrail. There were a row of large potted plants at the bottom of the steps, and white-painted bars in front of the window.

Lulu set the box on the ground and took out her keys. She unlocked the door, picked up the box and went inside. Conrad followed her as she flicked on the lights. There was a hallway running the length of the flat with doors leading off to the right to a bedroom, a sitting room, and a door at the end that opened onto the kitchen. She took the box through to the kitchen and put it on a pine table.

Beyond the kitchen was a small conservatory with sliding doors that opened onto the garden. The conservatory was the place Emily loved most, especially in the evening when the sun went down. She would sit there with a book and a glass of sherry and read until dinner.

Lulu sat down at the table and opened the box. Conrad jumped up and peered inside. 'There isn't much,' he said.

'Most of what she took in with her were clothes and shoes,' said Lulu. There were six sheets of paper on the top and she took them out. They were printouts of the photographs that Ildi had taken. She must have put them on the wall as she'd promised, because there were blobs of Blu-Tack on the reverse sides. Lulu smiled at the photograph of Emily with Conrad on her lap. 'That is such a lovely picture,' she said.

'I do photograph well, don't I?' said Conrad. 'The trick is to turn my good side towards the camera.'

'You have a good side?' asked Lulu, looking at him.

'Everyone has a good side.'

'You look perfect from every angle.'

Conrad gently headbutted her. 'That's such a nice thing to say.'

'It's true.' She put the picture to the side and looked at the second one. 'Ah, that's nice. That's Louise, Louise Baxter, she's one of Emily's bridge-playing friends. They had to stop because Emily's memory made it impossible to play. Sometimes she couldn't even remember the last bid. Emily loved cards so she switched to playing patience.' Lulu peered at the date stamp in the corner of the photograph. 'Oh, we just missed her. Louise was there on Sunday, an hour or so after we left.'

She looked at the third photograph and raised her eyebrows. 'Oh, that's strange.'

'What is?' asked Conrad.

Lulu showed him the third photograph. An elegant woman in her seventies with sunglasses perched on top of her dyed blonde hair was standing next to Emily, her hand resting on Emily's shoulder. It was a stiff posture, like a Victorian married couple being forced to stare at a camera. 'This is Celia Christopherson. They used to be friends but they fell out years ago. I mean years and years ago. Back in the nineties. Emily was a member of the Conservative Association and Celia was a member of the Labour Party. There was some argument over election materials being defaced or something and they ended up not speaking. They would literally cross the road to avoid each other. I think at one point there were lawyers involved.' Her frown deepened. 'I wonder why she visited. They don't look too happy in the picture, do they?' She squinted at the date stamp. 'That was on Thursday. In the afternoon, just before I was there. I wonder why Emily didn't mention it?' She shrugged. 'But then again, she was forgetting a lot of things, wasn't she?'

She put the sheet down and took out the next one. She

frowned when she saw who it was – her brother-in-law and his wife standing either side of Emily, who was sitting in her chair. 'So Richard and Maria were there this week,' she said.

She showed the picture to Conrad, who sniffed it gingerly. 'Your brother-in-law and his wife?'

'Yes.' Lulu looked at the date. 'They were there at noon, on Friday.' She frowned. 'I was there in the morning. I left at about eleven-thirty. You would have thought they would have phoned if they were in the area.'

Conrad's eyes narrowed as he stared at the picture. 'She's very pretty, isn't she?'

'Yes, she is. Stunning. I think she used to work as a model.'

'Where is she from? She's not English, is she?'

'She's Spanish. They used to live in Spain. They had a bar that closed during the Covid pandemic but I thought they would stay there. Richard was always in Spain. And he was in the Philippines before that. And Bali before that. He always enjoyed the sun and the sea. Maria is his third wife. It's good that she stuck with him.'

'Why do you say that?'

Lulu put the sheet of paper down. 'Richard is a dreamer, he always has been. Like Simon, he went to university to study law, but he left after the first year because he wanted to travel and, as he said, broaden his horizons. He journeyed around India and then Asia, funded by his doting father. Richard would always be chasing one dream or another. He'd want to set up a beach bar or a diving school or run one of those boats where you tow someone on a parachute. He'd ask his father to lend him the money to fund his schemes, but they were never really loans. There was a terrible predictability to it all. He would start up a business, funded by his father. And often the business would do really well. Richard is a charmer and he tended to succeed in any business involving people. But once the business was up and running, he'd lose interest. That was usually when he'd get involved with a woman. Or more than one. He'd be off having fun while the business floundered and then without fail the girlfriend – or wife – would leave him. Then he'd go quiet for a while and then he'd reappear with another business idea and ask his father to back him. And when Frank passed away, it was Emily who funded his schemes.'

'Frank is Emily's husband?'

Lulu nodded. 'Yes, he passed away fifteen years ago.'

'And Emily and Frank didn't mind? About Richard?'

'It's the prodigal son thing, isn't it? Simon never asked for anything; he earned his own money and made his own way in the world. I could see that Frank and Emily were proud of Simon, of course – why wouldn't they be? He was a very successful barrister. But there was a sparkle in their eyes when they talked about Richard. He was rarely here, but in their house he was always the centre of attention.'

'I'm sorry,' said Conrad.

Lulu shook her head. 'It doesn't matter. Simon knew they loved him. It was just that Richard was the favoured one. Simon was fine about it. At the end of the day, Simon was the successful one.'

The fifth photograph was of a couple who used to play bridge with Emily: John Eastman, who'd had a distinguished army career before retiring to Maida Vale, and his wife, Margaret – Maggie – who as a former ballerina had once danced with Nureyev. They were a lovely couple and popped in to see Emily several times a week. The photograph had been taken on Friday at four-thirty.

Lulu didn't recognize the man in the final photograph. He was in his fifties, and like John Eastman had a military bearing, a ramrod-straight back and slight tilt to his head as he looked at the camera. He was wearing a herringbone suit and a waistcoat and had a neatly trimmed beard.

Conrad put his head on one side as he looked at the picture. 'Who's that?' he asked.

'I don't know,' said Lulu. 'I don't think I've ever seen him before.' The date stamp showed ten o'clock in the morning on Wednesday.

'Your mother-in-law is holding his hand.'

'Yes, I noticed that.'

She put the photograph on top of the rest, then reached inside the box. She began taking out the framed photographs. There were twelve, in all. The first two were of Emily and Frank – their wedding picture, and a picture of the two of them standing in front of the Taj Mahal, taken when they were on their honeymoon. There was a photograph of Richard and Simon in their school uniforms. Richard must have been twelve and Simon eight; just four years apart but physically they were very different. Richard was tall and was already starting to fill out, but Simon was still very much a child with thin, spindly legs and a nervous smile. She took out the framed photograph of her and Simon's wedding, then there were several more photographs of Emily and Frank: at the races, at the opera, on a cruise ship. Lulu couldn't help but notice how happy they were in all the photographs, always smiling and always holding each other.

The final framed photograph was of Richard and Maria,

the two of them sitting at a nightclub table with a bottle of Cristal champagne in an ice bucket on the table. They were both tanned and were beaming at the camera as they held their glasses aloft. 'Where was that taken?' asked Conrad.

'Puerto Banus, near Marbella,' said Lulu. 'That's where Richard had his last restaurant. They were making money hand over fist back then. They had oligarchs coming in and spending ten thousand pounds on a bottle of wine. Then Covid hit and they had to close. Richard was never one to save money so they went out of business pretty quickly. I think Richard hoped to persuade Emily to lend him more money but her Alzheimer's put paid to that.'

Conrad peered at the photograph. 'Maria seems quite young.'

Lulu laughed.

'How old is she?' asked Conrad.

'You know, I'm not really sure. I only met her the once.'

'You didn't go to their wedding?'

'We weren't invited. No one was – no one from England, anyway. To be fair, a big wedding was never Richard's style and usually we'd find out after the event. I met her for the first time at Simon's funeral.'

'She looks . . . hard.'

'Hard?'

'Her eyes.'

'That's just the picture, I think. She's really nice.' She picked up the printout of the photograph of Maria, Richard and Emily and looked at it closely. Maria was smiling at the camera, her chin up to tighten the skin on her neck, one leg slightly forward to make her look slimmer. 'I see what you mean about the eyes. But that's not how she looks in real life.'

'When you look at the pictures of Emily and Frank, or

of you and Simon, you can feel the love. You really can. The way you look at each other. But Maria, it's as if it's the camera she loves.' Conrad wrinkled his nose. 'Maybe I'm overthinking it.'

'Richard seems happy with her, and to be honest that's all that matters,' said Lulu. 'I think she's really good for him.' She put the printout back on the pile, then delved into the box and pulled out a ziplock plastic bag filled with toiletries, and another containing two hairbrushes, a comb and half a dozen clips. 'Why would they do that?' asked Lulu.

'Do what?' said Conrad.

'Send me her used toothpaste and hand cream and deodorant. That's just ridiculous. It's not as if I'm going to use it, is it?'

'I suppose they'd be worried that they'd be accused of theft,' said Conrad.

Lulu reached back into the box and took out a carriage clock that usually stood on Emily's bedside table. 'She loved this clock,' said Lulu, placing it next to the framed photographs.

She took out another ziplock plastic bag, this one containing Emily's medications, including painkillers, vitamins, antacid tablets and her blood pressure medicines. There were three EpiPen packs in another bag.

The next item was a small silver trinket box. Emily had kept it on the sideboard with the framed pictures, where it had contained some of her jewellery. Lulu opened it. There was a gold bracelet, two gold necklaces, the locket she wore around her neck, several pairs of earrings and her wedding ring, engagement ring and eternity ring. Lulu shuddered as she looked down at the rings. Emily would have been wearing them when she died and someone must have removed them. She took the locket from the box. It was exquisite, almost two hundred years old, solid gold with ornate engraving. Lulu clicked the catch at the side. Inside were two photographs, a teenage Richard on the left, Simon's graduation picture on the right.

'They look so handsome,' said Conrad, peering around her shoulder.

'Good genes,' said Lulu. 'Emily was quite beautiful when she was younger and Frank was a very good-looking man.' She closed the locket and put it back in the trinket box. Then she had second thoughts and put it around her neck.

The final items were books – the John Grisham novel Emily had been reading, a copy of a Richard Osman book that didn't appear to have been opened yet and a well-thumbed old Bible.

'Was she religious?' asked Conrad.

'Oh yes,' said Lulu. 'Before she went into the home, I used to take her to church every Sunday. St Saviour's, the one near the Colonnade Hotel.'

'Are you religious?'

'That's a tough question,' said Lulu.

'It isn't really,' said Conrad. 'Either you are or you aren't.'

'But it's not as simple as that.' Lulu held up the Bible. 'Do I believe everything written in this? No, of course not. I know the world wasn't built in seven days. And I know we aren't all descended from Adam and Eve. But do I believe in God? The logical part of me says no, how could I, when there is so much evil in the world? How could God allow children to suffer?' She shrugged. 'But then I walk into a church and I feel . . . safe. As if there's a greater power watching over me. When I was really grieving for Simon, when I couldn't eat or sleep or do anything, I'd go and sit in the church and I'd feel better. I just would. So . . . I don't know. I don't think I can answer the question. But I know that Emily believed in God, most definitely.' She put the Bible down and smiled at him. 'You do like having serious conversations, don't you?'

Conrad purred. 'I am a curious cat.'

'Well, you know what curiosity did to the cat, don't you?'

'That's a myth.'

'I do hope so.' Lulu sat back and looked up at the ceiling. 'I suppose I should check the house while I'm here,' she said.

'When was the last time you went inside?' asked Conrad.

'Two weeks ago,' said Lulu. She brushed her hair behind her ear. 'No, actually. Closer to three weeks.'

Conrad tilted his head to one side and looked at her. 'Are you okay?'

'Yes, of course. Conrad, I'm not scared of going inside, I just don't feel comfortable there, that's all.'

'I'll be with you.'

Lulu smiled. 'Yes, you will.'

She put the things back into the box, leaving the framed photographs on the side. Lulu let them out and they went up the stone steps to the pavement. 'Didn't your mother-in-law have trouble with these?' asked Conrad.

'No, she was absolutely fine. Physically she was as fit as the proverbial fiddle. We had to be careful on icy days but there's a handrail and she was strong. That was what made the Alzheimer's so much worse for us – she wasn't in the least bit frail physically.'

They reached the front door of the main building and Lulu took out her keys. There were two locks and she unlocked them in turn, then pushed open the door. The hallway led to the kitchen and for a crazy moment she imagined Simon standing by the sink, holding a coffee mug. She gasped and then felt her cheeks redden in embarrassment. Conrad walked in, his tail high, his whiskers twitching. He stopped and looked into the sitting room, with its overstuffed sofas and baby grand piano. 'Do you play?' he asked.

'I don't, but Emily does. Emily used to, I mean. That was one of the awful things about her illness. She was a concert pianist when she was in her twenties and then she became a music teacher and she did that until she was in her late seventies. But then bit by bit it went. All those pieces she'd spent a lifetime learning just evaporated, one by one. She stopped playing about five years ago. In a way it was better that we couldn't move it down to her flat because it would only remind her of what she'd lost.'

As she closed the door she saw the wire basket behind the letter box was pretty much full. She lifted the lid and took out the letters. Most were addressed to Simon.

She went down the hallway to the kitchen. 'Would you like a drink?'

'I would,' said Conrad, jumping up onto the island in the middle of the kitchen.

'Evian?'

'You spoil me.'

'Or, I tell you what I do have that you might like. It's a Welsh spring water. Tŷ Nant, it's called.' She opened the fridge, took a blue bottle out of the fridge and showed it to him. 'Simon loved it.'

'I'll give it a go,' said Conrad.

Lulu picked up a saucer off the draining board and put it on the island in front of him. She opened the bottle and poured water into the saucer. She stood and watched as Conrad delicately sniffed the water and then lapped at it. He raised his head and nodded. 'Nice,' he said. As he resumed lapping, Lulu put the bottle back in the fridge and switched on the kettle to make herself a cup of coffee. She sat down on one of the stools at the island.

'This is a nice house,' said Conrad, looking around.

'It's a lovely house,' said Lulu. 'But I always thought of it as a home rather than a house. Simon and Richard lived here as children. The family moved in during the sixties, when property was quite cheap here. Now it's worth a fortune. After Frank passed away we tried to get Emily to move to somewhere smaller but she wouldn't have it.' Her eyes widened in surprise. 'Oh, my goodness, I hadn't thought about that before but she is the exact opposite of me.' She forced a smile. 'I don't like the fact that everything in the house reminds me of Simon. But she loved that Frank's presence was here. She'd talk to him sometimes. Not when she thought we were in earshot, but you could tell she was having a conversation.' She grinned at Conrad. 'A bit like you and me, I suppose.'

'I'm real, Lulu. I'm here.'

'Yes, but you only ever talk to me when there's no one around. The point I'm making is that being in the house made her feel closer to Frank, but for me it just reminds me of what I've lost.' She felt tears welling up in her eyes and she tried to blink them away. The kettle switched itself off so she made herself a mug of Gold Blend, then sat down again and reached for the letters she had taken from the wire basket. Most of them were bills or flyers.

'You know what's missing, right? From her belongings?'

'No, what?' Lulu put down the letters.

'The chocolates.'

'The chocolates?'

'The box she had on her bedside table. You had one, remember? So did that Ildi lady.'

'Maybe Emily finished them.'

'No, she said she only had one, last thing at night.' Conrad stared at her, his tail twitching from side to side.

'Oh my goodness,' said Lulu. 'The chocolates. Maybe there was something wrong with the chocolates.'

'Do you think so?'

'It's possible. That would explain why Emily was fine when they checked on her. She might have eaten the chocolate afterwards, when she was alone in the room.' She put her hand over her mouth. 'That would be awful. Truly awful.' She frowned. 'I don't think they put sesame seeds in chocolates, do they?'

'We could ask,' said Conrad.

'Ask who?'

'The people who made the chocolates, of course. It isn't rocket science, Lulu.'

Lulu laughed. 'Right, fine. But the chocolates were hand-made, weren't they? And for the life of me I can't remember the name of the company that made them.'

Conrad's ears flicked forward. 'Isn't the box in the picture that Ildi took?'

'Of course, yes!' She took the printouts from her handbag and found the one of herself, Conrad and Emily. She squinted at it and tutted. 'The resolution isn't good enough.'

Conrad sighed. 'Your phone.'

'My phone?'

'Ildi sent you a copy, remember?'

Lulu put down the printout. 'How did you get so smart?'

Conrad shrugged. 'I eat a lot of fish. The Omega-3 in fish can boost your IQ by more than three points.'

'I didn't know that.' Lulu took her phone out of her handbag and scrolled through the photographs. She found the one that Ildi had sent her and expanded it so that she could get a better look at the box of chocolates on the bedside table. 'Bellissimo Chocolates of Covent Garden,' she said.

'I love Covent Garden,' said Conrad. 'The buskers are so much fun.'

'We can get there on the Tube.'

'That's how I usually get there.'

Lulu's jaw dropped. 'Are you serious? You travel on the Tube?'

'It's the law,' said Conrad. 'Cats and dogs are allowed, though they recommend that we're carried on the escalators.'

'You mean you travel alone on the Tube?'

'Sometimes. I don't have a ticket, obviously. But I can walk under the barrier and it's easy enough to get on and off the trains.'

Lulu shook her head in astonishment. 'I've never seen an unaccompanied cat on the Tube.'

'But you've seen pigeons, right?'

'Sure. Sometimes.'

'Well, a pigeon has a brain the size of a grape. Why are you so surprised that a cat, with a much superior intellect, would use public transport?'

Lulu realized she didn't have an answer for that.

9

They caught the Tube at Warwick Avenue and changed at Piccadilly Circus to catch a Piccadilly Line train to Covent Garden. Conrad rode on Lulu's shoulders all the way. Lulu was surprised at how quickly she had become used to carrying him around. She was barely aware of his weight and he seemed to be able to shift his position at will so that he was always perfectly balanced.

Most passengers who saw him were entranced and would smile and wave, but she did get a number of disapproving looks, probably from dog-lovers. She returned the smiles and ignored the glares.

As they walked out of the Tube station they heard a roar in the distance. Lulu walked down James Street and crossed over King Street to the main Covent Garden mall. A fire-eater in a top hat and tails was entertaining a large crowd in the main courtyard while a pretty girl in a basque corset and fishnet tights was collecting money in another top hat. From what Lulu could see, most of the people handing over money were men and they were more interested in watching the pretty girl than the fire-eater.

Lulu stopped and watched for a while. The performer switched to juggling, then to juggling on a unicycle. The pretty girl appeared in front of Lulu and Lulu dropped a few coins into the top hat. 'I love your cat!' said the girl.

'Meow!' said Conrad.

'OMG, he talks! How adorable.'

'Meow,' said Conrad.

'He's a regular chatterbox,' said Lulu.

The fire-eater was building to a climax, combining all three of his skills by juggling flaming axes while bobbing back and forth on his unicycle. Lulu walked across the Piazza to the Market Building. Bellissimo Chocolates was in the middle of a line of shops, between a cruelty-free make-up outlet and a shop selling designer silver jewellery.

As Lulu pushed open the door a small bell tinkled and a woman in a blue and white striped uniform with a straw boater on her head blocked her way. 'I'm sorry, animals aren't allowed inside,' said the woman. She had a badge on her shirt with her name: Chloe.

'Oh, he's a seeing-eye cat, I'm blind,' said Lulu, with as straight a face as she could manage. She heard a slight chuckle from Conrad.

Chloe's face creased into a frown and Lulu reached out and gently touched her on the arm. 'I'm sorry, my dear, just my little joke. Of course he can wait outside.'

'It's health and safety,' said Chloe, still confused. 'No animals allowed on the premises.'

'It's fine,' said Lulu. She crouched down and Conrad jumped down off her shoulders. Conrad looked around, his tail straight up in the air. He sniffed a couple of times and then walked, stiff-legged, out of the door.

'Won't he run away?' asked Chloe.

'No, he's very well behaved,' said Lulu.

Conrad snorted and sat down on the pavement.

'So how can I help you today?' asked Chloe.

'Actually, I just have a question,' said Lulu. 'About sesame seeds. Do you use them in your chocolates?'

'No, definitely not. Why, are you allergic?'

'No, but a friend of mine is. So you are quite sure?'

'One thousand per cent,' said Chloe. 'We are very careful about labelling anything that people might be allergic to. Everyone is, after that poor girl died from eating a sandwich with sesame seeds in the bread, do you remember? She bought a sandwich at an airport and then had a seizure on the plane.'

'Yes, I do remember that.'

'Is your friend allergic to anything else?' asked Chloe. 'The reason I ask is that half the people who are allergic to sesame seeds are also allergic to nuts. And a lot are allergic to dairy.'

'No, just sesame seeds.'

'Then you can give them anything in the shop. If your friend was allergic to dairy then I would recommend anything from our vegan range. So far as nuts go, we do special batches that are guaranteed nut-free. Cross-contamination is always an issue so our chefs do a deep clean before each batch.'

'You sound very thorough.'

'We are.' She flashed a wide smile. 'So, what can I get you?'

Lulu really didn't want any chocolates but Chloe had been so helpful that it would have been churlish to have left the shop without buying something. She looked over at the trays of chocolates and the silver and gold packages, tied up with red and blue bows. 'How does it work?' she asked.

'You can buy one of our pre-boxed selections, or you can choose what you want to go into a box of six, a dozen or two dozen.'

'I'll just take a box of six, please.'

Chloe bent down, took one of the small boxes and put it into a very pretty bag. Lulu held up her bank card. 'Contactless?'

'Perfect.'

Lulu tapped her card on the reader and Chloe took the receipt, slipped it into the bag and handed it to her. Lulu went outside. 'I bought chocolates,' she said to Conrad, showing him the bag.

'Meow,' he said.

She bent down and he jumped gracefully up onto her shoulders. He was purring contentedly as she walked back to the Tube station. The fire-eater had been replaced by a spindly ginger-haired man with ornate sleeve tattoos who was balancing on a slack rope some six feet above the piazza cobbles. 'I can do that,' Conrad whispered into her ear.

'I'm sure you can,' said Lulu.

10

Lulu poured boiling water on the sprigs of mint and sniffed the aroma. 'That smells so good,' said Conrad. He was sitting on the sofa watching her. They had walked to *The Lark* from Warwick Avenue Tube station.

'Do you want to try some? I could cool it down for you.'

'Unfortunately, mint is toxic to cats. I do like the aroma but the essential oils would play havoc with my digestive system.'

Lulu sat down on the sofa and placed her cup on the shelf next to her. She picked up the box of Bellissimo chocolates and nodded as she looked at it. 'It's beautifully presented, isn't it?'

'A work of art,' said Conrad, wrinkling his nose. 'But I have to say, I'm not a fan.'

'Oh, I love chocolate,' said Lulu, as she placed the box on her lap and undid the bow.

'You know that chocolate is toxic to cats, right? Worse than mint.'

'I didn't know that. I'm sorry.' She stopped undoing the bow. 'I knew that chocolate was bad for dogs, but I hadn't heard about it being a problem for cats.'

Conrad nodded. 'It's the same. Chocolate contains caffeine and theobromine. It can mess up your heart rhythm and cause tremors and seizures. So I'll pass.'

'Well, obviously you'll pass,' said Lulu. 'That's just awful.'

She finished untying the box, then lifted the lid. There were three milk chocolates and three dark. Each was a different design. There was a small card in the lid of the box with a map showing the six sections and identifying the chocolates. She picked up the card. 'Strawberry Fondant, Coffee Cream, Salted Caramel Crunch, Apple Fudge, Orange Delight, Mint Surprise.'

'The surprise being you throw up and die,' said Conrad. He pretended to vomit onto the sofa.

Lulu's jaw dropped. 'Conrad, that's a terrible thing to say!'

Conrad's ears pricked up, then he wrinkled his nose. 'I'm sorry, I was joking, about cats. I didn't mean your mother-in-law.' He stood up and lowered his head. 'I'm sorry. That was a stupid thing to say.' She reached out and stroked him behind the ears. He began to purr softly. 'Sorry,' he said again.

'It's okay, I guess I overreacted. And cat-wise it was funny.'

'I'll think before I speak, next time.'

'No, I don't want that. You made a joke and I took it the wrong way, it was my fault, not yours.' She held up the box of chocolates. 'The girl in the shop was quite definite that they don't use sesame seeds, and that's the only thing that Emily was allergic to.' She picked up the Strawberry Fondant, sniffed it, and popped it into her mouth. She bit into it and immediately she tasted fresh strawberries and rich cream mixing with the flavour of the milk chocolate. She sighed contentedly.

'Good?' asked Conrad.

Lulu nodded enthusiastically. She chewed and swallowed and sighed again. 'Oh my God, that was so good.' She put the box on the shelf next to her tea. 'I'm going to have to ration myself or I'll wolf them all down.'

'Wolves are greedy eaters, it's true,' said Conrad.

Lulu looked over at the box of chocolates. 'Just one more won't hurt,' she whispered to herself. She reached for the box and helped herself to the Orange Delight. If anything, it was even more delicious than the first one. She closed her eyes and concentrated on the explosion of flavours in her mouth.

She felt Conrad jump onto the sofa next to her. 'You look so happy,' he said.

She opened her eyes and smiled. 'Oh, I am.'

He sat down and looked up at her with his big green eyes. 'Your aura is just amazing. So vibrant.'

'Chocolate will do that to a girl,' Lulu said. She put the box back on the shelf.

'So the chocolates couldn't have killed your mother-in-law,' said Conrad. 'Not if they were as sold at the shop.'

'Exactly.'

Conrad wrinkled his nose. 'Are you thinking that somebody tampered with them?'

Lulu frowned. 'No, I wasn't thinking that at all. But I am now.' She put her hand over her mouth. 'Oh my goodness, so are you saying that perhaps it wasn't an accident?'

'I'm just asking the question,' said Conrad. 'Your mother-in-law knew she had a sesame seed allergy. So did the home. We know there were no sesame seeds in the chocolates and the people at the home say that they always took care not to give her anything that might have sesame seeds in it.'

'So it could have been an accident? Somehow sesame seeds got into her food or the chocolates?'

Conrad scratched his right ear with his rear foot.

'So do you think it was an accident, or not?' said Lulu.

Conrad stopped scratching. 'Accidents happen, of course they do. It might have been an accident. Or it might have been something else.'

'That means you think that someone might have wanted to kill Emily?'

'I think that might be a possibility, yes. And I think you think the same. You just don't want to admit it.'

Lulu threw up her hands. 'But it wouldn't make any sense. Emily was almost ninety years old and everyone loved her. She didn't have an enemy in the world.'

'You said that she had fallen out with that woman in the photograph. The lady with the sunglasses.'

'Celia Christopherson? Well, yes, they didn't get on but that had been going on for almost thirty years. And I really don't see Celia doing anything like that. I mean . . .' She shook her head. 'Impossible.'

'So why did she suddenly decide to visit Emily?'

'That is a very good question.'

'Is it one you can answer?'

Lulu smiled. 'You are persistent, aren't you?'

'I don't like mysteries,' said Conrad. 'At least, I don't like mysteries I don't know the answer to. Where does Celia live?'

'Elgin Mews. Just around the corner from Maida Vale Tube station.'

Conrad looked at her and twitched his nose.

'You think we should go and talk to her?' asked Lulu.

'I think you should talk and I should just listen,' said Conrad.

'Ah, yes, probably best.' She picked up her glass of mint tea and sipped it.

'Is Celia the only person that Emily had a problem with?'

Lulu wrinkled her nose as she thought about the question, then she nodded. 'Yes. I think so. I mean, no one had a bad word to say about her. She helped run the local Conservative Association for years. She worked part-time in the Oxfam shop in Edgware Road and she always helped out with the St Saviour's fundraising. Everyone in Maida Vale knew her. She couldn't walk down the road without someone stopping her to say hello.'

'Okay,' said Conrad.

'I certainly can't think of anyone who would want to kill a ninety-year-old woman.'

'I only met her once. And yes, she seemed like a nice person. She had a lovely aura. I could see she was kind and empathetic and loving. I suppose there are always crazy people around, wherever you go, even in Maida Vale.'

'So now you think she was killed by a crazy person?' said Lulu.

'Maybe. I'm just considering all the options. Maybe someone who worked for the home did something. There have been lots of cases of nurses and doctors killing their patients.' Conrad scratched behind his ear again. 'And she did have a lot of visitors.'

'She did,' said Lulu. 'Two, sometimes three or four a day. I used to go most days. And several of her friends would pop in once a week. You saw what she was like, you couldn't do much more than sit and keep her company, but at times she was quite lucid and she'd tell me stories about when she was a child. It was funny, she often couldn't remember what she'd eaten for breakfast but she could recall something that happened when she was eight years old and she'd tell me every single detail.' She sighed. 'I can't believe she's dead.'

She sat in silence while Conrad groomed himself, licking his left rear leg with his rough tongue. She finished her mint tea, rinsed her glass in the sink and put it on the draining board, then turned to look at Conrad. 'Right, let's go.'

11

Elgin Mews was a short cobbled street running parallel to Elgin Avenue. It took just over six minutes to walk there, which made the feud between Emily and Celia seem all the more ridiculous. Celia Christopherson lived in a white Victorian house halfway along the mews. There was a white door with a brass letterbox and to the left a garage door which was just about wide enough for Celia's zebra-pattern Smart car. They could see the car parked outside the house when they walked into the mews from Randolph Avenue. 'Stylish,' said Conrad, who was sitting comfortably across Lulu's shoulders. 'Does she have a husband?'

'She did. Alfie. He died a few years ago. I didn't hear until afterwards or else I would probably have gone to the funeral.'

'Did she go to Simon's funeral?'

'No.' She forced a smile. 'Whatever her problem with Emily was, we were included.' She rang the bell and they heard a buzzing in the distance. They waited and Lulu was just about to press the doorbell again when the door opened. A brass security chain snapped into place and Celia peered through the gap. Her eyes widened when she saw Lulu. 'Oh my goodness,' she gasped. 'Lulu.'

'Hello Celia. So sorry to drop by unannounced.'

'No, no, don't be silly. I'm so happy to see you. Let me just get this chain thing off.' She closed the door and after a few seconds opened it wide. She was wearing skinny jeans and a white linen shirt and her skin was so tight across her cheekbones that Lulu immediately suspected surgery or Botox. Celia's blue eyes were sparkling and the Chanel sunglasses pushed back on her dyed blonde hair were clearly just for decoration. 'What a lovely surprise, come in, come in.' Her jaw dropped as she saw the cat around Lulu's neck. 'Oh how lovely? Did you train him to do that?'

'He trained me, actually,' said Lulu.

Celia stepped to the side and ushered Lulu into the narrow hallway. 'Come into the kitchen, I've just made some tea.' She closed the front door and followed Lulu into the kitchen. It was all gleaming marble and shiny stainless steel.

'It's a bit like the Tardis, isn't it?' said Lulu, looking around. 'It looks so much bigger inside.'

'They made good use of the space,' agreed Celia. She took a cup and saucer from a cupboard and poured milk and tea for Lulu, then waved for her to sit at a table by the window. 'So, what brings you to my humble abode? Did Emily tell you I had been to visit?'

Conrad jumped off Lulu's shoulder and sat down next to her chair. Celia looked over at Lulu when she didn't answer. Lulu grimaced. 'Oh I'm so sorry, you haven't heard. Emily passed away last night.'

'Oh my God, no.' Celia put a hand up to her mouth. 'Oh, that's awful.' She frowned. 'She looked fine when I saw her. Apart from the Alzheimer's, obviously. But she seemed healthy enough.' Her frown deepened. 'That sounds illogical, doesn't it?'

'No, it's exactly what I said to the doctor in the home. He said that he had put Alzheimer's as the cause of death on the death certificate and I said that Alzheimer's didn't actually kill people. I think at the end of the day my lack of a medical degree counted against me.'

'No, you're absolutely right. It's like Covid. It didn't matter if you had a stroke or a heart attack or got hit by a bus, if you had tested positive for the virus then it was recorded as a Covid death.' Celia folded her arms. 'Lulu, I'm so sorry for your loss. I know how close you were. She was like a mother to you.'

'Thank you.'

Celia shook her head. 'I can't believe she's gone. I mean, I could see how forgetful she had become – she clearly didn't know who I was – but she was sitting in her chair and when I left the nurse said they were going for a walk in the garden.'

'Celia, if you don't mind me asking, why did you suddenly decide to visit Emily? I know you two had been avoiding each other for years.'

Celia carried two cups of tea over to the table and sat down. 'It was a spur of the moment thing. A friend told me that Emily had gone into a home and I just thought . . .' She shrugged. 'Bygones be bygones, you know? Life's too short. I just wanted to make things right.' She held out her cup and Lulu clinked hers against it. 'To Emily,' she said.

'To Emily,' repeated Lulu.

They both sipped their tea.

'I don't know what I expected, really,' said Celia. 'I just wanted to clear the air, I suppose. There's no point in hanging on to bitterness as you get to the end of your life.'

'That's so true,' said Lulu. 'Did you take her a peace offering?'

Celia frowned. 'A peace offering?' she repeated.

'A gift. A present.'

Celia shook her head, still confused. 'No, I suppose I should have done. Flowers maybe.'

'Or chocolates?'

Celia grinned. 'Knowing Emily, I think she'd have preferred a bottle of Pinot Grigio.'

'Definitely,' said Lulu. 'Why did you and Emily fall out? It seems so silly, you two living so close together.'

'What did Emily say to you?'

'She said it happened when you were canvassing. Something about election material being defaced.'

'Oh my Lord, is that what she told you?' She laughed, and it was the harsh sound of glass breaking. 'That is so funny.'

'That wasn't it?'

Celia shook her head. 'No, my dear, that most definitely wasn't it.'

'So what then?'

Celia's eyes narrowed and her smile hardened. 'I'm not sure that I should tell you,' she said. 'Some dogs are best left sleeping.'

'Emily isn't here any more, Celia. And I really would like to know.'

Celia sipped her tea and watched Lulu carefully over the top of her cup. When she eventually spoke, her voice was almost a whisper. 'Lulu, my dear, some things are better not said. Ignorance truly can be bliss.'

'Was this secret, whatever it is, was it the reason you went to see Emily?'

'I wanted to make peace, yes. I wanted to put an end to the bitterness. Life is too short, isn't it?'

'Yes,' said Lulu. 'It most definitely is. And did you make peace with Emily?'

Celia forced a smile. 'I said what I had to say, and she listened, but I really don't think she knew who I was. At one point she thought I was Louise. And several times she called me by your name. I hadn't realized how far gone she was.'

'She had good days and bad days.'

'Well, when I went it was most definitely a bad day.'

'What exactly did you talk about?'

'You're asking an awful lot of questions, Lulu.'

Lulu laughed. 'I'm sorry. I was a detective for so long that it became a habit I can't break. And I hate mysteries.'

'You really won't give up until I've told you everything, will you?'

'Probably not.' She shrugged. 'That's probably why I was such a good detective.'

Celia sipped her tea and again she watched Lulu carefully over the top of her cup. 'I'm not surprised that Emily never told you what happened all those years ago,' she said. 'Sweet Emily, butter-wouldn't-melt-in-her-mouth Emily, Emily the wonderful.' There was a bitter note in her voice now.

Lulu looked down but didn't say anything.

'What you don't know, what she obviously didn't tell you, is that darling Emily had an affair with my husband. An affair that took place over almost six months. An affair that only ended when I caught her in bed with my husband. In my bed. In my house.'

Lulu's mouth fell open in astonishment. She looked over at Conrad and he seemed equally surprised.

Celia emitted the harsh laugh again. 'The look on your face,' she said. 'You're never going to think of her the same way again, are you? That's why sometimes it's best to let sleeping dogs lie.'

'When was this?' asked Lulu.

'When I found them? The third of November 1997. At three o'clock in the afternoon. When did it start? The second of May 1997. The day that Tony Blair was elected prime minister. I often wonder if that was why Emily did it, as some sort of perverse revenge for the Conservatives losing. She campaigned so hard for John Major, even though she was never really a fan.'

'How do you know when it started?' asked Lulu.

'Alfie told me everything,' she said. 'I made that a condition of my not divorcing him. He said that he loved me and didn't want to lose me so I made him tell me everything. And I made him dispose of the bed. And sell the house.' She flashed Lulu a tight smile. 'I made him accept the first cash offer we had. Ended up selling it for ten per cent less than the market price, but I didn't care. That's when we moved here. I didn't want to sleep in the place where he'd been unfaithful.'

'I'm sorry, Celia. I had no idea.'

'Nobody did,' said Celia. 'Oh, I thought of telling Frank and making him feel as bad as I did, but what would have been the point? And anyway, how stupid would I have looked? It was best just to cut all ties. Which is what I did.' She picked up her cup again and took another sip of tea. This time her hand was shaking. When she replaced the cup on its saucer, she flashed Lulu an uncomfortable smile. 'Part of me wanted to leave Maida Vale, but why should I? I've spent my whole life here. I wasn't going to let Emily run me out of town, as if I was in the wrong. So I just ignored her. It was as if she no longer existed. I'd see Frank around and if he was on his own I'd maybe say a few words, but generally I just avoided them.'

'And Frank never knew what happened?'

'I didn't tell him. I've no idea if Emily ever did. I suspect not.' Her eyes were hard. 'She slept with Alfie in their house, too. Many times. And they went to stay at a hotel in Brighton. Alfie told me it was for work. I don't know what she said to Frank.' She shrugged. 'I tried not to think about it too much.'

'So why did you go to see Emily now, after all these years?'

Celia lowered her eyes and shifted uncomfortably in her chair. 'I suppose I wanted to clear the air.'

'After almost thirty years?'

Celia met Lulu's gaze. Her eyes were brimming with tears. 'I heard that she was in the home, and that she wasn't getting any better. I suppose I wanted to end the bitterness. We could never put things right, obviously, but when you reach the end of your life, it makes no sense to be bearing grudges. Alfie has been dead for going on eight years, Frank passed away ages ago. We didn't go to the funeral, I didn't want to see Alfie with Emily, but with Alfie gone and Emily in the home, it just seemed time.' She shook her head. 'Of course, as it turned out I needn't have bothered. She didn't know who I was. As I said, she called me by your name, and she asked me when Simon was coming.'

'She didn't remember you at all?'

Celia shook her head. 'That nurse, the Hungarian one, took a picture and said she'd put it up on the wall and that sometimes that helped spark a memory, but I didn't plan on going back. It's immaterial now, of course. Now that she's dead. But at least I was able to tell her that I had forgiven her.' She forced another smile. 'Not that she knew what I was forgiving her for.'

'You did the right thing, Celia.'

'Thank you.'

'And even though her Alzheimer's was getting worse, she would have known that you were with her and that you cared about her.'

'I hope so.' Celia drained her cup and refilled it from the teapot.

'I still can't believe she's gone,' said Lulu. 'I was with her yesterday. She was forgetful but she was in good spirits. She gave me one of her chocolates.'

'Chocolates?'

'She had this box of handmade chocolates. Delicious. Did she offer you one?'

Celia frowned. 'I didn't see any chocolates.' She sipped her tea, pulled a face, and added some more milk. 'I do wish that I'd taken some wine in, though. Had a last drink with her.'

'Me too,' said Lulu. 'You never know, do you? When you're seeing someone for the last time.' She grimaced. 'It makes you realize just how precious life is. How fragile.'

'It does,' said Celia. 'It really does.' She raised her cup. 'To Emily. One of a kind.'

Lulu clinked her cup against Celia's. 'One of a kind,' she said.

12

Lulu stepped out into the street, with Conrad wrapped around her neck. Celia blew her a kiss and closed the door. 'She isn't well,' said Conrad as Lulu began to walk along the mews.

'She looked all right to me. In fact she looked really good.'

'No. There's a lot of blood red in her aura, and it's tinged with black.'

'That's not good.'

'No. It's bad.'

'So she's dying?'

Conrad nodded. 'I'm afraid so.'

'How long?'

'It's difficult to say. It's not an exact science. But weeks rather than months. Cancer, I think.'

Lulu sighed. 'So that's why she wanted to see Emily. It was nothing to do with Emily being in the home.'

Conrad nodded. 'I think so.'

'That's a bit sad, isn't it?'

'The sad thing is that Emily didn't really remember her. But I guess it made Celia feel a bit better.'

'Yes, you're right,' said Lulu. 'But we know for certain that Celia didn't want to hurt Emily. You saw how upset she was when we told her that Emily passed away.'

'You told her,' said Conrad. 'I didn't say anything, remember?'

'That's right. My silent partner.'

'But I take your point. She was very upset when she heard what had happened. And she didn't see the chocolates, did she?'

'That's right,' said Lulu. 'Where did the box of chocolates go?' she said quietly. 'And who gave them to Emily in the first place?'

'Two very good questions.'

'And do you perchance have any answers?'

'Sadly, no. But if somebody did use the chocolates to kill your mother-in-law, then it was probably them who took the box away.'

'Is that what you think happened? Really?'

'I think it's suspicious that the chocolates weren't among her belongings. I mean, they gave you back her used tooth-paste and hand cream and medicines – why wouldn't they give you back the chocolates? She can't have eaten them all; she said she only had one before she went to sleep. She can't have given them all away, surely?'

'I don't know. She did have a lot of visitors.'

'Not that many. And it's not as if anyone would take a handful, is it?'

'So you think that someone took them to get rid of the evidence?'

'Exactly,' said Conrad.

They reached the entrance to the mews and Lulu headed down Randolph Avenue towards the Warrington. 'So, some-body who wanted to kill Emily bought the chocolates and, what, pushed sesame seeds into them?' she said.

'Sesame oil,' said Conrad. 'They make oil from the seeds. You can buy it everywhere.'

'Oh my Lord. So you could just inject it into the chocolate with a syringe?'

'I think so. You wouldn't notice the taste.'

'When we were in Emily's room, I ate one, remember? And so did the nurse. Do you think they had the sesame oil in them?'

'If they had only added the oil to one, there'd be no need to take the box away,' said Conrad. 'So they must have done more than one. But probably only on the bottom layer.'

'Why do you say that?'

'Because it would be suspicious if Emily had died immediately after having been given the chocolates. But if the sesame seeds or oil had only been put into the chocolates on the bottom, there'd be a delay. And Emily would already have eaten several before she reached the dangerous ones.'

Lulu looked at Conrad. 'You know, I'm really starting to believe that this might have happened. But even if we know the "how", we're no closer to knowing who did it and why.'

'Well, so far as the "who" goes, it has to be either someone who works at the home, or someone who visited. We know it wasn't Celia.'

Lulu ran her hand through her hair. 'We should go back to the house and take a closer look at the photographs that Ildi took.'

'That sounds like a good idea,' said Conrad.

'I do have them on occasion,' said Lulu. She walked by the Warrington, and received several smiles on the way. Maida Vale was always a friendly place, more of a village than a part of London, but there was no doubt that having a cat on her shoulders got passers-by smiling more than usual. It was a warm day with just a few wisps of cloud overhead.

There were dozens of people sitting on the trestle tables outside the pub, drinking beer and wine and enjoying the sun.

They reached the house and Conrad jumped down from her shoulders and landed with a soft thud. 'Does that ever hurt?' asked Lulu.

'Of course not,' said Conrad. 'I have cat-like reflexes.'

Lulu laughed. 'Of course you do.'

Conrad looked up at her, his tail twitching from side to side. 'It's all in the elbows and knees.'

'I shall remember that.' She frowned. 'Do cats have elbows?'

'Of course. On our front legs.'

'I would have thought you'd have four knees.'

'You're getting cats confused with elephants.'

'Am I now?'

'It's a common mistake, so I won't hold it against you,' said Conrad. He padded down the stone steps.

Lulu followed him, chuckling, and unlocked the door to the basement flat. Conrad padded along the hallway to the kitchen while Lulu closed the door. By the time she reached the kitchen, Conrad was on the table sniffing at the cardboard box.

Lulu took out the photographs and spread them across the table. She checked the date stamps on each one, and then arranged them in order, first on the left, last on the right.

The first was of the man that Lulu didn't recognize. According to the date stamp, he was there the day before Celia and she hadn't seen the chocolates. If that was true, then he hadn't brought the chocolates, and Celia had said she hadn't either.

'Do you think that Celia was telling the truth?' asked Conrad.

'That's just what I was thinking,' said Lulu.

'I know. You were staring at her picture and frowning. I put two and two together. It's not difficult to guess what's going through your mind.'

Lulu smiled and shook her head. 'You are so darn smart.'

'Why, thank you.'

'And yes, that's exactly what I was thinking. If Celia had taken the chocolates and she had done something to them, she'd hardly be likely to admit to it. But in that case, she probably wouldn't have said anything about the affair, because that gives her a motive. But if the guy in the first picture, whoever he is, had brought them, she'd have said as much.'

'And it was Richard and Maria who visited after Celia?'

'Yes. Followed by John and Maggie Eastman.' She peered closely at the photograph of Richard and Maria with Emily. All three were looking at the camera. Richard and Maria were smiling but Emily seemed confused. Most of the bedside table was visible, though Richard was partly blocking the view of it. There was no sign of the box of chocolates, but it was possible that it was behind Richard. She looked at the next photograph. Emily was smiling broadly, and Maggie Eastman was looking at her with obvious affection. John Eastman was standing next to his wife and had his hand around her waist. Lulu held the picture closer to her face. The box of chocolates was on the bedside table. 'There it is,' she said, pointing.

Conrad moved closer to get a better look. 'So, we know that either the Eastmans or your brother-in-law brought them,' he said.

'Well, yes, either that or Celia lied and she gave them to Emily.'

'It didn't look as if she was lying,' said Conrad.

'Can you always tell if someone isn't telling the truth?'

'Oftentimes.'

'Good to know.'

'Can you call your brother-in-law?'

'I can, but it's going to be a strange phone call, isn't it? Calling out of the blue to ask about a box of chocolates. If they did do something to the chocolates, they'll know we suspect them. I think it's better that we pay a visit to the Eastmans. They're local.'

'Can I ride on your shoulders?'

'Of course you can.'

13

John and Maggie Eastman lived in a redbrick house in Ashworth Road, a short walk from the top of Warrington Crescent. Lulu had been there many times over the years. The house had a wonderful secluded garden behind it and the Eastmans regularly made it available for fundraising events for the local church, school and Conservative Association.

Five minutes after leaving Emily's basement flat, Lulu was ringing the Eastmans' doorbell. Maggie opened the door and her face broke into a smile when she saw Lulu. 'Oh my goodness, hello, wow, this is a surprise.' Then her eyes widened when she saw Conrad. 'Is that a cat? What a stupid question. Of course it is.'

'His name is Conrad, he's my new companion. I'm so sorry to drop by unannounced, but I don't have your phone number.'

'No, don't be silly, it's lovely to see you. Come on in. I've just made coffee.'

Conrad jumped down and landed gently on the carpet, then walked along the hallway with his tail in the air as if he owned the house. Lulu followed him. The wall to the left was filled with family photographs of the Eastmans, their three children and ten grandchildren. They had two sons and a daughter. The daughter, Paige, and one of the sons, Ralph, had followed their father into the military, and there were several photographs of them in the desert, dressed in fatigues and carrying big guns. The other son was a doctor, working in the States. Maggie ushered Lulu into the sitting room, where John was sitting in a comfortable winged armchair in front of a large cafetiere and two cups and saucers. 'Isn't this a nice surprise?' said Maggie.

'Oh crikey, yes,' said John, getting to his feet. 'Lulu, how wonderful.'

Conrad slipped into the room between Lulu's legs. 'I say, is that a cat?' said John.

'Obviously nothing wrong with your eyes, dear,' said Maggie archly.

Conrad walked into the room and looked around, his tail still high.

'Well, he's a fine fellow, isn't he?' said John.

'He seems to have adopted me,' said Lulu, smiling down at Conrad. 'And yes, he is a fine fellow.'

'I'll get another cup,' said Maggie and she headed to the kitchen.

John air-kissed Lulu on both cheeks and waved her to the flower-print sofa. It was a comfortable room with old oak bookcases filled with Maggie's favourite romance novels and John's thrillers and books on military history. John was an avid Dick Francis fan and had hardbacks of all his racing novels, many of them first editions. On one of the bookshelves stood their collection of bridge trophies, and his medals were on display on another.

'So how is Emily?' asked John as he sat down. His jaw tightened when he saw the look that flashed across Lulu's face. 'Oh God, no,' he whispered.

'I'm sorry,' said Lulu quietly. 'Can we wait until Maggie

gets back?' Conrad jumped smoothly onto the sofa and curled up next to Lulu.

John nodded. 'Of course.' He folded his arms and forced a smile.

Maggie returned with a cup and saucer which she placed on the low oval table in front of Lulu. She immediately sensed that something was wrong. 'What's happened?' she asked.

'I'm so sorry to have to tell you, but Emily passed away last night.'

Maggie put a hand on her chest and gasped. 'Oh, no.' She sat down on the sofa next to Lulu and looked over at John. 'Oh, no.'

He nodded. 'Sad news.'

Maggie looked back at Lulu, then reached out and took her hands. 'I'm so sorry, Lulu. She was a lovely lady. We'll miss her.'

'Thank you.'

'This is all so sudden. We saw her last week.'

'Yes, I know.'

'And she seemed healthy enough then,' said Maggie. She turned to look at her husband. 'Didn't she?'

'Right as rain,' said John. 'Her memory is getting worse. Was getting worse, I mean. But otherwise she was good to go.' He looked at Lulu. 'We even went for a walk. No mobility problems.'

'I know, I saw her yesterday and she was stroking Conrad and reliving old times.'

'It's funny how that works, isn't it?' said Maggie. 'She was telling us about things that happened just after the war and then she'd get John confused with Richard. Then she'd ask where Simon was and when we told her that Simon had passed away she said that we were wrong and that he'd been to see her. She wouldn't hear otherwise and she started to get upset so I dropped it.'

'She did get so confused,' said Lulu.

'But only about recent events,' said John. 'So far as her childhood was concerned, she was as sharp as a tack.'

'So what happened?' asked Maggie. 'It must have been sudden.'

'The doctor says it was Alzheimer's, at least that's what he put on the death certificate. But obviously it must have been something else, because you don't die of forgetfulness, do you?'

'Well, you might if you forgot to look both ways before you crossed a busy road,' said John.

'Johnnie!' said Maggie. 'What a terrible thing to say!'

'Why? Emily didn't get run over, did she, bless her?'

'No, she didn't,' said Lulu. 'They say it was dementia.'

'Well there you are then,' John said to his wife. 'I was just stating a fact.'

'Johnnie, that's how Simon, died, remember? The hit and run?'

The colour drained from John's face. 'Oh my God, I'm such an idiot.' He put his hand over his mouth. 'How bloody stupid of me. Lulu, that's not what I meant, obviously. Please forgive me.'

'It was a slip of the tongue, it's fine,' said Lulu. 'Don't even think about it.'

'I apologize for my husband,' said Maggie. She smiled at Lulu and squeezed her hands. 'We are so, so sorry for your loss, Lulu. Emily was a lovely lady and she had a wonderful, charmed life. She brought joy to so many people, she really did make a difference. And she will be sorely missed.'

'It's so sweet of you to say that,' said Lulu.

'It's the truth, and we all know it,' said Maggie. 'Emily would always go out of her way to help people, with her advice, with her time, and if necessary with her chequebook. She was a true humanitarian.'

'She was,' said Lulu.

Maggie looked over at her husband again. 'I really can't believe it.'

'It's a shock,' said John.

'Well, as I said I saw her the day before she passed away and I had no inkling that she was that ill,' said Lulu. 'She gave me one of her chocolates. She was really enjoying them. Did she offer you one?'

'She did,' said John. 'I couldn't, my diabetes is playing up again, but Maggie had one.'

'It was delicious,' said Maggie. 'Handmade. From that wonderful shop in Covent Garden.'

'Yes, Bellissimo Chocolates.'

'That's right, I was trying to remember the name.'

'I had one and loved it so much that I went and bought a box,' said Lulu. 'You don't happen to know who bought them for Emily, do you?'

'No, she didn't say. But Jenny had just been to see her. Maybe she dropped them off.'

'Jenny?'

'Jenny Tyler.'

Lulu frowned. Jenny Tyler had been one of Emily's oldest friends; they had been at primary school together, so had known each other for more than eighty years. But her picture hadn't been in the box.

'Something wrong?' asked John.

'No, no. I just haven't seen Jenny for a few weeks. How is she?'

'She seems fine. We passed her in reception, you know Jenny, busy-busy-busy. You'd never guess she was almost in her nineties. I don't know where she gets her energy from.'

Lulu sipped her coffee. If Jenny had visited without her photograph being taken, there could have been others. That meant she had no way of knowing exactly who had been in to see Emily. Unless she could take a look at the nursing home's visitors' book, of course.

'So, Lulu, what about the funeral?' asked Maggie. 'When will it be? We'll both be there, obviously.'

Lulu put down her cup. 'You know, I haven't been involved in the arrangements. It's being handled by Richard.'

'She'll be buried alongside Frank, of course,' said John.

'Oh yes,' said Lulu. 'No question. I'll find out and let you know the details.'

'I thought Richard was in Spain with wife number three,' said John. 'Or is it four? I tend to lose count.'

'He's back in England now.'

'Another business failure?' asked John.

'I'm afraid so.'

'That man has the opposite of a Midas touch, doesn't he? Everything he touches turns to . . .'

'John!' said Maggie sternly

'I was going to say stone,' said John. 'The opposite of gold, anyway. He always manages to snatch defeat from the jaws of victory, that one.'

'They came back from Spain and are in Beckenham now.'

'And the latest wife is Spanish?' asked John.

Lulu nodded. 'Maria. She's quite nice.'

'Younger than him?' asked John.

'A bit.'

John laughed. 'He has a type, doesn't he?'

Lulu nodded. 'But Maria seems to be sticking with him through thick and thin.'

'Why is he handling the funeral arrangements?' asked Maggie. 'Surely you should be doing that.'

'Man couldn't organize a piss-up in a brewery,' muttered John, but fell silent when his wife flashed him a warning stare.

'He was down as Emily's next of kin, which of course he is, or was, so the home called him and he made the arrangements.'

'Do let us know,' said Maggie. She sighed. 'I can't believe it,' she said. 'It's so sudden.'

'It was a shock to me, too,' said Lulu. 'I was with her yesterday afternoon and she was sitting in her chair and reminiscing about Jeffrey Archer's champagne and shepherd's pie.'

'Oh yes, we've heard that story so many times. It's funny how Alzheimer's works.' Maggie shook her head. 'It's an awful illness. John and I have set up living wills, making it clear that they can't keep us alive just for the sake of it.'

'But that was the thing, Maggie. Physically she was fine. She loved her food, she went for walks, she was reading a John Grisham book, though she had to keep starting again because she couldn't remember what she'd read. I said goodbye to her, everything was fine and then this morning she'd . . .' Lulu smiled sadly. 'You never know, do you? You never know how long you've got your loved ones for.'

John reached over and held Maggie's hand. 'That's why you've got to treasure every second you have.'

Maggie squeezed his hand. 'That's such a nice thing to say.'

'I mean it.'

'I know you do. That's what makes it so nice.'

Lulu finished her coffee and put down the cup. 'It's been lovely seeing you both again, despite the circumstances, obviously. And I know that Emily would want me to thank you both for your friendship over the years, especially once she went into the home.'

'We loved going to see her,' said Maggie.

John nodded in agreement. 'I'll miss our visits,' he said.

Lulu looked down at Conrad. 'Time we were off,' she said.

He jumped up onto the arm of her chair and then onto her shoulders. John and Maggie stared in amazement. 'How long did it take you to teach him to do that?' asked John.

'He just does it,' said Lulu. 'To be honest, I think it's simply laziness.'

'Meow!' said Conrad, settling down around her neck.

'And he talks!' said Maggie.

'You don't know the half of it,' said Lulu. She air-kissed John and hugged Maggie, then they both took her down the hall and showed her out.

'They're nice,' said Conrad, as Lulu walked slowly down the street.

'Please don't tell me you saw something wrong with their auras.'

'No, their auras are lovely. Lots of yellow and pink. Nothing amiss.'

'They make a lovely couple. He was a soldier. He was a colonel when he retired. Saw action in the Falklands and had some close calls in Northern Ireland.'

'And she was a ballet dancer?'

'How do you know that? Did you see that in her aura?'

'No, I saw the photographs of her wearing a tutu on the wall.'

Lulu laughed. 'Of course you did,' she said. She reached Elgin Avenue and stopped. 'You heard what they said about Jenny Tyler visiting Emily?'

'She wasn't in any of the photographs, was she?'

'No, she wasn't. Which means that Ildi didn't photograph everyone who visited Emily.'

'So even though your friends saw the chocolates, that doesn't mean it was your brother-in-law who gave them to her.'

'Exactly.'

'So what do you want to do?'

Lulu sighed and looked towards St John's Wood. 'I have a plan,' she said. She looked at her watch. 'But it's getting late; it can wait until tomorrow.'

On the way home, Lulu popped into the Coastline Galicia in Abbey Road and bought two sea bass, which she asked the fishmonger to fillet for her. Once she was back on *The Lark*, she dredged them in a mixture of flour, sea salt and freshly ground black pepper and fried them in a little olive oil and butter. She put them on a plate and then added some white wine to the pan, then some butter followed by chopped herbs from her plot by the towpath, some water and a dash of lemon juice. She added a little more butter, then poured it over one of the fillets and served it with some fresh salad from the fridge. The other fillet was for Conrad, so she put it on a plate with no sauce or salad.

He was waiting for her on the back deck, where she had left him with a bowl of Evian water. She took up his plate first and put it on the deck, then went down to fetch hers and a glass of wine.

Conrad took several bites, then looked up at her. 'This is good,' he said. 'Really good.'

'You sound surprised. I can cook.'

'You most definitely can.' He went back to eating.

A young couple walked by with a Staffordshire bull terrier on a chain lead. He couldn't see Conrad but he could clearly smell him because he began to sniff loudly and tried to get over to the boat. The man pulled hard on the lead. 'Sorry,' he said.

'He probably smells your food,' said the woman. She was in her twenties with chrome piercings in her eyebrows, nose, lips and ears. And goodness knows where else, thought Lulu.

She smiled brightly. 'I suppose he probably does.'

The man yanked hard on the chain again. He had a tattoo of a cobweb across his neck and red and green streaks in his hair. 'What is wrong with you?' he shouted. He managed to pull the dog away. The girl waved apologetically.

Conrad finished his fish and jumped up to sit next to Lulu. He stared after the dog. 'Why would anyone want to own an animal like that?' he said.

'They're loyal. Dependable. They can offer protection.' Lulu shrugged. 'I don't know. I've never seen the attraction.'

'And you have to follow them around picking up their poop,' said Conrad. 'How disgusting is that?'

14

Lulu woke at eight. The stove had gone out but the radiators were still warm. Conrad was sleeping on the floor by one of the radiators, curled up with his tail under his chin. She showered and pulled on a flowered wrap dress with long sleeves. She smiled as she knotted the belt, remembering what Emily always said – 'On the side, never in front, and don't even think of tying it in a bow.'

Conrad woke up as she was making herself a mug of coffee and she poured him a bowl of water. 'You said you had a plan,' said Conrad. 'What did you mean?'

'We need to get a look at the visitors' book, and you can help,' said Lulu. She explained what she needed him to do as they walked along the towpath and headed towards St John's Wood.

There was a florist's opposite Maida Vale Tube station. Lulu stopped and looked in the window. 'I need some flowers.'

Conrad jumped off her shoulders and landed gracefully on the pavement. 'I'll wait for you outside.'

'What's wrong?'

'The shop is full of lilies.'

'So?'

'Really? You don't know about cats and lilies?'

'Well obviously not.'

Conrad sighed. 'The whole plant, leaf, pollen and the

flower, are poisonous. Just a couple of leaves will kill a cat, and even licking a few pollen grains can give a cat acute kidney failure.'

'Well, you live and learn,' said Lulu.

'Yes, with any luck. But plenty of cats have died after eating a leaf or licking some pollen. Trust me, it's not a pleasant way to go.' Conrad shuddered. 'I've heard of cats taking up to a week to die after coming into contact with a lily, and there's nothing that can be done.'

'Oh, Conrad, that's horrible. I won't go in, then. I'll take some fruit instead.'

They walked along to a small grocer's with a display of fruit outside. Lulu picked up a couple of pears, a bunch of bananas, some grapes and an apple and took them inside to pay for them. When she came out with the fruit in a carrier bag, she bent down so that Conrad could jump back onto her shoulders.

It was a lovely, sunny day and there was a warm wind rustling the leaves of the trees they passed. Lulu was getting so used to Conrad on her shoulders that she was barely aware of his weight any more. Several times passers-by smiled at her and she wasn't sure why until she realized that they had spotted him.

When they reached the home she opened the door and went into the reception area. Gary was behind the counter, sitting at a desk and tapping on a calculator. He kept his head down as Lulu walked up, even though she was sure he had heard her arrive. The visitors' book was on the counter, next to a ballpoint pen. Conrad jumped down from her shoulders and landed on the counter. He mewed at Gary, who finally looked up.

'Hello, Gary, I'm here to see Mrs Watson,' said Lulu.

'Mrs Watson?' said Gary, frowning as if hearing the name for the first time.

'Shirley Watson.' She held up the bag of fruit. 'I brought these for her.' Shirley was one of Emily's friends in the home and they often strolled together in the garden. Shirley had lung problems after a lifetime of smoking and was always connected to an oxygen tank. She had no living relatives and no friends outside the home, so although Lulu felt guilty about using Shirley to get into the home, at least it meant she would have a visitor.

'Right, okay, sure,' said Gary. 'If you sign the visitors' book. I'll get your badge done.'

'Of course,' said Lulu, putting down the fruit and pulling the book towards her. Right on cue, Conrad jumped onto the floor, dashed by Gary and rushed into the office. 'Oh, I am so sorry, Gary. He never does that.'

'I'll get him,' said Gary, putting down his files and heading after Conrad.

Lulu took her iPhone from her bag, switched to camera mode and took a photograph of the open book. Then she flicked the page and took another picture. And another picture. She heard a thump as something fell to the ground and then a crashing sound and then a curse from Gary. She turned the page and took another photograph, and another, and another. Then she heard footsteps and she slipped the phone back in her pocket and picked up the pen. She was filling out her details when Gary appeared with Conrad in his arms.

'I'm so sorry, I've no idea what came over him,' said Lulu. 'I hope he didn't make a mess.'

'He knocked a tub of pencils off Mrs Fitzgerald's desk, but I picked them up,' he said.

'I'm so sorry,' said Lulu again. She took Conrad from him and held the cat's face just inches from hers. 'You're a very naughty boy,' she said.

'Meow,' said Conrad.

'He's okay, I think he just got confused,' said Gary.

'Oh, no,' said Lulu. 'He knew exactly what he was doing.' She lifted Conrad onto her shoulders and he wound himself around her neck.

Gary filled out a badge for her and she slapped it onto her chest. 'Mrs Watson is just along from Mrs Lewis's room,' said Gary. 'I mean, Mrs Lewis's old room. Sorry.'

'I understand, Gary. It's okay.'

She picked up the fruit and went through the door to the right and up the stairs. She felt her pulse quicken as she approached the door to the room that Emily had used. It was open. There was a new name in the card holder by the door: BECKY NEESON. Lulu couldn't help but glance in as she walked by. A grey-haired lady was sitting in the chair, knitting. She smiled up at Lulu. 'Hello, my lovely,' she said. 'Are you here to see me?'

'No, I'm sorry.'

'Never mind,' said the lady, and she went back to her knitting. The chair was the one that Emily used to sit in, but the hospital bed had been replaced with a regular one.

Lulu walked on by. 'That was quick,' she whispered. 'Emily's barely cold.'

'It's a business,' said Conrad.

'I know, but even so. I assumed they would . . . I don't know . . . redecorate or something.'

'It's a hospital but with more comfortable furniture,' said Conrad.

'I suppose so,' said Lulu.

The door to Shirley's room was closed so Lulu knocked and opened it gently. Shirley was sitting in her armchair staring at the carpet. 'Shirley?' said Lulu. 'It's me, Lulu.' She lifted up the bag. 'I come bearing gifts.'

'For me?' There was a green oxygen cylinder standing next to Shirley's chair and a clear tube led to a nasal oxygen cannula. Lulu knew all the technical terms; her father had needed a similar set-up during his final weeks.

Lulu walked over and handed the bag to her. Shirley reached in and took out a pear. She sniffed it. 'Lovely,' she sighed. 'My Reg brings me fruit and flowers, every Friday after work. Regular as clockwork.'

'That's nice.' Shirley's husband had been dead for more than ten years but she always spoke as if he was still around. Lulu sat down on the edge of the bed. 'I just wanted to pop by and say hello. I know you'll miss your walks and chats with Emily.'

Shirley frowned. 'Who is Emily?'

'Emily Lewis. Your friend.'

Shirley shook her head and smiled, showing a complete absence of teeth. 'Emily isn't my friend. Alice is my friend and she likes Eddie but Eddie doesn't like her; he likes Betty. Eddie can run really fast.'

'Well, that's interesting,' said Lulu. Conrad dropped down to sit next to her on the bed.

'Oh, a cat!' exclaimed Shirley, seeing him for the first time and clapping her hands together like an excited child.

'Do you want to hold him?'

'Yes, please!'

'Is that okay, Conrad?'

'Meow,' said Conrad, standing up.

Lulu picked him up and gently placed him on Shirley's lap. Shirley giggled and began to stroke him. 'He's lovely,' she said. 'So smooth.'

Conrad purred and settled down in her lap. Lulu smiled at the obvious enjoyment that Shirley was getting from stroking him. She had a blissful smile and a faraway look in her eyes. 'His name is Conrad.'

'That's a nice name. He's a handsome boy.'

'Yes, he is.'

Lulu sat on the bed and watched Shirley stroke Conrad. She seemed much more relaxed and her breathing had slowed. Conrad was purring like a two-stroke engine and pushing his head against her hand. Lulu couldn't help but smile. She had only intended to say hello and drop off the fruit, but she ended up staying for almost an hour. Conrad seemed content to sit on Shirley's lap and Shirley was clearly delighted to have the cat to play with. From time to time Shirley would start talking about something that had happened to her, more often than not when she had been at school. She would ramble on about playground romances or which teachers she really liked and school trips she had been on. Her memory for events that had happened more than seventy years ago was crystal clear, but every now and again she would squint at Lulu and ask who she was.

Eventually Lulu said that she had to go. She let Shirley give Conrad a final cuddle, then gathered him up. 'You will come again, won't you?' asked Shirley as Conrad settled around Lulu's neck.

'Of course,' said Lulu.

'I was talking to Conrad.'

Lulu smiled. Of course she was.

'Meow,' said Conrad.

Shirley laughed girlishly. 'He said yes.'

'He did, didn't he?' said Lulu, letting herself out of the room. 'You take care, Shirley.'

15

On the way back to *The Lark*, Lulu decided to stop off at the house in Warrington Crescent. She wanted to pick up a photograph of Emily to use at the funeral. There was a lovely one in the sitting room, taken when she was in her fifties. Conrad rode on her shoulders as Lulu walked up to the front door and unlocked it. As she closed the door she noticed that there was a single large white envelope in the wire basket. It was addressed to Simon and had BY COURIER typed at the bottom. She looked at the address in the top left-hand corner. It was from Emily's solicitors, Savill, Smith and Schmeling. She ripped it open and read it quickly.

'Is it important?' asked Conrad.

'It's about the reading of the will. It's this afternoon.'

'I thought the reading of the will came after the funeral,' said Conrad.

'Only on the TV and in the movies,' said Lulu. 'In real life, it usually comes before the funeral, mainly because the deceased often puts details of his or her wishes for the funeral in the will. Whether they want to be cremated or buried, what music they want played, whether they want flowers or money donated to charity. All those sort of things.'

She walked to the sitting room and Conrad stuck to her heels. 'What did Emily want? What were her wishes?'

'To be buried next to Frank. With money going to cancer charities.'

'And music?'

Lulu smiled and sat down on one of the overstuffed sofas. '"Nimrod" from *Enigma Variations* by Elgar. Chopin's *Nocturne in E-Flat Major*, "The Lord Is My Shepherd", and "You'll Never Walk Alone" by Gerry and the Pacemakers.'

'Nice,' said Conrad. He gestured at the letter with his chin. 'It came quickly, didn't it?' said Conrad. 'The letter.'

'You'd be surprised how efficient the death industry is. It's actually a well-oiled machine. Everyone knows exactly what they're doing and you're guided through the process so smoothly that before you know it, it's all over.'

'Well, yes, I am sure it is. But Emily only passed away the day before yesterday, didn't she?'

'That's what they said. Sometime in the night.'

'Right. So that letter must have been written this morning at the latest.' Conrad put his head on one side. 'The point I'm making is that somebody must have told the solicitor that Emily had died. And they must have done that very quickly.'

'As I said, it's all very efficient these days.'

'So do you think that Mrs Fitzgerald or somebody from the home informed the solicitor?'

'Yes, maybe.'

Conrad wrinkled his nose. 'It just doesn't seem to be the sort of thing that the home would do. They didn't even inform the police, did they? They just called the doctor and then called your brother-in-law as next of kin.'

Lulu nodded thoughtfully. 'So you're suggesting that Richard called the solicitor?'

'That sounds more likely,' said Conrad. 'And, again, you have to wonder why he did that so quickly. I mean, what was your first thought when you heard that Emily had passed away?'

'To get a drink.'

'Exactly. At no point did you decide to call her solicitor.'

'That's true,' said Lulu. 'Though I did call the police. Phil Jackson, anyway.'

'Yes, you did. But you didn't think about phoning Emily's solicitor to get the reading of the will up and running.'

Lulu nodded thoughtfully. She took out her iPhone from her handbag, called the nursing home and asked to speak to Mrs Fitzgerald. The call was put straight through. 'Hello, Lulu, how can I help you?'

Lulu could hear the tension in her voice. She was obviously expecting a problem, so Lulu tried to sound as cheerful as possible. 'I'm so sorry to bother you, but I'm just checking to see who has been told about Emily's passing and who still needs to be informed.'

'Okay . . .' The hesitation was still there.

'So, obviously the funeral director was called, and Dr Khan signed the death certificate, but does the home do anything else in the way of notifying people?'

'I'm not sure I follow you.'

'Well, Emily's banks, for instance. Would you inform them? Or her solicitor? Would the home call her solicitor to tell them that she had passed away?'

'Oh, I see. No, that wouldn't be our responsibility. Because the death occurred on our premises, we register it at the Registrar of Births, Deaths and Marriages at the Register Office. We normally do that within five days. But everything else is up to the next of kin – in this case your brother-in-law, Richard Lewis.'

'Oh, so it would have been Richard who arranged for the funeral director?'

'Oh yes, absolutely. When he was called to be told of Emily's passing he would have been asked to make arrangements with a funeral director. We can supply a list of reliable firms if necessary but he already had a firm in mind. They came and collected the body within hours. Is there a problem?'

'Absolutely not,' said Lulu. 'I just want to make sure that nothing has been missed. There's so much to do, isn't there?'

'Well, yes, there is, but it is all very straightforward. You can google what needs to be done and you'll find lots of useful lists. Have you spoken to Richard? He should be able to give you more information.'

'I will do, yes, I just wanted to check that there wasn't going to be any duplication.'

'I understand. Other than registering the death and informing the next of kin, everything else is then done by the next of kin, usually.'

Lulu thanked her and ended the call. 'The home didn't call the solicitor,' she said to Conrad. 'It has to have been Richard.' She put the phone in her bag.

'Which brings me back to my point – he was very quick off the mark.'

'Yes, he was.' Lulu's eyes narrowed. 'You think that he was expecting it? He knew that Emily was going to die?'

'As you said, your first thought wasn't to call a solicitor, was it? Most people would be in shock, and a solicitor would be well down the list of things you'd think about.'

Lulu nodded. 'I think you're right. Would you like to come to the reading of the will this afternoon?'

'Try stopping me,' said Conrad.

Lulu stood up and went over to a low mahogany side-board. There were more than a dozen framed photographs, including Lulu and Simon's wedding photograph in a silver frame, a larger copy of the one that Emily had had in the home. Next to it was the photograph she was looking for. Lulu picked it up and showed it to Conrad. 'Wow, she was pretty,' he said.

'She was beautiful,' said Lulu. 'This was taken at her fiftieth birthday party at the Ritz. One of her friends was a professional photographer and he took it. Frank loved it, it was his favourite picture of her.' It was too big to put in her bag so she tucked it under her arm and picked up her handbag. She bent down so that Conrad could jump onto her shoulders, and then let herself out of the house.

They walked back to *The Lark*. As soon as they were on board, Lulu put the framed photograph on a shelf and made herself a cup of coffee. Conrad sat on the sofa and watched her. 'Do you want a drink?' Lulu asked.

'No, I'm good, thank you. I'm just eager to see who visited Emily.'

'Me too,' said Lulu. She sat down next to him and took her iPhone from her handbag. She tapped on the screen to call up the photographs she'd taken of the visitors' book. She flicked through to the picture that had Sunday's visitors. On each line there was the date, the time, the name of the visitor, the resident they were visiting, and their signature.

Her own entry was there, showing her arrival on Sunday afternoon. Louise Baxter's entry showed her arriving later that afternoon. They were Emily's only visitors that day.

Lulu hadn't visited Emily on the Saturday. She'd arranged

to have the toilet emptied and the guy had promised to be there before noon. He had actually turned up at five o'clock in the afternoon. Emily had had three visitors, so she wouldn't have been lonely. Jenny Tyler had visited in the morning. Louise had been there at two o'clock. She worked in a local estate agent's so tended to visit at the weekend. Nancy and Donald Protheroe had dropped by at four. They were close friends of Emily's through the Little Venice Conservative Association and Donald had served on Westminster City Council for more than twenty years. There weren't photographs for Jenny or the Protheroes, so Emily guessed that Ildi hadn't been working on the Saturday. All of the visitors were long-time friends of Emily's.

Lulu found the entry for the Eastmans. They had arrived at four-fifteen on the Friday. She went through the entries prior to the Eastmans and found Jenny Tyler arriving at two-thirty on the same day. She frowned. So Jenny had been to see Emily on Friday and again on Saturday?

Lulu's own entry was there for Friday. She had gone in the morning and had left before Richard and Maria had arrived at noon.

She took a notepad and a pen from a drawer at the side of the sofa and wrote down the days of the week, then listed the times of all Emily's visitors. When she had finished she studied the list. Conrad jumped up and sat down next to her. 'She had a lot of visitors,' he said, as he looked at what she had written.

'She was a popular lady,' said Lulu. 'She had a lot of friends.' She tapped her pen on what she had written for Sunday. 'So, you and I visited Emily on Sunday afternoon and the chocolates were there then. I wasn't there on

Saturday, but I didn't see the chocolates when I visited Emily on Friday morning at ten-thirty. It's possible they were put away, but I doubt it. She seemed proud to have them. So that means she was given the chocolates between ten-thirty on Friday morning and when I got there on Sunday.' She tapped what she had written for Friday. 'Now the Eastmans were there at four-fifteen on Friday, and Emily had the chocolates then. That means they have to have been delivered between the time I left and the time the Eastmans arrived. That means it was either Jenny Tyler or Richard and Maria.'

'And Jenny was there after Richard and Maria, so you need to talk to her?'

Lulu nodded. 'Yes, you're right. But I can't believe that Jenny would do anything to hurt Emily. They sat next to each other at primary school. They were literally lifelong friends. So it looks as if it can only have been Richard and Maria.'

'Can you ask them?'

'Well I can, yes, obviously. But as soon as I do, if they have done anything wrong they'll know I'm onto them. I'm going to have to play this very carefully.'

'Maybe you can mention it at the reading of the will?'

Lulu nodded. 'That's a good idea.' She stroked the back of his neck and he purred. 'Thank you for staying with me.'

'There's nowhere else I'd rather be,' he said.

16

The offices of Savill, Smith and Schmeling were just off Baker Street, around the corner from the Sherlock Holmes Museum. It took half an hour for Lulu to walk there with Conrad on her shoulders and they were a few minutes early. Lulu had to press an intercom button to get inside. There was a reception area on the ground floor with the feel of an IKEA display. A receptionist looked up from her computer with a beaming smile that turned into a look of sympathy once Lulu had explained why she was there. 'Oh, you can go right up, first door on the left,' she said. Her eyes widened as she noticed Conrad. 'Oh my God, there's a cat on your shoulder.'

'There is indeed,' said Lulu.

'That is amazing.'

'He is an amazing cat,' said Lulu. She went up the stairs to where there was another seating area, this one with two blood-red leather sofas facing each other across an oak coffee table with magazines scattered over it. The door on the left was open and she heard a man's mumbled voice. She went to the doorway and looked in. She almost gasped as she recognized the man standing behind a large antique desk – he was the stranger in the photograph that had been on Emily's wall, the man whose hand she had been holding. He looked younger than he had appeared in the picture, but he was wearing the same herringbone suit and waistcoat.

Conrad dropped down from her shoulders and the man

turned when he heard the sound of his paws hitting the carpet. The man frowned. 'I'm sorry, you are . . . ?'

'Lulu Lewis,' she said. 'I'm here for the reading of Emily Lewis's will.'

'I'm sorry, Mrs Lewis. But this isn't a public reading.'

'Emily Lewis was my mother-in-law.'

'Yes, I'm sure she was. But only the executor has the right to attend the reading of the will.'

'And you are?'

'I'm Thomas Turnbull, a solicitor. I'll be going through the will.'

Lulu frowned. 'I thought Mr Smith handled Emily's affairs?'

'I'm afraid Mr Smith passed away two years ago. Most of his clients became my responsibility. Please, you are going to have to leave now, we're about to start.'

Lulu moved to the side and saw Richard and Maria sitting on wooden chairs facing a desk. Richard stood up and walked towards her, arms outstretched. 'Lulu, how are you? Sorry we haven't had the chance to get together, but obviously it's been frantic.' He was less tanned than the last time they'd met; there was obviously not as much sun in Beckenham as there had been on the Costa del Sol. He was wearing a leather bomber jacket with some sort of gold eagle design on the back, tight blue jeans and shiny black shoes with pointed toes.

'I'm sorry for your loss,' said Lulu.

'Yes, right. Thank you. And you.'

'Look, Richard, Mr Turnbull here says I can't be at the reading of Emily's will.'

'Unless Mr Lewis gives his permission, in which case it would be perfectly fine,' said Turnbull.

Richard held out his arms. 'Of course it's fine. Absolutely no problem. The more the merrier.' His face tightened as he realized what he had said. 'I'm sorry. Bad taste. Please, come in and Mr Turnbull can get started.'

Lulu went into the room, followed by Richard and Mr Turnbull. Maria had stayed sitting and she offered her hand to Lulu. Lulu held it and wasn't sure if she was meant to shake it or not, so she gave it a gentle squeeze. Maria was wearing a blue dress with buttons down the front and a white cardigan, with her curly black hair hanging loose over her shoulders. 'Lovely to see you, Lulu,' she said, in her soft Spanish accent.

'And you, Maria.' She pulled away her hand. She wondered if Richard would get her a chair but he turned his back on her and went to sit next to Maria, who reached over and held his hand.

There was a chair next to a side table by the window, so Lulu sat there. Conrad padded over and jumped smoothly onto the table and turned to face Mr Turnbull. Mr Turnbull sat down onto a high-backed chair and flipped open a file. He had a pair of reading glasses hanging on a chain around his neck and he put them on. 'Right, so my name is Thomas Turnbull and we are here today to confirm the last will and testament of Emily Rose Lewis, which was signed by Mrs Lewis on the second of July 2009. The will is very straight-forward. There are five charitable donations to charities that I gather were close to her heart, each of ten thousand pounds. The rest of the assets, including all properties, contents thereof, shares and monies in various bank accounts, are to be split equally between Mrs Lewis's sons, Richard Francis Lewis and Simon Peter Lewis. In the event of either of the sons predeceasing Mrs Lewis, the entire estate goes to the surviving sibling. There is a list of properties attached, and a list of share accounts and bank accounts.' He looked up from the file. 'It is my understanding that Mr Simon Peter Lewis passed away three months ago,' he said.

'That's correct,' said Lulu. 'Simon was also listed as an executor, I believe.'

Mr Turnbull nodded. 'He is. Was. Yes. You are correct. Along with Mr Richard Francis Lewis, and myself, being a representative of Savill, Smith and Schmeling.' He looked down at the file. 'There is also a list of requirements for the funeral.' He looked up again. 'Who will be handling the arrangements?'

'We've hired Gilbert's in St John's Wood,' said Richard. 'I'll pass the list on to them.'

'Excellent,' said Mr Turnbull. 'Now, there is going to be a substantial inheritance tax payment which will have to be made within six months of Mrs Lewis's passing. My suggestion would be that we begin liquidating some of the shareholdings so that there is cash available to meet that deadline.'

'I'm sorry, I thought there was no tax to pay if the money was being inherited by children,' said Maria.

'No, that only applies to spouses,' said Mr Turnbull. 'So when Mrs Lewis's husband passed away, she received his estate without any inheritance tax being levied. But now the estate is being passed to your husband, inheritance tax has to be paid.'

'But we don't even live here!'

Mr Turnbull looked at her over the top of his glasses. 'I'm sorry, but the rules are the rules. On a more optimistic note,

I have spoken to our tax accounting people and there is more than enough money in the share-dealing and bank accounts to cover the tax bill, so it won't be necessary to sell the properties.'

'Oh, we'll be selling them,' said Maria. 'As soon as we can.'

'Maria . . .' said Richard plaintively.

She turned to glare at him. 'Well, it's true, isn't it? You don't want to stay in that stuffy old house, do you? You want a villa with a pool and a barbecue pit and a view of the beach. And decent weather. You won't get any of that in London.' She turned to the solicitor. 'So how much money is there in the accounts?'

'Maria . . .' Richard began again.

'We need to know, don't we?'

Mr Turnbull looked down at his file. 'Well, adding together the various share accounts, her ISAs and so on, at the last valuation which was two weeks ago, the total came to just over three million pounds.'

'How much exactly?' asked Maria.

The solicitor looked down at the file again. 'Three million, one hundred and seventy-five thousand, four hundred and sixty-eight pounds,' he said. He looked up and gave her a pained smile. 'And thirty-three pence.'

'And the bank accounts? How much is in there?'

Mr Turnbull sighed and looked down at the file. 'There are four accounts, with a total of two hundred and twenty-eight thousand, four hundred and seventy-two pounds. And eighteen pence.'

Maria clapped her hands. 'That's almost three and a half million pounds!' she said.

'Well, yes, but as I explained, there will be a substantial inheritance tax liability.'

'How much?'

'Well, we are still working on that calculation. A lot will depend on the valuation of the properties, furniture and artworks, and so on. And some of the investments are in a trust fund that Mr Frank Lewis set up some thirty years ago. Because of the nature of the trust, there will be no tax to pay. But you won't be able to liquidate the trust. It is, I'm afraid, rather complicated.'

'Surely you can give me an idea. What is it you call it? A ball-park figure?'

'Ball-park? Yes, well, I suppose, somewhere in the region of two million pounds.'

Maria frowned at him. 'What? Two million pounds?'

'As you say, that's a ball-park figure.'

'We have to pay two million pounds to the government?' Her voice had gone up an octave.

'Well, yes, that's how inheritance tax works.'

'But why is it so much?'

Mr Turnbull sighed. 'Yes, I agree that it does sound rather a lot. But in fact if it wasn't for the trust, it would be considerably higher. Also, a portion of her residence is tax free because it is going to her son. I have to say, with hindsight, that there were ways that the tax bill could have been reduced further still, but for whatever reason, that wasn't done.'

'You mean because she didn't bother speaking to an accountant, we have to give away two million pounds?'

'Maria, please!' said Richard.

'But this is our money, they're trying to steal it from us.'

'Honey, you're being unreasonable. Just calm down and we'll talk about it later.'

Maria opened her mouth to snap at him but then she obviously had a change of heart. She smiled and reached over to pat him on the leg. 'I'm sorry,' she mouthed. She leaned over and rested her head on his shoulder.

'I'm sorry, Mr Turnbull, my wife and I have been under a lot of stress over the last few days. Please go on.'

'I understand,' said Mr Turnbull. 'It's a stressful time for everybody. As I said, I think you and I and a member of our taxation department should sit down and go through the various shareholdings to see which assets are best liquidated.'

'And the money in the accounts, how soon could we have access to that?' asked Richard.

'Probate usually takes between four and twelve weeks, depending on the complexity of the estate. As there is only one beneficiary, that simplifies things. For instance, if there were several beneficiaries we would probably have to sell the properties and distribute the funds, but that won't be necessary in this case.'

'So four weeks?'

'That should be achievable, yes.'

Richard put a hand around Maria's shoulders and hugged her, then whispered in her ear. She nodded.

'So I'll arrange a time for you to come in and go through the share accounts,' said Mr Turnbull. 'I'll phone you later.'

'Thank you,' said Richard. 'And what about the trust fund?'

'That's a relatively simple matter,' said the solicitor. 'All that happens is that you are registered as the beneficiary of the trust in place of your mother. The trustees can approve that this week.'

'Who are the trustees?' asked Maria.

'There are three and they are all employed by our firm,' said Mr Turnbull.

Maria narrowed her eyes. 'Are you a trustee?'

'No, I'm not,' he said. 'It's a separate department.'

'Okay, but once the trustees have said it's okay, we can access the money in the trust fund?'

'No, the fund will pay you a monthly income.' He looked down at the file, flicked over a few pages, and then looked up again. 'Mrs Lewis was receiving four thousand pounds a month.'

'And how much is the fund worth?' Maria asked.

'In total?' He flicked over another page. 'At the last valuation, just under three million pounds.'

'That's quite a small payout for such a large fund.'

'That was the amount decided upon by Mrs Lewis's late husband.'

'But what if we needed more?'

'Then you would apply to the trustees and they would consider your request.'

'And could we liquidate the whole fund?'

'Maria, please,' hissed Richard. 'We can talk about this later.'

'I just want to know,' she said. 'I have the right to know, don't I? It's my money.' She caught herself and flashed him a smile. 'Our money,' she said. She reached over and squeezed his hand. 'I meant our money.'

'I would have to look at the terms of the trust, but I very much doubt it,' said Mr Turnbull. 'I am fairly sure that the rules of the trust would prohibit its liquidation. But let me get back to you on that.' He sat back in his chair. 'That is probably all for today,' he said. 'Unless there are any questions?' He looked over at Lulu. She just smiled and gave a small shake of her head. She had questions, but none that she wanted to ask in front of her brother-in-law and his wife.

'Very well,' said the solicitor, removing his glasses and closing the file. 'Thank you all for coming, and I'll be in touch with Mr Lewis later today to arrange the inheritance tax meeting.'

Richard stood up. Maria was smiling but her eyes were hard. She looked over at Lulu and gave her a tiny nod, then kept her eyes down as she walked out of the office. Richard had his arms around her shoulder. He thanked the solicitor, then looked around at Lulu. 'I'll call you about the funeral,' he said.

'Thank you,' said Lulu, but he had already gone through the door. Conrad jumped down off the side table and rubbed against her legs. Mr Turnbull was waiting for Lulu to leave, but she stood up and stayed where she was. 'Mr Turnbull, could I have a quick word with you?' she said.

The solicitor grimaced. 'I'm not sure if that would be appropriate,' he said. 'If you have any problems with the will as I outlined, then you need to talk to your own solicitor. And not one from this firm, obviously.'

'Oh, you think I want to contest the will?' She smiled and shook her head. 'No, no, that's not what I wanted to discuss. It is about Emily, though.'

Mr Turnbull pursed his lips and for a second Lulu thought he was going to refuse to talk to her, but then he forced a smile, closed the door and waved her to a seat. She sat on the chair that Maria had been using and waited for Mr Turnbull to sit down. Conrad stayed where he was, watching them both with unblinking eyes. 'You went to see my mother-in-law last week,' said Lulu. 'On Wednesday. Wednesday morning.'

Mr Turnbull frowned. 'Did Mrs Lewis tell you that?'

'No, I saw your picture. One of the nurses was taking photographs of Emily with her visitors to put on the wall as a way of jogging her memory.'

'Ah yes. I remember telling the nurse what a splendid idea it was.'

'And that was on Wednesday.'

'Yes. In the morning.'

'Can you tell me why you were there?'

'I'm not sure that I can,' he said. 'Client confidentiality.'

'Yes, I understand that, but Emily has passed away.'

'Indeed. But client confidentiality survives even when the client has passed.'

'Right. But can you tell me if the meeting was your idea, or hers?'

'Oh, hers. Quite definitely hers. It came out of the blue. She left a message saying that she needed to see Mr Smith. Obviously that caused some confusion seeing as how she had been informed of Mr Smith's passing at the time. Of course when I got out there, I realized what the problem was.'

'She had become very forgetful?'

'Indeed.' Mr Turnbull sat back in his chair. 'In fact, when I turned up, she had no idea who I was. She kept calling me Richard. I explained who I was but it didn't seem to register with her.'

'I know exactly what you mean,' said Lulu. 'In the picture she was holding your hand.'

Mr Turnbull smiled awkwardly. 'Yes, she kept holding on to me tightly. She actually left me with marks. It seemed to comfort her so I didn't pull away. Anyway, I spent about half an hour with her but she was no more coherent when I left than when I'd arrived.' He sighed, then pulled a red handkerchief out and began polishing the lenses of his glasses. 'I feel I should ask, why did the family never have a Lasting Power of Attorney drawn up for Mrs Lewis?'

Lulu shrugged. 'We talked about it but she was never keen on the idea. And to be honest she was making all her own decisions up until a few months ago. My husband took over her finances but most of her bills were paid by direct debit so everything just ticked over.' She sighed. 'Obviously with hindsight, we should have. So you've no idea what she wanted?'

'When she called the office, she said she wanted to talk to Mr Smith about her will. That's all she said. We have no idea what she had in mind.' He put his handkerchief away.

'Well, presumably she wanted to change her will.'

Mr Turnbull threw up his hands. 'That would be pure conjecture and I really don't want to get drawn into a conversation about what she might or might not have wanted.'

'I understand,' said Lulu.

He lowered his hands and put the palms down on his desk. 'Having said that, because of the way she was, there would have been problems in her asking for a new will. Anyone who makes a will has to have what they call "testamentary capacity"; basically, they have to understand what making a will means and the effect it will have. She was clearly confused and was having issues with her memory, so I couldn't in all conscience have taken instructions from her. The state she was in, I just wouldn't be able to say that she had the mental capacity to make a valid will. The first step would be to get a doctor's statement that she was capable of understanding what she was signing, but as she was in the home because of dementia, that would be problematical at best.'

'So what would have happened, then?'

'Well, frankly, it would have been very awkward. If you had an LPA – a Lasting Power of Attorney – and you had a conversation with her that made it clear that she wanted to amend her will, then it could be done. But if she wasn't able to make her wishes clear . . .' He raised his palms. 'If she wasn't capable of signing a new will, it could be signed on her behalf. That's not the problem. The problem would have been getting her to explain what it was she wanted.'

'So how did you leave it?'

'I came back to the office here and talked it through with the partners. The only thing we could think of was to leave it for a few days and then go back and see if she was more coherent.' He smiled wryly. 'Obviously that is now moot. I do understand that you might have reservations about the will, but they were clearly the wishes of Mrs Lewis at the time.'

'No, it's fine, Mr Turnbull. I'm not a blood relative and Simon and I didn't have children, so it's only fair that her money goes to Richard.'

'Does Richard have children?'

'Three that I know of, with his previous wives. I hope that some of Emily's money will go to supporting them. That's what she would have wanted.'

'It's a pity that she didn't mention them in the will. They could have been named as beneficiaries. Also she could have left them a share in her residence, which would have been free of inheritance tax.'

'Hindsight is a wonderful thing,' said Lulu.

Mr Turnbull forced a smile. 'Indeed it is.' He leaned towards her. 'I am really sorry how this turned out,' he said. 'Off the record, if I had realized earlier that your husband had passed away then I would have raised the issue with Mrs Lewis with a view to redrafting her will, but I was never informed.'

'My husband was a QC and he used a friend to do all his personal legal work,' Lulu said. 'It's a firm in the City. They wouldn't have thought to have contacted you. It would perhaps have made sense for them to have had their wills drawn up by the same company. But, again, hindsight.' She frowned. 'But a letter was sent to Simon telling him about the reading of the will.'

'Ah, yes. A secretary would have sent that out as he was named as an executor. It was my fault for not mentioning that he had passed away. It was all a bit rushed.'

'No, I'm glad you sent the letter, otherwise I wouldn't have been here.'

Mr Turnbull nodded. 'Anyway, the first I heard of his passing was when I spoke to Mr Lewis on Monday.'

'He called you?'

'He called the firm. He asked for Mr Smith and was then put on to me. He informed me that Mrs Emily Lewis had passed away and asked for me to process the paperwork as a matter of urgency.'

'Those were his exact words?'

'Well, something like that. He said he and his wife wanted to return to Spain. By the sound of it they plan to sell everything and take the money with them.'

'There's nothing to stop them doing that, is there?'

'Well, no. But these things do take time and Mrs Lewis – Richard's wife – does seem in rather a hurry.'

Lulu sighed and got to her feet. Conrad padded across the carpet and jumped up onto the chair.

'He is quite the cat,' said Mr Turnbull.

'Yes, he is.'

'He's been listening to everything we've been saying. As if he understands every word.'

'I think he probably does.'

'Meow!' said Conrad.

Mr Turnbull laughed. 'There you have it,' he said. He stood up. 'I'm sorry about the way things worked out, and I'm sorry for your loss. For your losses. Your husband and your mother-in-law. I can only imagine how difficult it has been for you.'

Lulu bent down and Conrad jumped onto her shoulders. 'I'm just taking it day by day,' she said. 'And Conrad is a big help.'

Mr Turnbull frowned. 'Conrad?'

'The cat. Conrad the Calico Cat.'

The solicitor laughed. 'Oh, right. Yes. I see. Well it's been an absolute pleasure meeting you both.'

'Meow!' said Conrad.

'Conrad says it was a pleasure meeting you, too.'

'I love the way he talks.'

'Yes,' said Lulu. 'So do I.'

17

Richard was waiting on the pavement when Lulu stepped outside. He did a double-take when he saw Conrad sitting on her shoulders. 'He goes everywhere with you?' he asked.

'Pretty much, yes.'

'I didn't know you had a cat.'

'Richard, I haven't seen you since Simon's funeral. I didn't even know you were back in the UK.'

'Things weren't going well in Spain. We thought we needed a change. What's its name?'

'His name is Conrad.'

'Conrad? Nice.' He gestured at the door. 'What was going on upstairs?'

'It was the reading of Emily's will. You were there.'

He forced a smile. 'Your private chat with Turnbull. What was that about?'

'It's a private matter.'

'I'm one of the executors of the will.'

'It wasn't about the will.'

'Of course it was about the will,' snapped Richard. 'What else would you have to talk about?'

Maria was sitting in the passenger seat of a red Nissan Juke parked at the kerb, tapping on the screen of her smartphone.

Richard took a deep breath to calm himself down and tried to smile, though it looked more like a snarl. 'Lulu, darling, I'm so sorry about what happened in there. Maria was totally out of order.'

Lulu could hear the insincerity in his voice. 'She barely knew Emily.'

'I know you're upset, and I'm so sorry for what happened.'

Lulu shook her head. 'I really don't understand why you let her behave like that.'

'Oh now, be fair. I had no idea what she was going to say.'

'There's a time and a place, and so soon after Emily passing away really isn't the time. It's as if the money is all she cares about.'

'No, she loved Emily. There's no question of that.'

'Well, it didn't sound like that today.'

'And again I apologize for her behaviour.'

'To be honest, Richard, she's the one who should be apologizing.'

Richard looked over at the car, where his wife was still tapping away on her phone. 'Do you want a personal apology? Is that what you want? I'll tell her to come and say she's sorry in person.'

'Oh, of course not. She's not a child. Though she seemed to be acting like one in there.'

'It's her Spanish blood. She can be fiery.'

'Her ancestry is no excuse for her behaviour,' said Lulu.

'She knows she behaved badly,' said Richard.

'Really? She seems more interested in her phone.' She frowned. 'How long have you been back in the UK?'

'A few weeks. Why?'

'You didn't think to call me? Or drop by when you visited Emily?'

'It's all been frantic,' said Richard. 'Our business went belly up and we decided to come back to the UK for a while.'

'Beckenham?'

He squinted at her. 'Have you been checking up on me, Lulu?'

'Mrs Fitzgerald said you'd given an address in Beckenham, when you were signing up as Emily's next of kin.'

'We're renting a place. Temporary. I kept meaning to drop by but we've just been so busy.' Richard sighed. 'Lulu, you've got her all wrong. Really. Maria loved Emily. She was always happy to visit with me and she went on her own a few times.'

'How often? I'm there almost every day and I never saw you.'

'I've been going once a week. Maria has been a few times. Not that Emily knows who we are. She is – was – pretty far gone.'

'And you took her chocolates?' She watched him carefully for his reaction.

'Yes, we did, actually.' He frowned. 'How did you . . . ? Oh, of course, you saw them when you visited.'

'Whose idea were the chocolates?'

'I really can't remember. We had dinner in Covent Garden and then we decided to buy her some chocolates from Bellissimo. The handmade ones.'

'And was it your idea or hers?'

'I don't know. We walked past the shop and one of us said we should buy a box for Emily. We went in and bought them. I paid for them, if that's your next question.'

'And when did you give them to Emily?'

'The next day. When we went around to see her.'

'Which was when?'

'Why are you so interested in the damn chocolates?' When she didn't answer, he exhaled in exasperation. 'Friday. About midday.'

'And did you both give her the chocolates, or just one of you?'

Richard laughed. 'My God, you really can't help being a copper, can you? It's never a conversation with you, is it? It's always an interrogation. I'm amazed that Simon put up with you as long as he did.'

Lulu's jaw dropped and she felt a physical pain in her chest as if she had been struck.

'Oh, God, Lulu, I'm sorry.' He reached out to hold her arm but she flinched and took a step backwards. 'I'm sorry, that was a terrible thing to say.'

'Just go, Richard.'

'I spoke without thinking. I'm sorry.'

'Well, that seems to be running in the family today, doesn't it?'

'Lulu, we're all under a lot of pressure here. A lot of stress. Things get said in the heat of the moment.'

'Not by me.'

'No, but then you've always had amazing self-control. No matter what happens, no matter what life throws at you, you always take it on the chin. Not everybody is as strong as you.'

Lulu shrugged and looked over at the car, where Maria was still focused on her phone. 'You heard what she said, Richard. About your own mother.'

'She spoke without thinking.'

'It sounded to me as if she was thinking all right – about money,' Lulu said sharply. She looked at Richard. 'From what I heard, she's far more concerned about your inheritance than she is about the fact that your mother passed away.'

'Families have always been difficult for her, Lulu. Her parents died when she was a teenager. She's had to take care of herself most of her life.'

'And now she's latched on to you.'

'She's my wife, Lulu.'

'So what's yours is hers?'

'You've got her all wrong.' He grimaced. 'Look, I know she spoke out of turn up there, but I have to say that I'm not happy to be giving the government two million quid to spend on gold wallpaper for the prime minister's flat. I agree, her tone and choice of words was unfortunate, but she does have a point. If my mother had done some half-decent tax planning we wouldn't be in this situation.'

'So now Emily's death is a situation?'

Richard sighed and shook his head. 'There's just no talking to you.' He turned and began walking towards the car. He stopped and looked round. 'I'll call you about the funeral arrangements? Okay?'

Lulu nodded but didn't say anything. Richard went over to the car and climbed into the driving seat.

'Calm down,' Conrad whispered in her ear.

'I can't believe he's defending her,' said Lulu.

'She's his wife.'

'And Emily is his mother. Was his mother.' As the car pulled away, Lulu took her phone from her handbag and took a quick photograph of it. 'Come on, let's go home,' she said.

'Tube?'

'No, I want to walk. I need the fresh air.'

18

Lulu made herself a glass of fresh mint tea as soon as they got back to *The Lark*. She poured Evian water into a saucer for Conrad. 'Well, that was an unpleasant experience,' she said, dropping down into the armchair.

'I suppose no one enjoys a will-reading,' said Conrad.

'Well that awful woman certainly didn't,' said Lulu.

'You said you'd met her once before, didn't you?'

'Yes, she and Richard flew over for Simon's funeral. To be honest, I didn't pay her much attention at the time.' She forced a smile. 'I had other things on my mind, obviously.' She inhaled the fragrance of her tea and then sipped it. 'How could she be so insensitive? And why didn't Richard stop her?'

'To be fair, he did tell her to be quiet.'

'She shouldn't need to be told.' She sighed and shook her head. 'And I'm going to have to see her again at Emily's funeral.'

'Were you surprised at the will?' asked Conrad. 'Did you expect Emily to leave everything to Richard?'

'Well, strictly speaking, that's not what happened. She left her estate to be split between her sons. Both of them.'

'But when Simon died, she should have changed her will, surely?'

'To do what?'

'Well, to leave money to you, obviously.'

'But I'm not a blood relative.'

'No, but you took care of her.'

'I know, but it's not as if Simon and I had children. Richard does, and it's only fair that her money goes to them.'

Conrad snorted. 'You think his wife will allow that? She wants to keep every penny she can.'

'Well, that's Richard's problem, not mine. I'm not short of money, Conrad. When we moved into the house in Warrington Crescent we sold our home in Islington, so that money is still in the bank. Simon was always very clever with his money – not like his brother. When Frank died he gave both boys two hundred and fifty thousand pounds each. Richard invested his money – though I'm not sure that's the right word – in an upmarket expat magazine in Marbella. He blew it all in less than six months and was then back asking Emily for more. Simon, though, opened up a new share-dealing account and called it the Frank Fund.' She smiled at the memory. 'He bought shares in all the companies that made the things that Frank enjoyed. Distillers because of their whiskies. Various restaurant groups. Rolls-Royce. The Savoy. It was done as a way of remembering him, but over the years the Frank Fund trebled in value.'

'Frank had a Rolls-Royce?'

Lulu laughed. 'No, he never drove. But he always loved to see them. True British craftsmanship can't be beaten, he always said, though of course they're made by BMW now. Frank used to say he felt safer in a plane powered by Rolls-Royce engines. He had a lot of quirks like that. Anyway, the point I'm making is that I'm not short of money. I've no problems at all with Emily's estate going to Richard.' She sipped her tea again. 'Mind you, I'm not thrilled with the idea of Maria spending Emily's money.'

'And it means the house goes to Richard.'

'That's okay, I don't think I'll ever want to live there again.' She looked around the boat. 'I like it here. It's . . . compact.'

'That's a word estate agents use when they mean small.'

Lulu laughed. 'It's manageable, that's what I mean. The house in Warrington Crescent is just too big. It was always meant as a family home, the perfect house for Emily and Frank to raise their boys. There were so many memories there, they were happy to live there after the boys had left. And Emily, she never wanted to leave. If it hadn't been for the Alzheimer's she'd be there still. But it was always too big for me and Simon.'

Lulu's phone rang and she picked it up and looked at the screen. It was Phil. She answered the call.

'Evening, boss. I hope I'm not disturbing you.'

'I'm retired, Phil. What's to disturb?'

'It's just that we've got something on your Dr Khan that I thought you should know ASAP.'

'I'm all ears.'

'Well, he's not Dr Khan, for a start. The real Dr Khan is working at the Wockhardt Hospital in Mumbai Central, where he's been for the last twelve years.'

'Wow. Now that's a surprise. My goodness.'

'Yeah, I thought I'd do a little digging just to cover my bases and found out straightaway that Dr Khan has never left India. We haven't yet worked out who the man in the home is but we'll arrest him, and his DNA and fingerprints should ID him pretty promptly. I have a guy pulling all his death certificates at the moment and we'll see where that leads us.'

'You think he was . . . you know . . . ?'

'I don't think anything at the moment, boss, I'm taking it one step at a time. But I can tell you for sure that the man working at the home is not Dr Khan. We'll pick him up tonight, sweat him in the cells and then question him first thing in the morning. I'll keep you in the loop, obviously.'

'I can't thank you enough, Phil. Thanks.'

She ended the call and realized that Conrad was watching her expectantly. She ran through what the inspector had told her. 'So do you think Dr Khan did something to Emily?' he asked once she had finished.

'It's too early to say,' said Lulu. 'You have to let the evidence guide the investigation. If you assume guilt, your subconscious starts to edit out the facts that don't back up your case. Phil is going about it the right way.' She smiled at Conrad. 'He was trained by the best.'

'That would be you?'

She picked up her glass of tea and toasted him. 'Indeed it would.'

19

Lulu was washing down the roof of *The Lark* again with the long-handled brush when her mobile phone rang. She pulled the phone from the back pocket of her jeans and looked at the screen. It was Richard calling. She really was in no mood to talk to him, but she took the call.

'Lulu, hello, how are you?'

'I'm as well as can be expected, Richard,' she said frostily. Conrad was sitting on the grass next to the towpath, basking in the morning sun.

'I just wanted to apologize again for what happened at the solicitor's office. Maria is truly appalled at her behaviour. She's going to write to you to say exactly how sorry she is.'

'There's really no need, Richard. Water under the bridge.'

'She is really mortified.'

'Tell her it's forgotten. Please.'

'That's very good of you, Lulu. I will. And I'm also calling to let you know that the funeral will be next Wednesday.'

'That's rather quick, isn't it?'

'Well, everyone is here in London, pretty much. It's not as if people will be flying in from around the world.'

'No, but people have diaries. And people often have trips pre-booked. Theatre tickets. People need notice, Richard.'

'I'm sure people will reassess their priorities,' said Richard.

'Anyway, it's all booked now. We'll be at the St Marylebone Crematorium on the East End Road. We're there at eleven a.m. and they're asking us to be prompt as they have a full card that day.'

Lulu's mouth fell open. 'What?' she said.

'St Marylebone Crematorium. It's a beautiful building. Lovely setting. And they are very reasonable.'

'Richard, Emily always wanted to be buried with Frank. In Kensal Green Cemetery. You know that.'

'Yes, I know that. It's in the will.'

'So what the hell are you doing taking her to a crematorium?' she snapped. She was gripping her phone so tightly that her knuckles had turned white.

'Lulu, don't fly off the handle, please. Emily's wishes are that she be buried next to her husband. And she will be. The will doesn't mention a coffin or a casket. All it says is that she wants to be buried in the same grave, so that's what will happen. Her ashes will be taken from the crematorium and they will be buried next to my father's grave.'

'But that's not what she wanted.'

'I've already spoken to Mr Turnbull and he says that I'm quite right, the wording is such that burying her ashes is in complete agreement with her wishes.'

'But it so obviously isn't!' said Lulu. 'She wanted a coffin, she wanted to be lowered into the ground and to be next to Frank. That's what they both wanted. Frank bought the plot more than thirty years ago.'

'Lulu, I don't understand why you're getting so upset. I'm sure if Emily was alive she'd be more than happy to be cremated. Burials are so wasteful; cremation is better for the environment, it's a more efficient use of resources. Nearly eighty per cent of bodies are cremated – that's just the way it is. Simon was cremated, remember?'

'Of course I remember, I'm not senile. Yes, Simon was cremated. That's what he wanted. And I'll be cremated, too, when the time comes. But it's not what Emily wanted. And with the greatest of respect, you barely knew Emily.'

'How can you say that? She was my mother.'

'Yes, and how many times did you see her over the last thirty years?'

'That's not a fair question. I was abroad. I was an expat.'

'Yes, and the only time you came to London was when you wanted money.'

'That's uncalled for, Lulu.'

'But it's the truth. How many times have you visited your father's grave?'

There was no answer, and that was because, as Lulu knew, the answer was never.

'Emily visited Frank's grave every Sunday to lay fresh flowers and keep it looking nice. I often went with her. So did your brother. And every time she was there she would talk about joining him. So please don't tell me that she would be happy to be cremated. She wouldn't.'

'Well, clearly we are going to have to agree to disagree about this,' said Richard. 'As I said, the cremation will be at eleven o'clock sharp. It's up to you whether you attend or not.'

He ended the call, leaving Lulu fuming. She took a couple of deep breaths to calm herself. Conrad jumped onto the bow and then leaped onto the roof. 'Are you okay?' he said, looking up at her anxiously.

She dropped the brush on the roof and sat down, her eyes

brimming with tears. Conrad padded over to her and gently butted his head against her arm. She gathered him up and hugged him, pressing her face against his fur. 'I'm sorry,' she said.

'It's okay,' said Conrad.

'He's being so horrible.' She explained what Richard had said.

'Can he do that?'

'He's the executor. And he says he has checked with Mr Turnbull already.' She sniffed. 'I know what Emily wanted and she wouldn't want to be burned into ashes and dumped next to Frank as if she were a pile of rubbish.'

'What can you do?'

Lulu sniffed again. 'I don't know. I really don't know.' She pressed her face harder against Conrad's fur. 'I wish Simon was here. He'd know what to do.' She began to sob. 'I miss him so much.'

'I know you do,' whispered Conrad. She closed her eyes and held him close as he rubbed his head against her chin. 'Stay strong,' he said.

'I'll try.'

'I'm here for you,' said Conrad.

Lulu sighed. 'Thank you.'

'I've an idea,' he said. 'Why don't you take me to all the places Emily liked? The places around here that meant a lot to her. You said she liked afternoon tea at the Colonnade Hotel – why don't you show me her other favourite places?'

She put him down and wiped away her tears. 'Like a tour? An Emily Lewis tour?'

'Yes. Exactly.'

'I love it,' said Lulu. 'And I shall take a glass and a bottle and drink a toast to her at every stop.'

'You might be drunk by the time you finish,' said Conrad.

'Now that definitely sounds like a plan.' She stood up and wiped her eyes again. 'Right. Let me get organized.' She bent down and opened the fridge door. 'I think Pinot Grigio,' she said, taking out a bottle and putting it on the counter. She opened a drawer and took out a corkscrew, then retrieved a crystal wine glass from a cupboard. She wrinkled her nose. 'I can't be seen carrying an opened bottle of wine through the streets of Maida Vale, can I?'

She took her large Louis Vuitton bag from a cupboard and put it on the sofa. She put the glass in the bag, then frowned and took it out and wrapped it in a scarf. She looked at Conrad and smiled. 'This is quite exciting, isn't it?'

'It's an adventure, yes,' said Conrad.

Lulu opened the bottle of wine with the corkscrew, then unscrewed the cork and slid it back into the neck of the bottle. She put the bottle into the bag and slung it over her shoulder. 'Right, off we go,' she said. She went up the steps to the rear deck, waited for Conrad to join her and closed the door.

'Don't you ever lock it?' asked Conrad.

'If I'm away overnight, yes, but not if I'm only gone for a few hours,' she said.

'You're a very trusting person.'

'It's Maida Vale,' she said. 'Very low crime rate.'

She bent down and let Conrad jump onto her shoulders, looked both ways, and then stepped onto the towpath.

'So where are we going?' asked Conrad, as they walked towards Blomfield Road.

'Not too far,' said Lulu. 'Just a few hundred feet, in fact.'

Conrad walked with her around the corner to a line of shops and restaurants. Lulu stopped outside the Red Pepper, which despite the name had a blue awning above the pavement. 'A pizza place?' said Conrad.

'Emily loved pizza,' said Lulu. 'Frank was a real gourmet, he loved his food and was a regular at all the Michelin star places in London. Alain Ducasse, Marco Pierre White, Gordon Ramsay, Heston Blumenthal – he knew them all. Emily shared his love of fine dining, but she loved pizza too. She brought me here for the opening night, back in 1994. And she stayed a regular, usually when Frank was away on business because he was never a fan of pizza.'

'What did Frank do?'

'His family made their money during the war, in engineering,' she said, taking the bottle from her bag. 'They had a factory that made car parts and they switched to making components for aircraft like the Spitfire and the Hurricane. Frank was a child then, but in the fifties he used the family's money to buy up bomb-damaged property. That turned a small fortune into a much larger one and he stayed in property development but started investing in restaurants and West End shows.' She took the cork out of the bottle and sloshed some into the glass. She raised the glass at the window. 'I'll miss you, Emily,' she said. 'I already do.' She drank the wine, flicked the dregs onto the pavement and put the glass back into her handbag. She recorked the bottle and put that in the bag, too.

She turned onto Castellain Road, lined with four-storey mansion blocks, crossed over Sutherland Avenue and walked to Lauderdale Parade, a small cluster of shops and delis. On the corner was Le Cochonnet. 'Emily sure liked her pizza,' said Conrad, as Lulu sat down on a wooden bench overlooking the restaurant. There were only a few tables occupied and a waitress was carrying two large pizzas over to one of them. Two chefs were standing next to an impressive pizza oven.

'We were at the opening of the Piglet, back in July 1985. Emily always called it by its English name. It was mobbed. Hundreds of people came and they spilled out into the street. Peter and Graham, who owned the building, had run restaurants before and they had loads of celebrity friends. Simon and I had only just got married and we went with Frank and Emily.'

'You said that Frank wasn't a fan of pizza?'

'Ah, back then it wasn't a pizza place, it was a French bistro. Lovely food. The pizza oven came later.' She took the glass from her bag, uncorked the bottle and poured in some wine. 'I was a DS back then, a detective sergeant. I could see people drinking and then getting into the cars and driving home and Simon kept telling me I had to let it go. We got into a bit of a fight. Well, an argument, anyway. We never really fought. He was a criminal barrister back then so he was trying to keep the bad guys out of prison and I was trying to keep them in.'

'Did you enjoy being a policeman? Policewoman?'

Lulu laughed. 'They stopped calling women WPCs in the seventies. Nowadays it's officers. Or policeperson, for all I know.' She sipped her wine. 'It was a whole different world back then. It wasn't so much a glass ceiling as a metal one with rivets and studs. I made it to superintendent, but I was a rarity in the Met. The idea of having a female commissioner would have been pure fantasy. A lot has changed.' She took another sip of wine. 'Not always for the better.' She raised her glass towards the restaurant. 'I miss you so much, Emily.'

She drained her glass and shook it to get rid of the dregs, then recorked the bottle and put it and the glass in her bag. She smiled at Conrad. 'Onwards and upwards,' she said. 'You should jump on my shoulders, we'll be crossing Elgin Avenue and they tend to speed there.'

Conrad did as he was told and made himself comfortable around her neck. Lulu stood up and walked to the zebra crossing opposite the City of Westminster College. A white van stopped to let her cross and she flashed the driver a smile. She walked down Morshead Road to Paddington Recreation Ground, then through the gates and along the path that circled the main grassy area. A dozen or so people were jogging at various speeds around the blue running track.

'Did you know that most outdoor athletics tracks are red?' asked Conrad.

'I have to confess, no, I didn't.' She walked past the quiet garden and around the small bandstand, towards the south side of the park.

'It's the most UV stable colour and takes longer to react and fade in the sunlight,' said Conrad.

'Well, now I know,' said Lulu. 'The one here used to be red but they changed it to blue some years ago.'

'It's usually indoor tracks that are blue,' said Conrad.

Lulu chuckled. 'Do you think someone made a mistake?'

'I do,' said Conrad. He shrugged. 'Mistakes happen.'

Lulu reached a vacant bench and sat down. Conrad climbed down and sat next to her, looking out over the cricket pitch. Three women were exercising their dogs together in the middle of the pitch – an Alsatian, a Great Dane and a Rhodesian ridgeback. The dogs clearly knew each other and were chasing around and play-fighting.

'Emily and Frank had dogs for most of their lives,' said Lulu.

'Everyone has their faults,' said Conrad.

Lulu laughed. 'They loved spaniels. They had four in all, over the years. No, five. They usually had two, a younger one and an older one.'

'So that when one died they still had one left?'

'They never said as much, but yes, I think that was the idea.' She poured a small amount of wine into the glass. This was going to be a long tour and she wanted to be still standing at the end of it. 'They used to bring the dogs here for exercise. If Frank was working, then Emily would come alone. Every day, at least twice a day, rain or shine.'

'See, the great thing about cats is that we don't need to be walked.'

'True.' She sipped her wine and then gestured with her glass at the pavilion to their left and the running track beyond. 'This is where Roger Bannister trained before he broke the four-minute mile,' she said. 'He was a medical student at St Mary's Hospital and he trained here every day until he broke the record in 1954. He did the actual run in Oxford, but Emily saw him run here many times. She was a teenager, still at school.' She chuckled. 'I think she had a bit of a crush on him.'

'Did she have a dog before she went into the home?'

'No. They had one when Frank passed away. A springer spaniel called Milo. Milo was quite old and they'd been thinking about getting another puppy but then Frank got sick and they didn't. Milo died a few years later and Emily said she'd had enough of dogs. She was in her eighties then and the twice-daily walks rain or shine had become a bit tiresome.'

'She should have got herself a cat.'

'Emily was always a dog person.' Lulu finished her wine, shook the glass, and put it in her handbag.

'Well I can assure you that she was very much a cat person, too,' said Conrad. 'The way she allowed me to sit on her lap and the way she stroked me told me all I needed to know. And her aura.'

'You liked her? That's good.'

'I liked her a lot.'

Lulu stood up. 'Okay, on we go,' she said, putting her bag on her shoulder.

It was a twenty-five-minute walk back through St John's Wood to Lord's Cricket Ground. 'Frank was a member of the MCC – the Marylebone Cricket Club,' said Lulu as they walked up to the main entrance. 'For going on thirty years. He always wore their egg-and-bacon tie.'

'Egg and bacon?' repeated Conrad.

'It's red and yellow. The MCC tie. Emily would buy him a new one every Christmas.' She smiled. 'She carried on buying them even after he passed away. Every Christmas morning, under the tree, there'd be a wrapped tie for him.'

There wasn't a match on and the gates were shut. Lulu peered through them. 'Emily loved cricket almost as much as Frank did. They spent a lot of time here. And then when Frank died, she used to come here with Simon. I'd often tag along, though I know next to nothing about cricket.'

'We're closed!' said a voice. A large black man in a high-vis jacket walked towards them on the other side of the fence. 'Next match is on Saturday,' he growled.

'That's okay, Joe,' said Lulu, recognizing him. 'Just having a look.' Joe was a big West Indian man who had worked at Lord's for more than twenty years and before that had been a paratrooper who had served in Northern Ireland until a bullet in the thigh had ended his army career.

Joe peered through the fence. 'Oh, hello, Lulu. Not seen you for donkey's. How's Emily? Not seen her for a while, either.'

'I'm sorry, Joe. Emily passed away.'

'Oh my God, no. That's terrible. When?'

'Sunday night. I'm just taking Conrad around her favourite places.'

Joe looked through the fence. 'Conrad?'

Lulu pointed at the ground. 'My cat.'

Joe looked down and laughed when he saw Conrad looking up at him. 'Well I never. I didn't know you had a cat.'

'He's just adopted me.'

Joe spotted the bottle in her hand. 'What's the story with the wine?'

'Oh, nothing. I'm just raising a glass to Emily in the places she loved.'

'That's such a lovely idea,' he said. He unbolted the gate. 'Come on in.'

'Are you sure?'

'The bosses are all away on some diversity and inclusion in the workplace training course,' he said. 'We've got the place to ourselves.'

'Get yourself a glass,' said Lulu. 'You can join me.'

'Can't do a glass, but I've got my mug.'

He closed the gate after them and disappeared into the security office, reappearing with an Arsenal mug a few seconds later. 'You know, to do this right we should do it where she liked to sit. The Tavern Stand, right?'

Lulu nodded. 'That's where she and Frank always sat.'

'Come on then.' He took them around the stadium to the Tavern Stand and Lulu led the way to Emily's favourite seats. She sat down and Joe sat next to her. Conrad jumped up onto the seat next to Emily.

'I'm so sorry for your loss,' Joe said.

'I'm still in shock, Joe.' She took the glass from her handbag, and uncorked the wine. She poured some into Joe's mug and half-filled her glass. 'To Emily,' she said, and clinked her glass against his mug.

'To Emily,' echoed Joe. 'A lovely lady. Salt of the earth. She always asked about my boys and, that time I was in hospital with my knee, she came to visit and brought me home-made chicken soup. I'll miss her.'

They both drank. It was definitely cricket weather – an almost cloudless blue sky and a soft breeze coming from the pavilion off to their left.

'What happened, if you don't mind me asking?' said Joe.

'She'd had problems with Alzheimer's for quite a while. I thought she was okay but apparently not.'

'Yeah, my mum had Alzheimer's,' he said. 'My dad did all he could but eventually she had to go into a home. She kept getting sick. Pneumonia mostly. She made it through the Covid and then got bad flu.' He forced a smile. 'Getting old sucks.'

'It does, yes,' said Lulu. 'But it's better than the alternative.'

Joe frowned as he tried to work out what she meant, then realization dawned and he smiled. 'Yes, I suppose it is.' He stood up. 'Right, I'll love you and leave you. You let yourself out.' He smiled down at the cat. 'Pleasure to meet you, Conrad.'

Conrad looked up at him. 'Meow.'

'No, we'll be off,' said Lulu.

'Where are you headed?' asked Joe as they walked towards the gate.

'The Lisson Gallery.'

'Oh, nice. I sometimes pop in after work if there's an interesting exhibition there.'

Joe let them out of the gate and Lulu started walking towards Edgware Road Tube station. The Lisson Gallery was in Bell Street, just around the corner from the station. It was just over a mile from Lord's and Conrad walked at her heels all the way. The gallery was a four-storey brick building. It had been converted from a derelict shell in the sixties and now had fifteen thousand square feet of space, often given over to new and exciting artists, more often than not with a conceptual or minimalist slant.

'Emily and Frank used to love coming here,' said Lulu. 'They probably bought a dozen or so paintings over the years.'

There was nowhere to sit so she juggled the bottle and the glass and poured herself a small drink. She toasted Emily and downed the wine in one go. 'Cheers, Emily,' she said. 'I'll always be grateful for the way you opened my eyes to art.'

'Any paintings of cats?' asked Conrad.

'Rarely,' said Lulu. 'Though I did once see a painting of dogs playing poker.'

Conrad looked up at her. 'Really?'

'I'm joking,' said Lulu. She shook the glass and put it back into her bag. 'Come on, back to Little Venice.'

The quickest way to the Bridge House was along Edgware Road, but it was a noisy, polluted thoroughfare, so instead Lulu took a meandering route along St Mary's Terrace and across the Rembrandt Gardens. It was a twenty-minute walk, and a pleasant one, and for most of the route Conrad stuck to her heels.

'I'm guessing Emily wasn't at the opening of the Bridge House,' said Conrad, looking up at the white three-storey pub. It was on the corner of two wide roads, with a small terrace to the right of the entrance.

Lulu laughed. 'Hardly. This goes back to the eighteen hundreds,' she said. She looked at her bottle, which was now half empty. 'Are you hungry? They do a lovely fried squid. And a delicious mackerel pate. We could share.'

'Either sounds great,' said Conrad.

The outside tables were generally commandeered by smokers, but it was still early so they were unoccupied. Lulu sat down and Conrad jumped up onto the adjacent chair. A waitress appeared almost immediately. She was one of the regular staff, a charming West Country girl with dyed red hair and eyelash extensions that gave her the look of a cartoon fawn. Lulu held up the wine bottle and smiled apologetically. 'Briana, I know this is a little naughty, but I'm working my way through this bottle. Is there any way I could finish it at this table?'

'That is naughty,' said Briana. 'But I don't think it's a problem. Maybe keep the bottle in your bag just in case the boss walks by.'

'You're an angel,' said Lulu. She uncorked the bottle and poured herself some wine.

'And you brought your own glass,' said Briana. 'I hope you're not going to make a habit of this – you'll put us all out of business.'

'No, this is a one-off. We're on something of a pilgrimage, you see.'

The waitress frowned. 'We?'

Lulu waved her glass at Conrad. 'My date.'

'Well isn't he a fine-looking cat,' said Briana. 'A calico. I love calicos. But aren't all calicos female?'

'Conrad is a very special calico cat,' said Lulu, putting the cork back into the bottle and sliding the bottle into her bag.

'And you're on a pilgrimage, you say?'

Lulu nodded. 'My mother-in-law passed away. Emily.'

'Oh, good Lord, no. Oh that's awful. I'm so sorry to hear that. She was a lovely lady.'

'Yes, it was quite sudden. So Conrad and I are visiting all the places she liked, and she always loved it here.'

'She used to go to the review upstairs all the time.' Briana patted her chest. 'I can't believe it. That's just terrible. I'm so sorry for your loss, Lulu.'

'Thank you.'

'Can I ask what happened?'

'Alzheimer's. That's what the doctors say, anyway.'

'Oh, my grandad had that. It was terrible. It drove my gran crazy. Towards the end he forgot everything. He'd say something and then five minutes later he'd say it again. And again. He thought my gran was his mum and he thought I was his gran. He was so sweet most of the time, but then he'd get angry because he couldn't remember something.'

She grimaced. 'I'm sorry, listen to me rambling on. Would you like to eat something?'

She offered Lulu a menu but Lulu waved it away. 'I was going to choose between the squid and the mackerel pate and then I thought, what the hell, let's have both.'

'Good choice.' She looked at the cat. 'And anything to drink for you?'

Conrad pricked up his ears. 'Meow,' he said.

'Water,' said Lulu. 'Evian, if you have it.'

'I got that,' said Briana, with a smile. She went back inside.

'So Emily was a regular here?' asked Conrad.

'She was, it's a lovely pub,' said Lulu. 'It's very theatrical with lots of original features. And there's a gorgeous red velvet curtain covering the entrance to the toilet. But the main reason she and Frank came here was to attend the Canal Cafe Theatre upstairs. They do a really funny news review show that changes regularly so that it's always topical. It's in a small room with a tiny stage and a piano so you really are up close and personal. After Frank passed away she used to come on her own, or with me and Simon. We'd have dinner in the pub and then take a bottle of wine upstairs. Great fun.'

Lulu heard a noise behind her and saw it was Briana returning with the water. Her cheeks flushed as she realized that Briana must have heard her talking. The waitress sensed her embarrassment and flashed her a reassuring smile. 'I always talk to my dog,' she said. 'Sometimes I swear he understands every word.' She poured the water into a glass bowl and placed it on the ground next to the chair Conrad was sitting on.

'Ah, but does he talk back?' asked Lulu.

'Actually, he does,' said Briana. 'He puts his head to one

side and he makes a woofing noise or a growl. And he has one sort of woof when he wants food and another for when he wants to go out.' She gestured at Conrad. 'What about him? Does he talk?'

'Oh yes, he's a regular chatterbox. Say something to the nice lady, Conrad.'

Conrad looked up at the waitress, pricked up his ears and said 'Meow.'

'Brilliant,' said Briana.

Lulu sipped her wine and watched the waitress walk away. 'Can I ask you a question?' she said.

Conrad looked over at her. 'Sure,' he said. 'But nothing to do with history. I'm terrible at dates.'

Lulu chuckled. 'Do you talk to anyone else, the way you talk to me?'

'I'm very selective,' he said.

'And very evasive.' Lulu raised her glass to him. 'If you don't want to tell me, it's okay.'

'No, I can tell you,' he said. 'As I said before, if too many people know what I can do, it'll end badly. The scientists will want to know how it works so they'll begin by testing me and eventually they'll want to start cutting me up.'

'Oh, they won't. Don't be so paranoid.'

'They still experiment on animals, Lulu. Mice and dogs and cats and pigs and even monkeys. Sure, they'll start off talking to me, but there'll come a point when talking isn't enough. Then they'll reach for the knife.'

'Nonsense,' said Lulu. 'There are scans they can do. X-rays. All sorts of non-invasive things.'

'So let me get this straight. My life can follow two paths. Path One: I am locked in a lab where I am prodded and poked by men in white coats who probably aren't even cat lovers. Or Path Two: I live on a lovely narrowboat in Little Venice with a lovely lady who takes me for walks and feeds me at wonderful restaurants. Hmmm, let me think, which one do I prefer?'

Lulu laughed. 'Okay, I hear you.'

Conrad stared at her with unblinking green eyes. 'Seriously, though. People claim to be animal lovers but really they're not. Ask cows and chickens and pigs if they think humans love them. Love to eat them, maybe. But that's not real love. When humans claim to love animals they really mean they love pets.'

'I can't argue with that,' said Lulu. 'By rights I should be a vegetarian. Or a vegan.'

'No, don't get me wrong,' said Conrad. 'I eat meat. And I've killed my fair share of mice and birds. It's just that I'm not a hypocrite.'

Lulu gasped. 'So you're saying I'm a hypocrite? That's not very nice.'

'Now don't go getting all sensitive on me, Lulu. That's not what I meant. I can see from your aura that you are a genuine animal lover.'

'I always buy organic.'

'I'm sure you do. And I know you wouldn't stand to see any animal suffer. But not everyone has a good heart like you, Lulu. So I am very careful who I speak to.'

'I'll never let you down.'

Conrad purred loudly. 'I know that.'

Lulu took another sip of wine. She was starting to feel a little light-headed. The Bridge House was going to be the last stop on her tribute walk; *The Lark* was only a few minutes away. She was just about to thank Conrad for suggesting the walk when the waitress appeared with their food, so she just smiled. Briana placed two plates on the table and a bowl of water. 'Can I get you anything else?' she asked.

'No, this is perfect,' said Lulu. 'Thank you.'

The waitress looked down at Conrad. 'What about you, sir?'

Conrad gazed up at her. 'Meow,' he said.

Briana chuckled as she walked away.

'You have a fan there,' said Lulu, picking up a piece of squid and placing it in front of Conrad.

He sniffed it delicately. 'She has a good aura,' he said. 'For a dog person.' He licked the squid and then took a bite. Lulu stabbed a piece with a fork and sighed appreciatively as she chewed.

20

Lulu crawled off the bed and padded along to the galley to put the kettle on. The stove was still hot and the embers cast a warm glow across the cabin. She showered and pulled on jeans and a polo-neck sweater and returned to the galley just as the kettle began to whistle. She made herself a cup of instant coffee and put a bowl of Evian water down for Conrad. 'How's your head?' he asked.

'Surprisingly good,' she said, sitting on the sofa. 'But then I've never really got hangovers from wine, especially white wine.' She sipped her coffee. 'Plus we were walking from place to place so I think that burned off the alcohol. I'd hate you to think that I drank like that every day.'

'It was a nice day. I learned a lot about Emily.' Conrad lapped at his water, then sat down and looked up at Emily. 'How do you feel?'

'As I said, no hangover. I'm good to go.'

'I didn't mean that,' said Conrad. 'I meant how do you feel about your mother-in-law passing?'

Lulu shrugged. 'Wow, that's a tough one. My mind's in a bit of a whirl at the moment.' She frowned as she drank her coffee. 'Emily was old and I knew she wasn't going to live forever, obviously. So I was getting used to the idea that she was reaching the end of her life. But it happened so suddenly, you know? One moment she was here and then I'm told she isn't here.' She sighed and brushed away a tear with the

169

back of her hand. 'When my father passed away, it was a gradual process, you know? He was old and bit by bit his body just failed. His last few days weren't easy but he was at home and they kept him on morphine and when he was conscious he was able to recognize me and even say a few words. I'm not saying I was happy when he finally passed away – he was my dad and I loved him with all my heart – but at least he wasn't suffering. He'd lived a good life and it was time to go.'

'What about your mother? Is she still alive?'

Lulu shook her head. 'No, she passed away two years before my father. And again it was a slow process. She fell and broke a hip and was taken to hospital and then she got pneumonia. The doctors said she probably wouldn't recover and we all had the chance to say goodbye to her. It was all long before that Covid nonsense so we could all go and see her, and my father and I were with her when she passed away. It was actually quite peaceful, despite all the machines around her.' She paused. 'I think that's what's upsetting me, the fact that it was so sudden.'

'Like when Simon died? The hit and run?'

Lulu looked at him over the top of her coffee mug and frowned. 'I hadn't thought of that,' she said quietly.

'Maybe you had, but subconsciously,' said Conrad quietly.

'You're right. Yes. Oh, my God. Yes. It is the same.' She raised her eyebrows. 'You are one clever cat.'

'I think it's more about empathy than intelligence,' said Conrad. 'I feel your unhappiness and I understand it.' He jumped up onto the sofa and gently headbutted her.

'It was the suddenness of it,' said Lulu softly, almost to herself. 'Simon was on his way home. I was cooking dinner.

We were having dinner with Emily that evening. Emily was already with me and we'd opened a bottle of Pinot Grigio. I'd phoned him to let him know it was almost ready and he said he'd be right there. Those were the last words he ever said to me. And my last words to him were "See you soon." That was it. I didn't even say that I loved him. He didn't see me soon, and after half an hour and his dinner was on the table I phoned him and a policeman answered, and that's how I found out that he was dead.' She put a hand up to her head. She felt suddenly faint.

Conrad gently butted her again. 'It must have been terrible.'

'Oh, it was,' said Lulu. 'It was as if I'd been punched in the face. I just collapsed. The policeman was so matter-of-fact about it. It was only later that I realized he was probably still at the scene. Simon was lying in the road and the policeman was trying to deal with it all.' She shuddered.

'And when you got to the nursing home, it was the same, wasn't it? That silly boy was so matter-of-fact about it.'

'He was embarrassed, I understand that. But yes, it was another shock. I was looking forward to sitting with Emily and having a chat and then – bang! She's dead. Dead and gone. And they've taken her away so that I can't even see the body. Alive one second, dead the next.' She sighed and brushed away another tear. 'I never got the chance to tell Emily how much I loved her, how much she meant to me. That walk you and I did yesterday was wonderful, it really was, but I should have done it with her. I should have taken her to all those places and talked about why they were so special to us.' She sniffed. 'What were my last words to her? "I'll see you tomorrow." It means nothing. And it was a lie.

And her last words to me were asking who I was? Remember? She asked me who I was and I told her my name and then I said I would see her again.' She shook her head sadly. 'I should have told her that I loved her.'

'She knew.'

'You think so?'

Conrad nodded. 'I'm sure so. I could tell. She was full of love for you. She knew who you were, she just couldn't remember the name. And she knew how much you loved her.'

'I hope so. And I hope Simon knew, too.' She wiped away another tear. 'I just don't understand why this is happening. First Simon. Now Emily. It's just awful.'

'It's the circle of life,' said Conrad.

Lulu's jaw dropped. 'What?'

'You know. The circle of life.'

Lulu laughed out loud. 'So now I'm talking to the Lion King, is that it? The circle of life?' She sighed. 'Oh Conrad, you do make me laugh sometimes.' She sipped her coffee.

'What's wrong?'

She lowered her mug. 'What's wrong? Life isn't a circle. It's a straight line. There's a beginning where you are born, a middle bit where, with any luck, you enjoy your life, and there's the end, where it all stops. There's no circle.'

'I guess the circle is the bit about having children.' He fell quiet and lowered his head. 'Oh,' he said eventually.

'That's right. Simon and I never had children. So there's no circle.'

Conrad walked over and pressed himself against her side. He arched his back and she began to stroke him.

'Is that why you're here, Conrad? To help me get through this?'

He turned his head to look at her. 'Do you mean did I know that Emily was going to die? No.'

'But cats can tell, right? I told you about the cat at the nursing home who used to lie down next to residents before they died. As if she knew and wanted to help them pass away.'

'Sure, we can see from a person's aura when they are about to die. But that's not the same as predicting the future. Emily's aura looked great when I saw her. I told you that.'

'She was fine, wasn't she?'

Conrad nodded. He stopped arching his back and sat down next to her. 'She had the aura of a healthy person. Yes. I could see that she was forgetting things, but that happens when people get older, doesn't it?'

'Often times, yes.'

Conrad pushed his head against her arm and she began stroking him again. He purred loudly.

'So you coming along is a coincidence?'

'Serendipity, I'd call it. Happenstance, maybe.'

'Happenstance? Yes, I like that. So you're not an angel, then?'

Conrad chuckled. 'An angel? I'm a cat, Lulu. A calico cat. Do you see wings and a halo and a harp? No, you don't. You see whiskers and fur and a tail.'

'And a very smart cat you are, too.' Her phone rang and she picked it up. It was Phil Jackson. 'Hi Phil, how are things?' she said.

'All good, boss. You okay to talk?'

'Go ahead.' She smiled at Conrad and stroked his back. He purred with pleasure.

'We need to talk, boss, and the way the world is at the moment it's probably best face to face.'

'I understand, Phil. Walls have ears.'

'And loose lips sink ships.' He laughed. 'Is the Devonshire Arms okay? I was planning on lunch around one.'

'I'll see you there, Phil. And thanks.' She switched off the phone and smiled at Conrad. 'I've got to meet him in Kensington,' she said. 'How are you in taxis?'

'Very well behaved,' he said.

'So you'll come with me?'

He softly butted his head against her arm. 'Of course.'

21

The Devonshire Arms was a traditional English pub with a cream frontage and a pretty terrace to the side. Phil Jackson had always been a smoker, so Lulu wasn't surprised to see him sitting outside with a pint of beer in front of him and a lit cigarette in his hand. She had caught an Uber taxi from Blomfield Road and Conrad had sat in her lap all the way. Conrad walked by her side as she went over to greet Phil with a hug.

'You're looking well, boss,' said Phil.

'You, too.' His unruly hair had more grey in it than the last time she'd seen him and his smoking habit was doing his teeth no favours, but he was still a good-looking guy with deep-set dark brown eyes and a strong chin. His skin was the colour of burnished mahogany, reflecting his father's Barbadian roots, and he had his Irish mother's ready smile and sense of humour. He was in his late forties but was still trim and lacking the pot belly that tended to afflict most detectives after a decade or two of pub lunches and after-work curries. 'White wine, boss?'

'Chardonnay would be perfect, Phil, thanks.'

Phil put his half-smoked cigarette onto an ashtray and nodded at Conrad. 'Is he with you?'

'He is indeed. His name is Conrad. And if you don't mind, I'm sure he'd love a bowl of Evian.'

'Not tap water?'

Conrad looked at him. 'Meow!' he said.

'Right,' said Phil. 'Evian it is. Do you want to eat? They do a great Scotch egg.'

'Definitely,' said Lulu.

Phil looked down at Conrad. 'What about you, mate? They do beer-battered cod goujons, we could peel off the batter.'

'Meow!' said Conrad.

'I'll take that as a yes,' said Phil. He went off into the pub. Conrad jumped up onto the seat next to Lulu.

'He's a nice guy,' said Lulu.

'Meow,' said Conrad.

Lulu realized that there were two men at the neighbouring table, smoking roll-ups and drinking cider, and they had obviously heard her talking to Conrad. She smiled over at them and they raised their glasses. 'I talk to him all the time,' she said.

'He's a lovely-looking cat,' said the older of the men, who had long grey hair tied back in a ponytail and a straggly grey beard.

'Thank you.'

'What do they call that colour?' said the second man. He was in his thirties with a flat cap atop a mop of ginger hair.

'Calico,' said Lulu.

'That's right. You see it with horses, too, don't you?'

'Yes, you do,' said Lulu.

'And llamas,' said the ginger man.

The older man turned to look at him. 'Are you serious?'

'Yeah, it was an answer in a pub quiz I did once.'

'Well, you live and learn,' said Lulu.

Phil returned with a glass of wine and a bowl of water.

He gave Lulu the glass, put the bowl on the table and sat down. 'Food's on the way.' He leaned across the table and lowered his voice. 'Sorry about the cloak and dagger, boss, but they're looking for any excuse to get rid of dinosaurs like me. They bug our phones, and that's not a joke. They check all our emails and God forbid you try to crack a joke on Facebook or Twitter.'

'Are you on Facebook and Twitter?'

Phil chuckled and shook his head. 'Of course not.'

'That's what I thought.'

'What about you, boss?'

'I've never seen the attraction of social media,' said Lulu. 'Anti-social media would seem to be a better name.'

Phil nodded. 'I've lost count of the number of guys who've been kicked out of the job for something they said, often in jest. The bosses were encouraging us to use WhatsApp groups to share intel but then they started spying on the groups. Worse than that, they were getting guys from Professional Standards to join under false identities and then they'd start egging people on.'

'Entrapment?'

'With a capital E, boss. I mean, the job is a minefield now, you can't afford to put a foot wrong. I can remember back in the day when you might describe a young tearaway as a bit of a monkey – you'd get the sack for that now.'

'Things have changed, Phil. You know that.'

'Tell me about it,' said Phil. 'Soon as my pension is locked in, I'm off.'

'Where to?'

He laughed. 'Well, that's the question, isn't it? My dad left me a plot of land in Barbados, not far from the sea, so

I was thinking of building a house there. I've an uncle who works for the Bridgetown cops, and he says they could always use me.'

'Nice,' said Lulu.

'On the other hand, I've loads of relatives on my mum's side in Galway. Spent most of my summers there as a kid and I was always happy there. Plus my Irish passport gives me access to the whole of Europe.'

'You're spoiled for choice, Phil.'

He smiled ruefully. 'Not really. Barbados is too bloody hot and it's always raining in Galway.'

'I've never really had to make a decision like that. West London, born and bred.'

'Yeah, you see, I've always been a visitor. I was born in Hastings and only moved to the Big Smoke to work. I never really saw it as a permanent move.'

'And how many years have you been here?'

He chuckled. 'Yeah. Going on twenty. It's like John Lennon said, right? Life is what happens while you're making plans.' He sipped his pint and then put down his glass. 'So, to the matter in hand. Dr Kamran Khan. Or the man passing himself off as Dr Khan. His real name is Samesh Gupta. He's not a doctor but he is a qualified nurse. He worked with the real Dr Khan in Mumbai.'

'So he came over pretending to be Dr Khan?'

Phil shook his head. 'Bit more complicated than that. I like to think that the Home Office would have spotted a bogus application, but these days, who knows. No, Sammy – that's what he calls himself – was issued with an education visa to come to London and study for some nursing quali-fication. So he came in quite legally – his photograph and prints are on file so we had no problems identifying him. And he came clean straight away. Admits to it all.'

'He admits to killing patients?'

Phil threw up his hands. 'No, no, no,' he said. 'Nothing like that. No, he admits to pretending to be Dr Khan and getting jobs under false pretences. He actually finished his nursing qualification – top of his class, as it happens – but instead of returning to Mumbai he took over Dr Khan's identity and got a job with a nursing home in Reading.'

'And they didn't check?'

'He'd put a lot of planning into it. He'd stolen Dr Khan's passport a year before he came to the UK. It was cancelled and Dr Khan applied for a new one, so Sammy couldn't use it to enter the country. But once he was here he could use it as ID. He doesn't look too dissimilar to the real Dr Khan, and the way Sammy tells it, the nursing home in Reading was so short-staffed that they didn't bother checking references, they just took him on. Initially he was providing cover for when their regular doctor was away but then he quit and Sammy – Dr Khan – was hired.'

'And no one realized that he wasn't a real doctor?'

Phil shook his head. 'He never put a foot wrong. The way he explained it is that the people in those homes aren't there to get better. So no one is expecting a cure, just that they are kept comfortable. He'd prescribe anti-depressants for the depressed ones, tranquillizers for the hyper ones, and pain-killers for the ones who were hurting. He was a good nurse so he knew his medications and he knew how to behave like a doctor.'

'Did many patients die under his care?'

'So far as I can see, the death rates at the homes he worked at were no different to any other home. In fact, it looks as if he actually saved lives.'

'How so?'

Phil took another swallow of his beer. 'The home he worked at before the one in St John's Wood was in Croydon. He was there during the Covid pandemic. Seems that Sammy got wind of what was going to happen and brought in his own PPE. Gloves, overalls, face masks, the works, for himself and for staff dealing with the most vulnerable patients. He set up a no-contact visitor policy and then arranged it so that visitors stayed outside the building and talked to their relatives through a window. And when the NHS hospitals started to send elderly patients who had tested positive for Covid back to the nursing homes, Sammy instituted a quarantine procedure. His bosses reckon that he saved dozens of lives. I mean, short-term, obviously, because the patients were all very old. But he made a difference.'

'Wow, that's not what I expected to hear,' said Lulu.

'I know,' said Phil. 'What he did was wrong, but he doesn't appear to have hurt anybody.'

'What did he do it for? The money?'

Phil nodded. 'Nurses get paid almost nothing in India. Doctors' pay isn't much better. He says he sent most of what he earned back to his family in Mumbai. He lives in a rented room in Kilburn and cycles to work.'

'Now I'm starting to feel guilty for drawing attention to him,' said Lulu.

'Well, what he did was wrong, no question of that. He's overstayed his visa, and he lied about who he was so that's fraud. And under Section 49 of the 1983 Medical Act it's a criminal offence to impersonate a doctor. But . . .'

'But?'

'Well, the CPS aren't too keen to prosecute. The worry is that all the places where he's worked think he's wonderful. If they get called as character witnesses he'll probably get off. The thinking at the moment is that if he's prepared to pay for his own ticket we just let him fly back to Mumbai.'

'It's a pity he can't stay.'

'That won't happen, and he's accepted that. He freely admits that he did wrong, but insists that he only had the best interests of his patients at heart. He genuinely enjoys helping people. He was advising the custody sergeant about his back, showing him some exercises he could do to pop his discs back into place.' He chuckled and took another drink from his pint.

'You're starting to make me feel really bad, here, Phil.'

He put down his pint and smiled. 'He'll be fine. The home in Reading asked for his number because they want to offer him a job again. They said they'll fix up a proper visa for him, the works, and he can work there as a nurse. The thing is, though, there's no sign that he hurt your mother-in-law. Or anyone else, for that matter.'

'I hear you.'

He leaned towards her. 'You seem so sure that something happened to your mother-in-law, but I really can't see anything that confirms that.'

Lulu sipped her drink. The simple fact was that she couldn't tell Phil why she was suspicious of Emily's death. It was one thing to say that Emily had seemed fine on Sunday afternoon, it was quite another to say that Conrad the Calico Cat had said that Emily had a strong aura that indicated she had a long and happy life ahead of her. She put down her glass and shrugged. 'Copper's intuition, Phil. That's all I've got.'

He grinned. 'I remember being told by a very wise detective that intuition played no part in a criminal investigation. That you had to let the evidence lead the way.'

She grinned back at him. 'Wise words indeed,' she said. 'And I meant them. But sometimes your subconscious picks up on something, lets you know that there's a problem. It just feels wrong. But that doesn't mean I'm jumping to conclusions.' She sighed. 'I take your point that Dr Khan – at least the man passing himself off as Dr Khan – wasn't in the business of hurting his clients. But I can't stop thinking about how well she looked the last time I saw her. The Alzheimer's notwithstanding.' She sipped her drink. 'I've spoken to Richard.'

'Your brother-in-law?'

Lulu nodded. 'He's been appointed the executor of my mother-in-law's will. And he's the only beneficiary, other than a few small bequests.'

'I thought you couldn't be an executor and a beneficiary?'

'No, that's fine. You can't be a witness to a will and be a beneficiary, but it's perfectly okay to be an executor and a beneficiary. Anyway, he's decided to have my mother-in-law cremated.'

'Is that a problem?'

Lulu grimaced. 'First of all, it's not what she wanted. Emily always wanted to be buried with her husband, Frank. They bought a double plot donkey's years ago and there's already a twin gravestone in place with space for her names and dates to be added. There is no way she would ever have wanted to be cremated. She said in her will that she wanted to be buried with Frank, but Richard says that means he can bury her ashes.'

'I've got to be honest, boss, I've always preferred cremation. I can't bear the thought of being eaten by worms. The fire just seems to be . . . I don't know . . . quicker.'

Lulu nodded. 'I'm the same. My husband was cremated and I'll be cremated too. But I know what Emily wanted and she wanted to be buried next to Frank. I made that clear to Richard but he basically told me to mind my own business.' She leaned closer towards him. 'He told me that eighty per cent of bodies are cremated. He must have googled that, right? Who does that?' She lowered her voice. 'I think he wants to get rid of the body.'

Phil frowned. 'What do you mean?'

'I mean I think he knows that whatever he did to Emily would show up in a post mortem. But if the body is cremated . . .' She shrugged.

'So now you're suspecting your brother-in-law?'

'Someone – I think it was him – gave Emily a box of chocolates on Friday. She died on Sunday night.'

'And what, you think they were poisoned?'

'Not poisoned as such. And anyway, they couldn't have been poisoned because I ate one myself on the Sunday. But my mother-in-law was allergic to sesame seeds.'

'Really? Is that a thing?'

'Oh, it's a big thing. Possibly worse than peanuts. It runs in their family. They have to avoid sesame seeds and the oil, and if they do get exposed to it, they need to jab themselves with an epinephrine pen. My husband had several attacks over the years.'

'But Dr Khan didn't put that down as the cause of death, did he?'

'No, but now we know that he isn't a real doctor, maybe we shouldn't be putting any store by his diagnosis.'

'Fair point.'

'So I'm thinking, the cremation is set for next Wednesday; is there any way we could get a post mortem done before then?'

'Is that what you want, boss?'

'I want to know what killed her,' said Lulu. 'And if it was something untoward, I want to know who did it and why.'

'Okay, let me put out a few feelers. What I can do is get the body looked at again. Not an inquest, nothing invasive, but obviously the death certificate is now invalid. We'll need another one. Signed by a genuine doctor.'

'You're a star,' said Lulu.

'Nothing to do with me, boss. We're going to have to redo every death certificate he signed – and there are dozens. Possibly hundreds.'

'At least we get a chance to get a second opinion,' said Lulu. 'I'm just grateful for that.'

22

The Scotch egg at the Devonshire Arms had been something of a treat, and Conrad had definitely enjoyed his cod goujons after Phil had patiently peeled off all the batter for him. After they'd finished, they said their goodbyes and Lulu ordered an Uber to go back to Maida Vale. She had the driver drop them outside Jenny Tyler's home. She lived alone in Randolph Avenue in a ground-floor flat; Lulu had been there several times with Emily. Jenny was an accomplished amateur baker and there was always something new and delicious to taste. Conrad followed on Lulu's heels as she walked up to the front door. The house had once been a family home on four floors but had been converted into flats during the seventies. There was an intercom with six buttons and Lulu pressed the one for Jenny's flat. After a few seconds there was a crackle of static, followed by Jenny asking who was there.

'Jenny, it's Lulu. Sorry to drop by unannounced.'

The lock buzzed and Lulu pushed the door open. As she and Conrad walked into the hallway, Jenny opened the door to her flat. She was wearing a long blue linen dress and had her grey hair tied up. 'Lulu, what a lovely surprise,' said Jenny. Her eyes widened when she saw Conrad. 'Oh, what a super cat. Is he yours?'

'He has sort of adopted me,' said Lulu. 'His name's Conrad.'

Jenny bent down and stroked Conrad. 'What a handsome boy he is.'

'Jenny, has Richard been in touch with you?'

'Richard? No. Why?' She straightened up and clasped her hands together as if she was at prayer.

'Oh, I'm so sorry to have to tell you like this, but Emily passed away on Sunday night.'

Jenny gasped. 'No! Oh my goodness, that's terrible. I saw her on Saturday morning.'

'Yes, I know.'

'What happened?'

'Natural causes, they say.'

Jenny put a hand against the wall. 'I feel quite dizzy,' she said.

Lulu closed the door and helped Jenny to the sitting room, which overlooked the street. She held Jenny's arm until she was safely sitting in a winged chair by the Victorian fireplace. 'Are you okay?' asked Lulu.

'My legs just went weak, I'm sorry.'

'Shall I make you a cup of tea?'

'Would you?'

'Of course. Conrad can keep you company.'

'Meow!' said Conrad, sitting next to Jenny's chair.

'Oh goodness, he talks.'

'Yes he does,' said Lulu. She went down the hallway to the kitchen and switched on the kettle. There was a delicious smell of chocolate brownies, and Lulu found them cooling on a wire rack, covered by a tea towel. She nibbled a piece as the kettle boiled. Jenny had a passionate dislike of teabags so Lulu used a teapot, and put it on a tray with three cups and saucers. She laughed when she realized what she was doing – Conrad wasn't a tea drinker. She took off one of the cups and added a jug of milk and a bowl of sugar, and two spoons. She carried the tray through to the front room, where Conrad was now sitting on Jenny's lap. Jenny was stroking him and he was purring loudly. Lulu put the tray down on the table in front of the fireplace. She poured two cups of tea, added some milk to hers, then took her cup to the overstuffed leather sofa.

Jenny added milk and sugar to her cup. 'Do you want some milk, Conrad?' she asked.

Conrad looked up at her and meowed. 'He prefers water,' said Lulu.

'I'll get him some.'

'No, you both look so comfortable, I'll do it.'

She went back to the kitchen, found a bottle of water in the fridge and poured some into a bowl. She put it down next to Jenny's chair and sat down on the sofa. 'So, Richard didn't call you about the funeral?'

'I'm not even sure that he has my number,' said Jenny. 'The last time I saw him was at Simon's funeral and we barely spoke. He was with his new wife, Mary?'

'Maria,' said Lulu. 'They're over here now, in Beckenham. Richard is the executor of Emily's will and is making the funeral arrangements.'

'Well, I'll be there, of course. When is it?'

'Next Wednesday.'

'Next Wednesday?'

Lulu nodded.

Jenny frowned. 'That's a bit of a rush, isn't it?'

'That's why I wanted to check that you'd been told.'

'I seem to remember Emily saying that Richard was never the most organized of people.'

Lulu nodded. 'He tends not to have an eye for detail.'

'Why aren't you handling the funeral?'

'I'm not an executor of the will. There's something else, Jenny. He's having Emily cremated.'

'He's what?'

'He's decided that she's to be cremated. At the St Marylebone Crematorium.'

Jenny shook her head firmly. 'No, that's not what she wanted at all. She wanted to be laid to rest with Frank. That was always what she wanted.'

'Yes, I know.'

'Well, then you have to tell him.'

'I did. He says that her ashes will be buried in the grave, so her wishes will be carried out.'

'No, no, no, her wishes are to be buried next to her husband. That's what she wanted.' Jenny frowned. 'We have to stop him. He can't be allowed to get away with this.'

'I'm looking into it.'

'We need an injunction or something. Something to force him to carry out her wishes.' She sighed. 'It's such a pity that Simon isn't here. He'd know what to do.'

Lulu forced a smile. 'I was thinking the same thing. The truth is that none of this would be happening if he was still here. He would have made sure that Emily got what she wanted.'

'You must fight it. And if there's anything you need, just tell me. I have a very good lawyer and I'm more than happy to get him involved.'

'Thank you so much,' said Lulu. 'I'm looking at options at the moment but I might very well take you up on that.' She sipped her tea as Jenny continued to stroke Conrad, who was purring loudly and clearly relishing the attention.

'This might sound a silly question, Jenny, but did Emily have some handmade chocolates when you saw her?'

'She did, yes. I had one. Absolutely gorgeous. From that shop in Covent Garden.'

'Bellissimo?'

'That's right.'

'On Friday or Saturday?'

'Both.'

'She didn't say who had brought them, did she?'

Jenny frowned as she tried to remember, then she laughed. 'Yes, she said that Simon had brought them. She wasn't having a great day. She kept forgetting who I was. Kept calling me Louise. I tried explaining that Simon had passed away but she wouldn't have it.'

'I was told not to contradict her, it only upsets her.' Lulu winced at the present tense.

'It's awful, dementia,' said Jenny quietly as she looked down at Conrad. 'Emily and I have known each other for ever. Since we were five years old. We've shared so much. I went out with her on her first date with Frank, as a sort of chaperone. I was a bridesmaid at her wedding. I held both boys in my arms just hours after they were born. We had I don't know how many legendary girls' nights out together. I remember everything we did and yet on Saturday she didn't even remember my name.' She shuddered and looked up at Lulu. 'I don't understand how it happens. Oh, I forget things, everyone does. But to have a lifetime of memories just wiped away.' She shuddered. 'I just pray it never happens to me.'

'You and me both,' said Lulu.

'It's the unfairness of it that upsets me. Emily was always

busy, always social, buzzing around here and there. You'd expect her to be the last person to get dementia.'

'I think it's a lottery, and Emily was just unlucky,' said Lulu. 'I met Margaret Thatcher at a Conservative function, during the 2001 election. She was starting to forget things, even then. You could tell she was beginning to slip away and of course by 2005 she had full-blown dementia. If someone with that amount of drive and energy can end up that way . . .' She shrugged. 'It's very depressing.'

'Well, you and I are just fine,' said Jenny. 'And Conrad here is an absolute delight.'

Lulu sipped her tea. 'So if you don't mind me asking, why did you visit Emily on Friday and Saturday?'

Jenny shrugged. 'Friday was just a flying visit, I was on my way to see a friend and popped in to say hello on my way. Little and often is best when it comes to visits, I always say. I hate to overstay my welcome.'

'I know what you mean. There's nothing worse than sitting there with nothing to say, is there?'

'Exactly. What matters is that she knows that you love her and care about her. If I could, I would have gone every day. We have been friends for ever.' She brushed away a tear with the back of her hand. 'I keep using the present tense, don't I? I'm going to have to stop doing that.' She forced a smile. 'Did you see the chocolate brownies in the kitchen?'

'I did. And I tried a piece. Mouth-watering.'

'Why don't you go and fetch them? Life always seems that much better when you're eating a chocolate brownie.'

Lulu chuckled. 'That's what I've always found.'

Conrad meowed and Jenny laughed. 'Oh look, he says he wants some.'

'No, that's not it at all,' said Lulu. 'He's telling you that cats can't eat chocolate, same as dogs. The caffeine can mess up their heart rhythm and cause tremors and seizures.'

'You understand what he says, then?'

Lulu laughed. 'Pretty much every word.'

23

Lulu spent an hour chatting with Jenny over tea and brownies. Jenny was right – life always seemed better when you were eating a chocolate brownie. Conrad had spent the entire time on Jenny's lap being softly stroked.

'She is a lovely lady,' he said, after they had left the flat and he was once more draped around Lulu's neck.

'She is,' agreed Lulu.

'She's a widow, too, right?'

'Yes, her husband Bill passed away twenty years ago. She and Emily were very close. I'm surprised she took it as well as she did.'

'She was hiding it,' said Conrad. 'She was keeping it all in. That's why I let her stroke me. I could feel her grief.'

'That was nice of you.'

'It was the least I could do.'

Lulu stopped. 'Jenny is okay, right? Nothing bad is going to happen to her, is it?'

'I don't foretell the future.'

'But her aura is fine?'

'Perfectly fine,' said Conrad.

Lulu's eyes narrowed. 'If you saw something bad in her aura, something worrying, would you tell me?'

'Of course.'

Lulu smiled. 'Okay. Thank you. I'm sorry if I sound paranoid, but . . .' She left the sentence unfinished.

'I understand,' said Conrad.

Lulu started walking again. They reached the Warrington Hotel and Lulu headed down Warrington Crescent. As they reached Emily's house, she saw movement in the sitting-room window and she stopped. 'Did you see that?' she asked Conrad, turning to face the house.

'See what?'

A figure moved across the middle of the room. 'That!' said Lulu.

'There's someone inside,' said Conrad.

'Exactly.' Lulu walked quickly towards the front door, taking her keys from her handbag. Conrad jumped down from her shoulders and landed on the horsehair mat. Lulu pushed the door open and Conrad ran into the hallway. 'Hey, let me go first,' said Lulu, closing the door and hurrying after him.

She had only taken a couple of steps when a figure emerged from the sitting room. Lulu gasped in surprise, but realized almost immediately that it was Maria. She was wearing a short black skirt, high heels and a tight white top that showed quite a bit of cleavage, certainly more than Lulu thought appropriate for a woman whose mother-in-law had just passed away. Maria smiled, showing brilliant white teeth behind glossy red lips. 'Lulu, hello! I did ring the bell but nobody answered.'

'So you let yourself in?'

Maria's smile hardened a fraction. 'Well, it is my house now,' she said.

'Richard's house, actually.'

'Well, I am Richard's wife, so I like to think that it's my house too.' She was holding a clipboard in her left hand and a pen in the right.

'What are you doing, Maria?'

'I'm compiling an *inventario*.' She frowned. 'What is the word?'

'Inventory?'

'Oh, you speak Spanish?'

'No, not really. I just guessed.'

Conrad walked past Maria, his tail brushing against her leg. She sneered at the cat. 'Does it go everywhere with you?'

'Yes, I suppose he does.'

'I don't like cats.'

'That doesn't surprise me.' Lulu gestured at the clipboard. 'Why do you need an inventory?'

'Richard wants to know what's in the house.'

'He knows exactly what's here, surely?'

'Well, he wants a list.' She walked into the sitting room and Lulu followed her. To the left was a large sofa and two armchairs, and in the middle of the room, under a glistening chandelier, was Emily's piano. 'That is a nice piece,' said Maria.

'Yes, Emily loved to play it.'

'It's a grand piano, right?'

'A baby grand.'

Maria lifted the lid to reveal the keys. 'Oh, a Steinway, that's a good make, isn't it?'

'Yes,' said Lulu. 'It is.'

'How much do you think it would sell for?' Maria's eyes stayed fixed on the piano, like a schoolgirl salivating over an ice-cream sundae.

'I really wouldn't know,' said Lulu.

Maria took out her mobile phone and tapped on the screen. After ten seconds or so her eyes widened and she made a whooping sound. '*Dios mio!*' she said. 'They sell for more than thirty thousand pounds!' She closed the lid and wrote something on her clipboard before walking over to look at the painting over the mantelpiece. 'Now this is nice.' She leaned forward and peered at the signature in the bottom right corner. 'Who painted it?'

'I really wouldn't know,' said Lulu. In fact she knew exactly who had painted it, and she had a rough idea of its value. Frank had bought the painting for a few hundred pounds shortly after he'd married Emily. He'd bought it because he loved the picture but it had proved to be a very good investment. Frank had always had a good eye for art and there were more than a dozen paintings on the wall which would sell for five figures apiece.

Lulu glanced over at Conrad, who had a look of disgust on his face.

Maria stepped back from the fireplace, tucked her clip-board under her arm and used her phone to take a photograph of the painting.

'Maria, what are you doing?' asked Lulu.

'I need to get them valued,' said Maria without turning around.

'You're planning on selling them?'

'They're old, Lulu. I wouldn't want to be looking at them every day, would you?'

Actually, Lulu loved the paintings. Simon had loved them, too. She opened her mouth to say something but then stopped. There would be no point. And Maria was well within her rights to sell anything she wanted. Or at least Richard was. As the sole heir, everything belonged to him. He had never been as attached to the house as Simon had been, and had probably only set foot inside it a dozen times over the last twenty years.

They heard footsteps coming down the stairs. 'Is that Richard?' asked Lulu. 'Is he here?'

Her question was answered when a tall black-haired man with piercing blue eyes appeared in the doorway. He had a couple of days of designer stubble on his broad chin and a diamond stud in one ear. 'This is my brother, Juan. He drove me here. I can never get used to driving on the wrong side of the road.' Juan was wearing a glistening black leather jacket over a tight white pullover that was stretched across his broad chest and six-pack abdomen. Like Maria, he was carrying a clipboard and a pen.

His face broke into a grin, showing brilliant white teeth. 'You are Lulu,' he said. 'My sister told me about you.' He moved to kiss her on the cheek but Lulu took a step back and offered her hand. He frowned at it, then looked at Maria. She said something to him in rapid Spanish and he laughed and shook it. 'Very English,' he said.

'I didn't realize Maria had a brother,' said Lulu.

'Oh yes, Juan managed the restaurant in Marbella,' said Maria.

'Are you staying with Richard and Maria in Beckenham?' Lulu asked Juan.

'Not with them, but not too far away,' he said. He grinned over at Maria. 'I need to make sure that my little sister stays safe.'

'He's very protective,' said Maria.

Juan spotted Conrad. 'How did that get in?' he said. He drew back his foot to kick Conrad but Maria hurriedly put a hand on his arm. 'No, Juan, that's Lulu's cat!'

Juan relaxed and flashed his smile at Lulu again. 'Lulu, I am so sorry. Forgive me. We were always having problems with stray cats at our restaurant. I was forever having to kick them out.'

'Well, there's no need to kick Conrad.'

Juan bent down and put his hand out to pat Conrad on the head. 'Nice kitty,' he said.

Conrad's ears went back and he hissed at Juan so loudly that the man took a step back and put up his hands defensively. 'He's a tough one, isn't he?'

Lulu wanted to say that Conrad was generally a good judge of character, but she held her tongue and just smiled.

'Juan, why don't you keep working on the bedrooms,' said Maria. 'I've still got a lot to do down here.'

'Sure, I just wanted to see who it was.' He smiled and nodded at Lulu. 'And now I know that it's Lulu and her charming cat. Nice to meet you both.' He flashed them a movie-star smile and left the room.

'Where is Richard?' asked Lulu.

'Oh, he has things to do, so he said Juan and I should start on the *inventario*. The inventory.' Maria frowned as she noticed the locket hanging around Lulu's neck. 'Isn't that Emily's?' she said.

'It was in the box of Emily's belongings, the one that you were too busy to collect.'

'Ah, yes. Richard and I had meetings all day.'

'Meetings?'

'Estate agents, antiques dealers, art dealers.' She rolled her eyes. 'We've been rushed off our feet, there's been so much to organize.'

Lulu felt a sudden surge of anger and her cheeks reddened.

Emily's body was barely cold and they were already planning to sell her belongings.

Maria reached out and held the locket. Lulu had to fight the urge to slap her face but she just stared at her, gritting her teeth. Maria looked at the locket and nodded. 'It is a lovely piece,' she said. 'Solid gold, isn't it?'

'It has great sentimental value,' said Lulu quietly.

Maria let go of it and it fell back against Lulu's throat. Maria scribbled something on her clipboard. 'Richard said we should allow you to choose some items of sentimental value, things you can remember her by.'

'That's very kind of him,' said Lulu, coldly.

'What about her watch? The rose-gold Cartier? The one she was wearing in the home.'

Lulu clenched her jaw, then took a deep breath to calm herself down. 'I don't know.'

'You collected her things from the home.'

'Yes, I did. Because Richard said he was too busy.'

'Well, Emily was wearing the Cartier watch when I saw her in hospital. Where is it now?'

'I told you, I don't know.'

'It's a very valuable watch, Lulu. It's rose gold, isn't it? Solid gold, not plate?'

'I know that it had great sentimental value to Emily. You know that Frank gave it to her when Richard was born?'

Maria wrinkled her nose. 'Lulu, do you know what I think? I think sentimental value is very over-rated. Everything has a value, and that value is the amount that somebody is willing to pay for it. Sentiment really plays no part in it.'

'Well, we are all entitled to our opinions, obviously,' said Lulu.

'You're not planning on keeping the watch, are you, Lulu? Like you're keeping the locket?'

'I already told you, Maria, I don't have the watch. It wasn't among her belongings.'

Maria's eyes narrowed. She stared at Lulu for several seconds, then nodded curtly. 'Fine,' she said.

'If you don't believe me, the box is downstairs – go and look for yourself,' said Lulu, but Maria was concentrating on her clipboard again. Eventually she finished scribbling and gave Lulu a cold smile. 'I know what you're worried about and, really, you don't have to give it another thought,' she said.

'Oh, really? What exactly am I worried about?'

Maria walked over, her high heels clicking on the polished wooden floorboards. She reached out and put a hand on Lulu's elbow. 'No one's going to throw you onto the streets, Lulu,' she said. 'The way the market is and the way solicitors always drag their feet, it'll be months before it's sold. You'll have plenty of time to find somewhere else.'

'Richard's definitely selling, is he?'

'Well, we wouldn't want to live here, would we? It's totally unsuitable. No, the plan is to sell it and buy ourselves a villa in Marbella. Something near the sea. With a pool. You'd be more than welcome to visit. As soon as we've got everything running smoothly.' She squeezed Lulu's elbow. 'I know you'll be fine. Simon left you a bundle, didn't he? And you sold your house in Islington, didn't you?'

'You're very well informed about my financial status,' said Lulu, archly.

Maria squeezed her elbow again, harder this time. 'Richard and I talk, obviously. Look, you've had a good run, living here rent-free, but all things have to come to an end. As I said, there's no pressure, but I'll be bringing estate agents around over the next day or two and we'll test the market.'

Lulu pulled her arm away before Maria could give it another squeeze. 'I'll leave you to it,' she said.

Conrad jumped up onto the back of an armchair and Lulu went over so that he could leap onto her shoulders.

'Does it always do that?' asked Maria.

'Do what?'

'Ride on your shoulders. I've never seen a cat do that before.'

'He's a very unusual cat,' said Lulu. 'And he's a "he", not an "it". I'll let myself out.' Maria had already turned her back and was examining another of the paintings.

Lulu headed to the front door and opened it. 'You didn't tell her you were living on the boat?' said Conrad.

'I thought I'd better not,' said Lulu. 'If she knew I was sleeping there, she'd change the locks in a flash.'

They went outside and Lulu pulled the door closed. 'She seems very well organized, doesn't she?' said Conrad.

'Yes, I noticed that.'

'She only found out two days ago that her husband is inheriting the house and already she's lined up estate agents and got people ready to value Emily's paintings.'

'Again, that did make me think, yes.'

They walked in silence for a while, towards the canal. 'I know you're not psychic, but I'm sure you know what I'm thinking, don't you?'

'I'm afraid I do, yes.'

'Do you want to talk about it?'

Lulu forced a smile. 'Not right now, no.'

'Okay.'

24

As soon as they got back to *The Lark*, Lulu made herself a glass of mint tea and poured water into a bowl for Conrad. Conrad jumped up onto the sofa and Lulu sat down next to him. She put the glass on the shelf and picked up the box of chocolates. She looked guiltily over at Conrad, who purred. 'Go on, you deserve to treat yourself,' he said.

Lulu laughed and opened the box. There were four inside. 'Eeny, meeny, miney, mo . . .' she began, but Conrad laughed.

'You're going to choose the Apple Fudge,' he said.

'How do you know that?'

'I just do.'

'I could choose another one, just to prove you wrong.'

Conrad snorted softly. 'But you won't, will you?'

She looked at him for several seconds, then her face broke into a smile. 'You really are a mind-reader, aren't you?'

'Maybe I am,' he said.

She picked up the Apple Fudge chocolate and put it in her mouth, then put the box back on the shelf.

'Good?' said Conrad.

Lulu nodded.

'I thought so.'

Lulu chewed slowly, relishing the chocolatey apple taste. There was a hint of spice in there, too. Eventually she swallowed and sighed. 'That was amazing.' She picked up her glass and held it with both hands and stared into the mint tea. 'Maria is clearly planning to sell that watch if she gets her hands on it.' She shuddered. 'Actually, I think I'd prefer that she did sell it. I couldn't bear the thought of her wearing it.'

'Is it very valuable?' asked Conrad.

'Now you sound like Maria.'

'I just wondered if it was worth stealing.'

'Maria wouldn't have to steal it. All Emily's belongings go to Richard and what's his is hers.'

'No, but someone else could have taken it.'

Lulu nodded thoughtfully. 'It was very valuable, that's for sure. I don't know what Frank paid all those years ago, but a new one would probably cost thirty thousand pounds or so. The vintage ones could go for a lot more.' She frowned. 'You think someone else took it?'

'Well, it wasn't in the box. You don't have it, so if Maria doesn't have it . . .' He left the sentence unfinished.

Lulu frowned. 'Someone else must have taken it.' She reached for her phone and called the home and asked to speak to Mrs Fitzgerald. Lulu was put on hold for several minutes but eventually Mrs Fitzgerald came on the line. 'Hello, Lulu, how can I help you?'

There was a tension in her voice again, as if she was expecting a problem. Lulu decided there was no point in any small talk, so she just asked if Mrs Fitzgerald had any idea why Emily's Cartier watch wasn't among her belongings.

Mrs Fitzgerald was quiet for a few seconds. 'Is it on the list?' she said eventually.

'What list?'

'You should have received a list of all her belongings.'

'I don't think I did. There was a box, which I took home, and there was a black bag containing her clothes, which Mrs Reynolds said would be given to charity.'

'Usually the list would be in the box.'

'No, there was no list. And no watch. Her jewellery was there, her rings and so on, but no watch.'

'That's strange.'

'I wanted to ask you about that. Who would have gathered her things together?'

'That would be Gary, usually.'

'And would Gary do things like removing the rings from her fingers? And the watch?'

'Good gracious, no. He wouldn't touch the deceased. That's not how it works.'

'How does it work, then?'

'The funeral director would gather her things together, and Gary would make a note of what there was. He would photograph any valuables, and then once the funeral directors had removed the deceased he would compile a complete list of all the belongings and that would be given to the next of kin when they came to collect them.'

'But Gary wasn't there when I picked up the box.'

'That shouldn't be an issue; the list should have been in the box.'

'And as I said, it wasn't. And neither was the watch.'

'I'm not sure what to tell you. We have a system in place and it has never failed us so far.'

'Can you ask Gary about the watch? And the list?'

'He's not in today. He should be back in tomorrow.'

'I never did catch Gary's surname.'

'Wilkinson,' said Mrs Fitzgerald. 'Gary Wilkinson.'

'Can you let me have his address? I'd really like to talk to him.'

'Oh no, I couldn't give that to you. Data protection. Even if I wanted to, it would be against the law.'

'So you don't want to give me his address, is that what you're saying?'

'No, no, that's not what I meant. I meant there's just no way I could let you have his address. But I will speak to him as soon as he comes in tomorrow.'

Lulu thanked her and ended the call. She told Conrad what Mrs Fitzgerald had said. 'I didn't see a list in the box, did you?' she asked him.

'I didn't.'

'If the list isn't there, it probably means that Gary didn't want us to see it.'

'I think you might be right. You could talk to the funeral director. If they removed her jewellery they must have seen the watch.'

'That's a very good idea.'

Conrad smiled. 'I do have them from time to time.'

She reached over and stroked his head and he pushed against her hand. 'I'm so lucky to have you here,' she said.

'Ditto.'

Lulu smiled. 'Simon always used to say that. If he was thinking the same thing I was thinking. Ditto.' She sighed, then shook her head. 'So, let's go and talk to the funeral director. What did Richard say they were called?'

'Gilbert's?'

'That's right. Gilbert's in St John's Wood. I know where they are.' She finished her tea and washed her glass. The sky was clouding over, so she took a dark blue North Face fleece from her wardrobe and slipped it over her pullover. She picked up the framed photograph of Emily and tucked it under her arm. They went out onto the back deck and Lulu bent down so that Conrad could jump onto her shoulder, before she stepped onto the towpath. A young woman was walking two springer spaniels and they both began to bark excitedly when they spotted Conrad.

'Sorry,' said the woman, pulling her dogs away. 'Lovely cat.'

'Thank you,' said Lulu. She walked to Blomfield Road and then headed towards St John's Wood.

Gilbert's had been in business for almost a hundred years and Lulu had been at several funerals they had arranged. They weren't the firm that had dealt with Frank's funeral, or Simon's, but Lulu had walked past their shop many times. There was a gold-painted sign in the window that said GILBERT AND SONS, and a display of silk flowers. 'Why don't you ever see coffins in the windows of funeral directors?' asked Conrad. 'That's what they're selling, right?'

'I think it would probably upset people,' said Lulu.

'But death is a part of life.'

'The circle of life, again? I'm starting to think that you've watched *The Lion King* too many times. The thing is, while the circle of life might be big in the jungle, death is still a scary prospect for most people and being confronted by a coffin in the window would make them uncomfortable.'

'Humans can be strange sometimes,' said Conrad, jumping down from her shoulders.

'Well, don't get me started on cats.' She pushed open the door and a small bell tinkled over their heads. There were several coffins on display to the left and a Regency desk to the right, on which there was an Apple computer and a pile of leather-bound albums. There were no fresh flowers on display, so no lilies for Conrad to worry about.

A side door opened and a small middle-aged woman in a dark grey suit appeared. 'Can I help you?' she asked. She had dyed blonde hair and her roots were just starting to show.

'Yes, I'm Lulu Lewis. I believe you are handling the funeral arrangements for my mother-in-law, Emily.'

'Yes indeed. I am so sorry for your loss.' It was a phrase she must have uttered several times a day but she said it as if she meant it and there was a look of sincere compassion in her eyes.

'Thank you,' said Lulu.

The woman spotted Conrad and she gasped. 'Oh. A cat. Is he with you?'

'Yes, yes he is,' said Lulu.

The woman crouched down and tickled Conrad under the chin. 'I just adore cats. I've got four. Well, five if you count the neighbour's tabby because he spends most of the day curled up on my sofa and I think she might have stopped feeding him.' She stood up and smiled apologetically. 'I'm sorry, rambling on like that.'

'I was wondering if Mr Gilbert was available?'

'Mr Gilbert Senior or Mr Gilbert Junior?'

'Mr Gilbert Senior, I suppose.'

'Oh, I'm sorry, Mr Gilbert Senior is at a funeral. He won't be back for a couple of hours.'

'Mr Gilbert Junior, then?'

'Certainly. I'll go and get him.' She gestured at a low-level leather sofa. 'Please take a seat.'

Lulu sat down and Conrad stood next to her as the woman disappeared back through the side door. 'She's nice,' said Conrad.

'You're just saying that because she's a cat person.'

'I can't dispute that, but she has a lovely aura. She's a very caring person.'

'I think you have to be, in this job,' said Lulu. 'People need reassuring and comforting when they've lost a loved one.'

Conrad rubbed his head against her leg and purred. 'Yes, they do,' he said.

Lulu reached down and stroked his head. 'Thank you,' she said. 'Thank you for getting me through this.'

The door opened again. A tall, thin man in a black suit appeared. Lulu had to force herself to stop smiling because Mr Gilbert Junior was in his sixties. He walked over and offered his hand. He caught Lulu by surprise and she didn't have time to get to her feet so she shook his hand while staying sitting. He reached out with his left hand and covered hers. 'Mrs Lewis, I am so sorry for your loss,' he said. He was as genuine and warm as the woman had been.

He released his grip on her hand and took a step back. 'So how can I help you?' he said. 'Richard Lewis is handling all the arrangements, I understand.'

'Yes, he is,' said Lulu. She gave him the framed photograph. 'We all love this photograph of Emily. Can it be on display during the funeral?'

'Of course,' said Mr Gilbert. He took it from her and smiled as he looked at it. 'She was lovely, wasn't she? So elegant. Beautiful.'

'Yes, she was,' said Emily. 'Mr Gilbert, can I ask you a

question? Did you collect Emily's body from the home, or was it your father?'

'That would have been me,' he said.

Mr Gilbert was still looming over Lulu and she wanted to be on her feet when she spoke to him, so she shuffled to the side and stood up. 'This is a bit embarrassing, Mr Gilbert, but I need to ask you. When you were preparing Emily's body, did you notice a watch?'

'A watch?'

'On her wrist.'

Mr Gilbert rubbed his chin, then his eyes widened. 'Oh yes, I did. I remember mentioning it to my assistant. It was a lovely Cartier. Rose gold, I think. It was a beautiful antique piece.'

Lulu smiled. 'Emily had had the watch since new, but yes, you're right, it was an antique.'

'Is there a problem?'

'Well, the watch wasn't among the belongings that the home gave to me.'

Mr Gilbert frowned. 'Well, that's a worry. But it was definitely there. We removed some rings, a bracelet, a locket, and the watch.'

'Yes, I was given everything other than the watch. So who was in the room when you took off her jewellery?'

'Myself. My assistant, Derek. And the chap from the home.'

'Gary Wilkinson?'

'Gary, yes. I didn't know his surname. Young chap.'

'And how does it work? You remove the items and put them in the box?'

'No, we use a tray. We remove any jewellery, watches and

so on and we put it on a tray. Derek takes a photograph, as does Gary. Then Gary adds it to the home's list of personal effects, clothing, and the like.'

'You take a photograph?'

Mr Gilbert nodded. 'It solves a lot of problems. We can show exactly what the deceased had on their person when they passed away. You'd be surprised how often it becomes an issue these days. Relatives start turning up and demanding this and that. But a lot of people in these homes have to pay for their own care, and as the bills start to mount they often sell off their valuables. Someone turns up and says their mum promised them her gold bracelet, but they don't know that Mum sold it or pawned it. They accuse the home or the undertakers of theft and it all gets very messy. By having the photographs, we can clear up any confusion.'

'So Derek would still have this photograph?'

'Of course.'

'Is he here, can I see it?'

'Derek is attending a funeral at the moment, but we'll have the picture on file. Please bear with me.' He went over to the desk and sat down. He put the photograph of Emily next to the computer and bent over the keyboard. He tapped on it, peered at the screen, then sat back in his chair. 'Here you are.'

Lulu walked to stand behind him and looked at the photograph on the screen. Emily's jewellery was on a blue tray, along with the rose-gold Cartier watch. 'Yes, that's it,' said Lulu. 'Thank you so much, I'm sorry to have bothered you.'

'It's not a bother: as I said, it happens a lot.'

Lulu started walking to the door, then stopped and turned to look at Mr Gilbert. 'Is Emily here, by any chance?'

'Yes, she is,' said Mr Gilbert. He stood up and clasped his hands together. 'She is in our Chapel of Rest. Don't worry, we're taking good care of her.'

'Would it be possible for me to see her? I never got the chance to say goodbye.'

'Absolutely. Of course.' He waved at the sofa. 'If you could just wait here while I get everything ready and I'll show you through.'

Lulu sat down on the sofa as Mr Gilbert picked up Emily's photograph and left the room. Conrad jumped up and sat next to her. 'Are you sure you want to see her?'

'Oh, I'm quite sure,' said Lulu. 'I just want to say goodbye to her. There'll be too many people at the funeral and, to be honest, I think I might not go. I can't see that I'll be comfortable at a cremation when I know that's not what she wanted. I think it's probably best that I say my goodbyes here.'

'Okay.'

Lulu could hear the doubt in his voice. 'You think it's a mistake?'

'I know how important funerals are to humans. And you loved her a lot.'

'I did, yes. But the thought of sitting in a church with Maria and Richard, knowing that they are planning to sell all her belongings and burning her body against her wishes, makes me feel quite ill.' She shuddered. 'I don't understand why Richard is doing this. He knows what Emily wanted. It's in her will, she made sure of that. And he was so mean when I confronted him with it. He just didn't care. And then at the funeral he'll sit there and pretend to be the grieving son until they take her away to burn her. He was at Frank's funeral and he has to remember how Emily stood at the grave and said that one day she'd join him.' She felt tears brimming in her eyes and she blinked. 'Am I being stupid?'

'No,' said Conrad. 'You're being emotional, and there's nothing wrong with that.'

'Emotional?' She wiped tears away with the back of her hand.

'In a good way,' said Conrad. 'You're empathizing with how Emily would feel. And you want to do what would make her happy.'

'I do,' she said. 'I want to grab Richard by the throat and shake some sense into him.'

'That would be the very emotional thing to do,' said Conrad. He butted his head against her side. 'There's still time for him to change his mind.'

'I don't think that's going to happen.'

'Don't count your chickens.'

Lulu smiled. 'Now, that is a very cat thing to say.'

The door opened and Mr Gilbert appeared. 'If you'd like to come this way, Mrs Lewis.'

'What about Conrad, can he come?'

Mr Gilbert frowned. 'Conrad? Oh, the cat.' His smile widened. 'Of course, bring him with you.'

Lulu bent down and picked up Conrad before following Mr Gilbert. They walked down a corridor lined with watercolours, mainly churches. 'These days we get a lot of people bringing pets in to say goodbye to their owners,' said Mr Gilbert. 'Most people pass away in hospitals where animals aren't allowed, so pets are often distressed when their owner goes away and doesn't return. But once they see the body, they do seem to understand what's happened.'

'Oh, I'm sure animals understand death,' said Lulu. 'Possibly better than we do.'

'Meow,' said Conrad.

'Good Lord, he speaks,' said Mr Gilbert.

'Yes, he does,' said Lulu. 'He's quite the chatty calico cat.'

'I always think it's dogs that are affected the most by death,' said Mr Gilbert. 'They'll look and they'll sniff and then they'll whine and even try to paw at the deceased, but cats seem to take it more in their stride. But cat or dog, they definitely seem to understand.'

There were two mahogany doors at the end of the corridor, left and right. Mr Gilbert opened the one on the left and stepped to the side to let them go through first. The air was chilled and Lulu couldn't suppress a shiver. Mr Gilbert had referred to the room as a Chapel of Rest and it was decorated with wall hangings and tapestries, and there were candelabras with flickering electric candles giving off a soft light; but in police terms it was a mortuary, a place to store bodies, and that required low temperatures. There were candles burning in the four corners of the room giving off a fragrant orangey scent. They looked lovely but Lulu knew their real purpose was to mask the smell of death. An Enya song was playing in the background. Another nice touch.

There were two coffins on pedestals at either side of the room: an ornate white one with gold trim and gilt handles, and a cheaper, more functional pine one. The pine one was open and Lulu's jaw tightened at the realization that Richard had clearly gone for the cheapest option. Mr Gilbert stood by the door so that Lulu could approach the coffin on her own. At first glance the floor looked as if it was made from highly polished wooden boards, but as she walked over to the coffin she saw they were wood-effect tiles. Mr Gilbert had put Emily's photograph on a table behind the coffin.

Emily's eyes were closed but there was a blush to her cheeks and she looked as if she was asleep. Lulu almost expected to see her nostrils flare as she breathed, but as she got close there was only stillness and the colour in her cheeks was expertly applied make-up. Emily's head was on a cream pillow that looked like satin, but considering Richard's budget, Lulu figured it was almost certainly nylon.

Lulu reached the coffin and clasped Conrad to her chest. 'She seems so peaceful,' whispered Conrad.

'Yes, she does.'

She put Conrad on the floor and leaned over the coffin so that her face was only inches from Emily's. 'I'm sorry I wasn't with you, I'm sorry you died alone,' she said. 'I wish I'd been holding your hand and that I had told you how loved you were. And I do hope that wherever you are now you know how much you meant to so many people. You brought so much joy into my life, Emily. You gave me your son, you welcomed me into your family, you taught me so much. You were such a good friend to me, Emily. You brought so much light into my life. I'll never forget the time we spent together.' She smiled. 'Yesterday Conrad and I walked around all your haunts. The Colonnade, Red Pepper, Le Cochonnet, the Bridge House. We went to Lord's, we went to the Lisson Gallery and to Paddington Recreation Ground. I actually raised a glass to you at all the places we went to. You should have been there, Emily, it was so much fun.' Lulu sighed. 'Whenever I go to those places, I'll always think about you.' She chuckled. 'Whenever I put on a wrap dress I always hear you telling me to tie the belt on the side, never in front, and don't even think of tying it in a bow.' Lulu smiled and shook her head. 'I will miss you so much.' She leaned forward and gently kissed Emily on the forehead.

She took a step away from the coffin and scooped Conrad into her arms. Mr Gilbert opened the door for her and stepped to the side to allow them through first. He followed them down the corridor and into the shop. 'Thank you so much for that,' said Lulu.

'My pleasure,' said Mr Gilbert.

'Meow,' said Conrad.

'And you are very welcome, too,' said Mr Gilbert. 'I hope to see you at the cremation on Wednesday.'

Lulu forced a smile but didn't reply. He opened the door for her and she stepped out onto the pavement, thanked him again, and walked away, still carrying Conrad in her arms.

'Are you okay?' Conrad asked.

Lulu sniffed. 'Yes, I am. I really did need that.' She began walking back to Maida Vale. She lifted Conrad so that he could sit on her shoulders.

'What do you think happened to Emily's watch?' he asked.

'Somebody at the home must have taken it,' said Lulu. 'I can't think of any other explanation.'

'I guess the question is, was the watch on the list? And why wasn't the list in the box? I know, that's two questions. My bad.'

'And they're both valid questions,' said Lulu.

25

Lulu thought about walking to the nursing home and talking to Mrs Fitzgerald about Emily's watch, but decided that a face-to-face meeting might be too confrontational. She stopped off at Starbucks opposite Maida Vale Tube station, ordered a coffee for herself and a bowl of water for Conrad. The barista suggested tap water but Lulu saw from the look of disdain on Conrad's face that tap water wouldn't be acceptable so she purchased a bottle of Evian.

They sat at a table outside and Lulu used her mobile to call Mrs Fitzgerald. 'I'm really sorry to bother you again,' said Lulu, 'but I'm still having trouble locating Emily's watch.'

'Well I'm sorry to hear that, but I'm not sure what else I can do. Gary won't be in until tomorrow evening. He's working the night shift. I did call him but he's not answering his phone.'

'I talked to Mr Gilbert and he says he definitely recalls seeing a rose-gold Cartier. And he showed me a photograph of it, along with her other things.'

'In that case the watch should have been in the box that you collected.'

'It wasn't, though. And there was no list.'

'I suppose the list could have been put in the bag with the clothing,' said Mrs Fitzgerald.

'Yes, I suppose it could have been. Do you have a copy of the list?'

'Not in front of me, no.' Mrs Fitzgerald's voice had a harder edge to it now; she was clearly on the defensive.

'No, but presumably there's a copy somewhere on the system that you could access.'

Mrs Fitzgerald grunted in annoyance and Lulu half expected her to refuse, but instead she asked her to hold the line. Lulu heard the tapping of fingers on a keyboard, and then silence. 'Well this is strange,' said Mrs Fitzgerald eventually.

'What is?'

'Well, I have the list on the screen in front of me and there is definitely no mention of a Cartier watch.'

'What about a picture?'

There was more tapping on the keyboard, then another silence.

'Well?' said Lulu.

'No, no photograph. And you are quite sure Mr Gilbert said he saw a Cartier watch?'

'One thousand per cent.'

'Mr Gilbert Senior or Mr Gilbert Junior?'

'Does that matter?'

'No, not really,' said Mrs Fitzgerald. 'I just wanted to know.'

'It was Mr Gilbert Junior. And he showed me a photograph of a blue tray with her valuables on it. Including the watch.'

'I have that photograph on my screen right now and I can assure you that there's no watch.'

'Then it's a different photograph. The one Mr Gilbert showed me definitely had a watch in it.'

'I really need to talk to Gary about this because something is clearly very wrong. Can you leave this with me?'

'I don't appear to have any choice, do I?'

'Rest assured, I will get to the bottom of this.'

Lulu thanked her and ended the call. 'The home has no trace of the watch,' she said to Conrad.

'That's strange.'

'Yes, isn't it? Somebody has taken it and my gut feeling is that it's Gary.' Her heart began to pound and she put a hand to her chest.

'What's wrong?' asked Conrad.

'I just had a terrible thought. What if Gary saw the watch and decided to do something to Emily? He had access, he'd probably be there alone, or just him and a nurse. It would be the easiest thing in the world for him slip into Emily's room.' Her eyes widened. 'Then once she was dead he'd be able to steal the watch.'

'But if he did that, he'd take the watch before the undertakers were there, wouldn't he?'

Lulu thought about it and slowly nodded. 'Unless he had crept in late at night and something happened and he had to leave and come back in the morning.' She put her hand up to her head. 'I'm getting a headache.'

'You've had a busy day.'

Lulu forced a smile. 'That's true.'

'And your blood sugar is probably low.'

'It probably is.'

'You should eat.'

She nodded. 'Okay, let me finish my coffee and we'll go and eat. What do you feel like?'

'I'm a cat, so fish is always a good bet. Or chicken. That's why I'm always comfortable on aeroplanes.'

'What on earth are you talking about?'

'That's always the choice in aeroplanes, isn't it? Fish or chicken.'

Lulu laughed. 'I suppose it is. Though when Simon and I travelled it was usually business class and occasionally first and we had a more varied choice. Simon was never a fan of economy.' She frowned as she stared into her mug. 'This is just so unpleasant,' she whispered.

'The coffee?'

She smiled despite herself. 'No. The situation. The whole Richard and Maria thing.' She sighed. 'Maria obviously knew she was going to get the house.'

'Well, yes, but you must have known that, too.'

'I suppose I did, yes. I mean, I knew what the law was, I just didn't really give it any thought. The law is the law. Simon was the beneficiary and if he died before Emily then everything that should have gone to him would go to Richard instead. That's the way the law works. If Emily had rewritten her will, things would have been different.' She shrugged. 'C'est la vie.'

'And you get nothing?'

'Well, yes, but then I'm not a blood relative.'

'No, but you're the one who moved in to take care of Emily. And you're the one who visited her every day at the home. You deserve whatever Simon was going to get.'

'It doesn't matter,' said Lulu. 'Simon left me well taken care of.'

'That's not the point,' said Conrad. 'They've taken what's yours.'

'I don't see it that way.'

'Emily should have changed her will. After Simon died, she should have changed his name for yours.'

'Well, in her state, she wouldn't have known that, and the thought didn't even occur to me,' said Lulu. 'I was too busy grieving for Simon. But even if it had been a priority there were all sorts of issues.'

'Because of her Alzheimer's?'

'Exactly. Simon was a lawyer and we did talk about it when Emily went into the home. It's just as Mr Turnbull said. First you have to get a medical opinion that they are capable of making decisions. They have to have what's called "testamentary capacity" which is a complicated way of saying that they know what a will is, what they will be leaving, and what their obligations are to their family. Now, when she first went into the home, she was fairly coherent most of the time. But we had seen the will and it was fine. There was no need to change it. When Simon died, Emily was already pretty far gone. I suppose with the benefit of hindsight I should have applied to the court to get the will changed so that I was a beneficiary but, as I said, I had other things on my mind.' She took another sip of coffee then lowered the mug as she saw that Conrad was staring at her with unblinking green eyes. 'What?'

'Nothing,' said Conrad.

'You look as if you want to say something?'

'I'm just worried about you.'

'Thank you.'

'And I don't want anyone to take advantage of you.'

'Do you think that's what's happening?'

'I don't know Richard and Maria well enough to make a judgement. We'll see.'

'Yes,' agreed Lulu. 'I suppose we will.'

26

Lulu woke up at nine, roused from a deep sleep by her phone's alarm. She rolled out of bed, showered and pulled on a pullover and jeans. She had planned on a morning of boat maintenance. There were always jobs to be done on a narrowboat but she never found them to be a chore. In fact she enjoyed working on *The Lark* and keeping her in good order.

She worked her way methodically through her mental checklist. She looked at the oil levels – they were fine – then she checked and cleaned the engine. She made sure the bilge pumps were working and inspected the three batteries. They didn't need any de-ionized water adding but there wasn't much charge left. She jumped off the boat and went along to the boat at her stern. It was called *Moor Often Than Knot*, which Lulu always felt was far too contrived a name. It was owned by two ladies in their sixties who lived in Sussex and came up several times a month. They had introduced themselves as Jo and Val. Lulu didn't know if they were friends, sisters or lovers, not that it mattered. They kept themselves to themselves and made no real attempt to be friendly, which was just fine with Lulu. She didn't want to annoy them by running the massive diesel engine for two or three hours to charge the batteries, but the boat was locked up so it wasn't a problem. She climbed back onto *The Lark* and fired up the engine.

Conrad appeared at the doorway. 'Are we going some-where?' he asked.

'Just charging the batteries,' said Lulu. 'Do you want a drink?'

'Yes, please,' he said. She took a bottle of Evian and poured some into a bowl, then made another coffee for herself before continuing her work. She checked that all bolts and pipes were secure, then inspected the cables and control equipment.

Maintenance over, she cleaned the boat from prow to stern and then changed the bed linen. After she had finished she felt grubby so she showered again and changed into a cream linen dress.

Conrad was lying on the sofa but he sat up and nodded. 'I like that dress.'

'Thank you, kind sir. Late breakfast?'

'Breakfast would be good.'

'Let's go, then.'

Lulu was walking along the towpath when her phone rang. It was from a landline, and she guessed it was Phil, although it was a different number from the one he had used for his last call. 'It's me, boss,' he said. 'Sorry about all the secrecy but I wasn't joking about Professional Standards listening in on our work mobiles. I just feel happier calling you from a landline.'

'No problem, Phil. So what have you got?'

'Well, bad news on the inquest front, I'm afraid. I spoke to Mr Gilbert at the funeral home and he was very cooper-ative.'

'Mr Gilbert Senior or Mr Gilbert Junior?'

'Sorry, what?'

'It doesn't matter, sorry to interrupt. Go on.'

'Okay, so Mr Gilbert let me send one of our police surgeons around to examine the body. Nothing invasive, but other than that our doctor was given free rein. The thing is, boss, is that there was nothing to suggest it was anything other than a natural death. The only bruising was where blood had settled after death; there were no contusions, no signs of violence and no signs of poison. Nothing at all to suggest that a post mortem was necessary.'

'You explained about Emily's sesame seed allergy?'

'I did, yes. The doctor – her name is Ashley – was pretty knowledgeable on the subject. She actually dealt with a case last year. The problem is that the symptoms of an anaphylactic shock tend to disappear soon after death. As I'm sure you know, the sesame seeds provoke a reaction and the airways seize up, making it difficult, even impossible, to breathe. Like a severe asthmatic attack. But after death, all the airways relax again. Often there's nothing to show what caused the death.'

'Which is why we need a post mortem. And why we can't allow Emily to be cremated.'

'I hear you, boss, and I ran that by Ashley. She said that the problem is that sesame seeds, or the oil, are actually a food, which means they are digested by the body. With inorganic poisons like cadmium, lead or arsenic, they're all readily detectable in the blood after death, and long-term exposure leads to traces in human hair and the like. But sesame seeds are organic and they're digested. And the thing about digestion is that it continues after death. The acid in the stomach keeps eating away at everything there. Now it's not as efficient because the stomach isn't moving, but it keeps on going. So with sesame seeds, if you do the post mortem within hours of the death then there's a chance you'll find them in the stomach. But after a day or two, they're gone. So the point I'm making is that a post mortem really won't tell us anything. I'm sorry to be the bearer of bad news. Ashley has signed a second death certificate, with dementia as the cause of death.'

Lulu sighed. 'I understand,' she said. She wanted to say more but knew that she was wasting her time. Phil had obviously done his best.

'You can pay for your own post mortem, get it done privately, but with the best will in the world you'll be throwing your money away.'

'Okay, Phil.'

'I'm sorry, boss. I wish I could do more.'

'No, I appreciate what you've done. I get that we've hit a brick wall.'

'You've still got that copper's hunch?'

'More than ever.'

'Well, if you get anything definite, anything at all, you call me.'

'I will, Phil. And I wonder if you could do me yet another favour?'

'Ask and you shall receive.'

'My mother-in-law's Cartier watch went missing from the nursing home. It's a rose-gold watch and it's quite valuable, though it's the sentimental value that's more important for me. The funeral director you spoke to saw it among her belongings but it wasn't in the box that they gave me. There's a young lad who works at the home – Gary Wilkinson – who was there when they were removing the jewellery from Emily's body. He was supposed to compile a list of everything, but the watch wasn't on the list. And he didn't put a copy of the list in the box, which he was supposed to.'

'So you think this Gary stole it?'

'I do, yes. Sorry.'

'I'll make some inquiries, boss,' said Phil.

Lulu ended the call and flashed Conrad a tight smile.

'Not good news?' asked Conrad.

'He's doing his best,' said Lulu. They headed towards Petite Cafe on Castellain Road, opposite Le Cochonnet. It was one of her favourite breakfast spots. It was a Lebanese cafe and did wonderful sweet pastries, but the downside was that they only used beef sausage and turkey bacon. But they still did a first-class full English with fried eggs, beans, mushrooms and hash browns, and Lulu assumed that Conrad would appreciate the turkey bacon – which he did, along with a slice of smoked salmon.

They sat at an outside table. Lulu was tucking into her breakfast when her phone rang again. She put down her knife and fork, took her phone from her pocket and looked at the screen. It was Richard. She answered the call. 'Yes, Richard?'

'Just what the hell do you think you're doing?' he shouted.

'I'm sorry?'

'You sent the police to the funeral home? What the hell were you thinking?'

'I don't like your tone, Richard.'

'Well, I don't like the fact that you went to the cops behind my back.'

'I simply wanted to reassure myself that there was nothing untoward about . . .'

'Untoward!' shouted Richard. 'What do you mean, untoward?'

'I'm still not sure what happened to Emily.'

'She died. Of Alzheimer's. There's a death certificate that says so.'

'Yes, well, apparently there are issues with the death certificate.'

'What do you mean?'

'The doctor who wrote the death certificate isn't a real doctor.'

'What? What are you talking about?'

'Look, it's a long story. But the first death certificate isn't valid.'

'This is because you don't want the cremation, isn't it? That's what this is all about. You always want to control everything. That's why you loved being a police officer.'

'That's a ridiculous thing to say.' She heard someone talking to Richard. A woman. Probably Maria. Then she heard a muffled male voice. Probably Richard replying to her. 'Are you there, Richard?'

'Listen, Lulu, Maria is very upset about all this. And frankly, so am I. My mother has passed away and you seem to be doing everything you can to make things more difficult. We're under enough stress as it is.'

'Richard—'

'No, don't Richard me. I am the executor of my mother's will, and I am handling the funeral arrangements. That's how it is, and if you're not happy with that – well, I'm afraid that's just the way it is. The funeral will be Wednesday next week, Emily will be cremated, and then her ashes will be buried next to my father. You are welcome to attend the funeral but if you do come, I would prefer it if you didn't approach me or my wife.'

Lulu opened her mouth to reply, but before she could speak, Richard ended the call. She glared at the phone and gritted her teeth for several seconds, then she took a deep breath, looked over at Conrad and forced a smile. 'How's the sausage?' she asked.

'Delicious. Are you okay?'

Lulu picked up her knife and fork, looked down at her plate and sighed. 'Now I've lost my appetite.' She put her knife and fork back on the table. 'Richard says that if – if, mind you – if I go to the funeral then I'm not to talk to him or Maria.'

'That's just ridiculous.'

'I know. What am I supposed to do? Hide at the back of the chapel like I'm the phantom of the bloody opera? Oh, he makes me so mad sometimes.' She stopped speaking as she noticed someone was walking close by. It was a woman in a long coat with a carrier bag in one hand and a leash connected to a Yorkshire terrier in the other.

'Lulu?'

Lulu looked up and realized it was Sue Thornton, one of her oldest friends. 'Oh, goodness, Sue. Hello. How are you?'

Sue frowned. 'I thought you were on the phone. But . . .' She smiled awkwardly.

'Oh dear, was I talking to myself again? I've been doing that a lot lately.'

'It happens to us all, darling,' said Sue. 'How have you been?'

'Not great, actually. Emily passed away and I'm just . . .' She shrugged. 'Trying to come to terms with it.'

'Oh, my God, what happened?'

'Alzheimer's, they said. The funeral is next Wednesday.'

The dog spotted Conrad and began to whine and tug at his lead. Sue held him back. 'Leave the nice cat alone, Benjy. You know you never know what to do with them even if you do catch them.'

'His name is Conrad,' said Lulu. 'He's been keeping me company.'

'Very nice to meet you, I'm sure, Conrad,' said Sue. 'You should have called me, Lulu. I'd have given you a shoulder to cry on. You're still on the boat, right?'

Lulu nodded. 'For the time being.'

Sue's eyes widened. 'I've an idea,' she said. 'Come around to mine. The weather forecast is for sun all day so we're having a barbecue. Zoe's coming with her new man, and as her godmother you really should be giving him your seal of approval before it goes any further.'

'No, that's okay, Sue. I'm fine. Really.'

'No, you're not fine, you're sitting outside a cafe muttering to yourself like a demented bag lady. I am sure Conrad is wonderful company but at times like this you need people around you. You need conversation and wine and laughter. Look, you'll know everybody there. And Colin from next door is bringing a couple of bottles of his Chateau Lafite, though frankly that's the only reason I invited him. Oh, come on, Lulu, please say yes. And Zoe is always asking after you. She'll be heartbroken if she finds out that I asked you and you turned me down.'

Lulu was about to shake her head and insist that she didn't feel like company, but then she caught Conrad staring at her. 'Meow,' he said.

Lulu laughed. 'Well, Conrad says I should go, so that's an end to it. Let me pay my bill and we're off.'

Sue laughed. 'Excellent,' she said. 'Conrad, I can see that you and I are going to become the very best of friends.'

'Meow,' said Conrad.

'He says . . .'

'I know exactly what he said,' interrupted Sue. 'Just because I'm a dog owner, doesn't mean I can't speak cat.'

27

Lulu sighed and looked at her watch. It was almost ten o'clock at night and she was dog-tired. She smiled at the thought. It was always dog-tired but never cat-tired, and yet it was cats who seemed to spend most of their time sleeping. Conrad was asleep on the armchair, his chest slowly rising and falling.

Sue's barbecue had been just what Lulu had needed to lift her spirits. Sue's flat backed onto a large communal garden with mature trees and bushes, and it was almost like sitting out in the countryside. There was plenty of good food and wine, and Colin had indeed brought two very nice bottles of Chateau Lafite with him. Lulu had known almost everyone there and it had been lovely to catch up with her goddaughter and meet her boyfriend, a banker who worked in Canary Wharf. He was dashing and handsome and very funny, and Lulu could see that he was besotted with Zoe. It had been a lovely afternoon, and evening, and Lulu had perhaps had too much to drink because Conrad had complained that she was swaying a little as she walked home.

She put down the magazine she had been reading and went over to the stove. It was already loaded with smokeless briquettes and she knelt down and lit them. It was still comfortably warm but there was always a night chill on the canal, so she needed the stove or she would wake up shivering. The stove also heated a water tank, which guaranteed her a hot shower in the morning. Conrad lifted his head to see what she was doing.

She closed the door to the stove and straightened up. 'Do you need to go out?' she asked Conrad.

'I'm good,' he said sleepily.

Lulu pulled the double doors closed and went along to the cabin. She stripped off her clothes and changed into thick red cotton pyjamas, then cleaned and flossed her teeth. She caught Conrad staring at her reflection.

'Cats never clean their teeth,' he said. 'Have you ever thought about that?'

'Cats never shower, either.'

'We don't have to. We lick ourselves clean. It's called grooming.'

'Not really an option for me,' said Lulu. She finished flossing and dropped the used floss into the rubbish bin.

'But it makes you think, doesn't it?'

'I suppose so. Dogs need their teeth cleaning, don't they?'

'Dogs are dogs,' said Conrad. 'What can you do?'

Lulu padded back to the cabin and got into bed. Conrad jumped up and lay at the foot of the bed, resting his chin on his front paws. There were six paperbacks on a small shelf to Lulu's right and she took one down. She was rereading *One Day in the Life of Ivan Denisovich*, one of her favourite books. Conrad closed his eyes and was soon asleep. His paws began to twitch, so he was clearly dreaming.

Lulu read for about half an hour but her eyes were heavy. She put the book down, switched off the light and closed her eyes.

She wasn't sure how long she slept. She knew that she was having a dream about swimming in the sea. The water was a perfect blue, almost matching the colour of the sky overhead. She was doing breaststroke, slowly and evenly, arms and legs working in perfect unison. She had no sense where the land was or in which direction she was heading. Her arms were growing tired and her lungs were starting to burn. She tried to take deeper breaths but she didn't feel as if she was getting enough air. She looked up at the cloudless sky, then looked left and right. No land. Her body was heavy now and every stroke was an effort. Her arms and legs were turning to lead and, no matter how fast she breathed, she couldn't get enough air into her lungs. She was panting now and her thoughts were slipping away from her. Something patted her on the nose and she shook her head. She took a deep breath but her lungs still felt empty. She was clipped on the nose again. 'Lulu!'

Her arms wouldn't move now and she could feel herself slipping below the water.

Something began hitting her on the cheek. 'Wake up!'

Lulu forced her eyes open. Everything was blurry. She tried to work out where she was but her mind wouldn't focus. She closed her eyes again and slipped back into the water.

'Lulu!'

The blows to her face became more insistent. Her eyelids flickered open. Conrad was looking down on her. 'Wake up!' he shouted.

Lulu sat up, shaking her head.

'Can you hear me?' said Conrad. His voice sounded as if he was at the end of a very long tunnel.

'What?' She could barely get the word out and the effort of speaking almost made her faint.

'You need to get out, Lulu! You're suffocating.'

Lulu shook her head. She had a blinding headache and everything looked blurry. She felt as if she was going to be sick and then her stomach heaved and she tasted bile at the back of her mouth.

'Lulu, you're dying!'

Lulu crawled off the bed. She was gasping for breath but it felt as if no air was getting into her lungs. She staggered past the shower and reached the galley. All the strength seemed to have gone from her legs and she slumped against the wall.

'We have to get out!' shouted Conrad. He batted at her leg with his paw. 'Come on!'

Lulu groped for the window by her head and slid it open. Cold air rushed in and she gasped. She moved along to the galley and slid open the windows on both sides. It had to be the stove, she realized. The fumes were filling up the cabin. She dimly remembered that carbon monoxide was slightly lighter than air so she dropped down onto her hands and knees. She grabbed a bottle of Evian water from the fridge, knelt by the stove and opened the door. She poured water onto the smouldering briquettes and white smoke billowed out. Her eyes began to tear and the smoke burned her lungs so she crawled to the double doors, still holding the bottle. She got to her feet, rushed up the steps, opened the doors and lurched onto the back deck, gasping for air. Conrad hurried after her.

Lulu sat down, sucking in lungfuls of the night air. Conrad jumped up and looked at her anxiously. 'Are you okay?'

'Thanks to you.' She reached over and stroked him. 'If you hadn't woken me up I don't know what would have happened.' She still had the Evian bottle in her hand and she drank some of the water.

'You were breathing strangely. You coughed in your sleep and that was what woke me up and I could tell you were having problems.'

'That'll have been the carbon monoxide. The stove, it was leaking carbon monoxide into the air.'

'You've got a detector, though. Why didn't it go off?'

'That's a very good question, Conrad.' She stood up and headed towards the doors.

'Where are you going?'

'It'll be okay now, the fumes will have dispersed.'

'Are you sure?'

'I'm sure.'

'Maybe give it a couple of minutes,' said Conrad. 'Better safe than sorry.'

'Okay,' said Lulu. She took another drink and then splashed water over her face. As she blinked away the water, she noticed that there were muddy streaks on the vents set into the doors. She bent down to get a closer look and realized that someone had forced mud into them.

After two minutes had passed she went down the steps and over to the carbon-monoxide detector, which was on the wall opposite the galley. She frowned as she looked at it. The indicator light was off, neither red nor green. She pulled away the plastic cover and her mouth opened in surprise when she saw that the batteries had been removed.

'What's wrong?' asked Conrad.

'Someone tried to kill me,' whispered Lulu. She picked up her phone. 'I can't believe it.' She scrolled through her address book to get Phil Jackson's number and pressed the call button.

28

Phil arrived at twenty to six, just as the sky was turning red. He was wearing a dark blue raincoat over his suit. Lulu had put on a pair of jeans and her North Face fleece over a pullover, and was wearing a pair of trainers. 'Did you call an ambulance?' he asked.

'I don't need it, my head's cleared and my headache's getting better. They'd only put me on oxygen and I've been getting plenty of fresh air.' She gave him a hug. 'Thanks for coming.'

'Are you kidding? Someone tries to kill my boss and you think I wouldn't be straight out here? Tell me what happened.'

'I'll show you,' she said. She stepped onto the back deck and made room for him.

Conrad was sitting by the rudder and Phil greeted him with a smile. 'Good morning, sir,' said Phil.

'Meow,' replied Conrad.

'I love the way he does that,' said Phil. 'It's as if he understands every word that's said to him.'

'Oh, he does,' said Lulu. 'Okay, so the heat for the boat comes from a wood-burning stove. That's in the main cabin. Most narrowboats have them; they're perfectly safe so long as they're used properly and the boat is well ventilated.' She pointed at the vents in the cabin doors. 'But while I was sleeping, someone slapped mud over the two vents here, effectively blocking them.'

Phil peered at the mud-splattered brass vents and nodded. 'Whoever it was also screwed down the mushroom vents on the roof so that the fumes couldn't escape that way.'

'Mushroom?' Phil repeated, frowning.

'They're shaped like mushrooms,' said Lulu. 'There are two of them. They're designed so that they can be screwed down when not in use. Or if the weather's really bad. Come on, I'll show you.' She stepped up onto the roof and helped him up, then walked past a skylight to the first of the two brass mushroom vents. 'This is in the fully closed position. I haven't touched it in case there are fingerprints on it.'

'I've already phoned forensics – they'll be out later today,' said Phil.

Lulu pointed at the second mushroom vent, close to the prow, situated over the berth where she slept. 'Both of them are closed. And I'd shut the windows already, so with all the vents closed, there was nowhere for the fumes to escape.' She moved back along the boat and pointed at the black metal chimney protruding from the roof. It was about two feet tall and the circumference of a small saucer. She put her hands inside so as not to leave any prints and lifted it off the flue. She placed the chimney on the roof and pointed at the metal-lined hole in the roof. 'I had a quick look, there's a rag stuffed in there and a load of leaves – more than enough to block it.'

'And there's no way that could have happened by accident?'

'It's basic boat maintenance, Phil. You check the flue regularly. The odd leaf might blow in, but a rag doesn't get in there by accident. And the mushroom vents can't close themselves.'

'Show me the stove,' he said.

Lulu headed to the rear of the boat and stepped down onto the back deck. She went down the steps and Phil followed, with Conrad bringing up the rear. Lulu gestured towards the black cast-iron stove.

'So, it's just a regular wood-burning stove?' said Phil.

'That's right. It's a Villager Puffin four-kilowatt multi-fuel stove. It's quite a small one but if you use it overnight it keeps the boat warm through two small radiators and heats up water for the shower.'

Phil pointed at the black metal pipe that led up from the stove for about two feet and then angled into the side of the boat. 'And the smoke and fumes go out here?'

'That's it.'

'You call that the chimney?'

'The flue.'

Phil bent down and peered at the stove. The door was open and inside was a mess of wet ash and half-burned briquettes. 'I opened the windows and put out the fire,' said Lulu. 'I didn't want to clear the flue until your forensics people have had a chance to check for prints and DNA.'

Phil straightened up. 'So, whoever it was blocked the door vents, screwed down the mushroom vents and blocked the flue?'

'That's it.'

'Presumably while you were asleep. What time did you turn in?'

'Ten. Ten-thirty.'

'And you called me at five o'clock. How long would it take for the boat to fill with fumes?'

'I really couldn't say,' said Lulu. 'It's a small stove and the boat is sixty feet long. Several hours, I'd say.'

'And was the fire on all day?'

'No, I lit it last thing at night.'

Phil nodded. 'So you lit the fire and went to bed, and the fumes started to build up?' He pointed at the carbon-monoxide detector in the galley. 'Then the alarm went off?'

Lulu shook her head. 'No. Someone had taken the batteries out.'

Phil took a pair of blue latex gloves from his jacket pocket and pulled them on. He unclipped the front of the carbon-monoxide detector and nodded when he saw that the batteries were missing. 'The forensics team will take prints from this and the vents. And the chimney. Yours will be on file still.' He put the cover back on the detector. 'It wasn't you who took the batteries out?'

'Of course not. There's always a risk of carbon-monoxide poisoning from these stoves, so the detectors are compulsory.'

'Who has been on the boat other than yourself? Who would have the opportunity to remove the batteries?'

'No one has been on the boat.' She held up a hand. 'Let me clarify that. No one has been on the boat while I've been here. But I have been away running errands and the like, and I tend not to lock the doors.'

'So anyone could get on board and remove the batteries?'

Lulu grimaced. 'I know it sounds irresponsible, but it's Little Venice; people don't steal from the boats. If I'm just popping to the shops or going out for coffee, more often than not I'll just close the doors and not lock them.' She frowned. 'Ah, yesterday I was out most of the day. I was at a barbecue at a friend's home. I didn't get back until late.'

Phil took off his gloves and shoved them back in his pocket. 'With any luck, the forensics will tell us who did it,' he said. 'Presumably the person who disabled the carbon-monoxide detector then came back in the night and screwed the mushroom vents down and blocked up the door vents?'

'Yes, and they shoved the piece of cloth and the leaves down the flue on the outside. The fumes gradually filled up the cabin and if I hadn't woken up I'd be dead.'

'You were lucky.'

'Yes. No question.'

'And you didn't hear anyone on the roof?'

'I was asleep. So was Conrad. And if they were careful, there'd hardly be any noise.'

Phil frowned. 'There's one thing I don't understand,' he said. 'If you were asleep when they sealed the vents, what woke you up?'

Lulu looked over at Conrad, who was lying on the sofa, grooming himself. She obviously couldn't tell Phil the truth, that Conrad the talking cat had woken her up and saved her life. She smiled at the inspector. 'I was lucky. I'm not sure what woke me. A noise in the street, maybe. A car horn. Who knows? But I woke up and I knew straight away that something was wrong. My throat was sore and I had a piercing headache. I was confused because the alarm hadn't gone off but I opened all the windows and put the fire out, and when I opened the doors I saw the vents there had been blocked. Later I checked the mushroom vents. Once I saw that the vents had been tampered with, I lifted the chimney and looked down into the flue.'

Phil nodded. 'It definitely looks like an attempt to kill you, boss.'

Lulu grinned. 'You ought to be a detective,' she said.

Phil laughed. 'Nice one,' he said. 'The big question is,

who would want to kill you? A face from the past, do you think?'

Lulu shook her head. 'I've only been here a few weeks, Phil. Anybody looking for me would maybe find my address in Warrington Crescent. I don't see they would trace me here.'

'They could have followed you here.'

'What, an old enemy spots me in the street and follows me to the boat? How likely is that?'

'I hear you, boss. I'm just doing what you taught me – always consider all the options and only let the evidence rule them out. Last thing we want to do is jump to conclusions.'

'You had a good teacher,' said Lulu, smiling.

'The best.'

'I've been thinking about it. In this case, my brother-in-law had the means, the motive and the opportunity.'

'Did he know you were staying on the boat?'

Lulu frowned. That was a good question. She hadn't told Richard or Maria that she had moved out of the house. She thought about it for a few seconds and then raised her eyebrows. 'I went to Emily's house in Warrington Crescent. Maria and her brother were there, making a list of the contents. They're obviously planning to sell everything. When I left they could have followed me. If they did, they'd know about the boat.'

'Did you see anybody on your tail?'

'No, but I wasn't looking. My days of being followed are long gone. Or at least I thought they were.'

'Okay. If we assume they followed you and saw the boat, and if we assume that they told Richard, what on earth would the motive be?'

Lulu sat down on her chair and waved for Phil to take the sofa. 'I told you before that I have reservations about the death of my mother-in-law. Emily Lewis.'

'Of course.'

'Well, the whole Emily thing is still bothering me. We had the reading of her will and everything goes to Richard. And it's a substantial estate. He had a lot to gain from her death.'

'You're suggesting that Richard killed his mother to get his inheritance? That doesn't make sense; she was dying anyway.'

Lulu shook her head. 'No, she wasn't. She was in a nursing home, that's true, and she did have Alzheimer's, but other than that she was healthy. She could easily have lived to be a hundred.'

'Okay,' said Phil, but Lulu could hear the uncertainty in his voice.

'It's worse than that, Phil,' she said quietly. 'My husband, remember? He died in a hit-and-run accident three months ago. At least, it was treated as an accident at the time. But what if it wasn't? It was a well-lit corner. No visibility problems. The driver didn't stop. And here's the thing – Emily didn't change her will after Simon died, so Richard inherits everything. Her whole estate, which is close to twelve million pounds, depending on the valuation of her jewellery and paintings.'

'That's a big chunk of change.'

'And Simon's death means that Richard is close to six million pounds richer.' She took a deep breath. 'If Simon was still here, then he would have half the house, and Maria wouldn't be in there with her clipboard compiling an inventory.'

Phil leaned towards her. 'You're not suggesting that Richard killed his own brother, are you?'

'Well someone did, Phil. And if it wasn't an accident, Richard had the most to gain.'

'But he'd need means, motive and opportunity. You've given me motive, but what about means and opportunity?'

Lulu ran a hand through her hair. 'Good point,' she said. 'They were in Spain when it happened. Richard and Maria flew over for the funeral and then decided to move back to the UK. They're in Beckenham now.'

'You're sure about that?' asked Phil. 'They definitely weren't in the UK when it happened?'

Lulu sighed. 'I didn't check, if that's what you mean. I just took them at their word.'

'Well, after what happened last night, we need to take a closer look at their movements. I'll give Jamie Hughes a call. He's an Interpol liaison officer based in Malaga now.'

'Jamie always did like the sunshine, didn't he? Are we still allowed to liaise with Interpol post-Brexit?'

'Interpol is fine; it's Europol that's proving difficult. Jamie has some good connections out there.'

'Give him my regards. It seems like only yesterday he turned up at Paddington Green wearing his Marks and Spencer suit and Brut aftershave.'

Phil laughed. 'Well he still wears the aftershave, but these days it tends to be Versace jeans and Ralph Lauren polos. I'll get him to check on their movements.'

'Maria's brother is here, too. Juan. I don't like the look of him.'

Phil took out his notebook and scribbled in it. 'I don't suppose you've got a mobile number for the brother? And for Richard and Maria? I can get a warrant to look at their phone records.'

'I only have Richard's number.' She gave it to him and he scribbled in his notepad again.

'Where was your husband killed?' he asked.

'Not far from here,' she said. 'Five minutes away. He was on his way home from the pub.'

'Do you mind showing me?' He looked at his watch. 'The forensics team will be a while yet.'

'You think I'm right?'

'I'm thinking you always had good instincts, boss. That's what made you such an effective copper.'

29

'This was the pub where he was meeting a couple of friends,' said Lulu. They were standing outside the Hero of Maida, once a traditional Victorian pub, now with the ground floor painted a dark blue-grey, the upper floors natural brick with white windows. There were tables on the pavement, most of them occupied by middle-aged women drinking coffee. 'He liked this place. The food is really good.' Conrad was sitting on her shoulders, looking up at the building.

'What time was it?' asked Phil. 'When it happened?'

'He went straight there after work, so he got here about six-thirty. He was here for about an hour. He had two glasses of wine, so he wasn't drunk.'

Phil took out his cigarettes and lighter. 'Do you mind?'

'Go ahead,' she said.

Phil lit a cigarette and blew smoke up at the sky before speaking. 'It would have been dark then, right?'

'At seven-thirty? Yes.'

'What about the people he was drinking with?'

'They stayed here. I was cooking duck confit, which he always loved. I phoned him to say it would be ready at eight.' She began walking along the pavement. 'This is the way he went.' They came to a junction and she stopped. 'And this is where it happened. There are no traffic lights or anything, but then it's never really busy here.'

Phil looked down the road. 'It's easy to see anyone about

to cross, isn't it? And there are plenty of streetlights, so even at night . . .'

'Well, yes, but you know what people are like these days. Everyone uses their mobile even though they're not supposed to.'

'Is that what happened? The driver was on the phone?'

'They don't know. The driver didn't stop, just kept on going. The police said the driver had probably been drinking and panicked.'

'I'm sorry, boss.'

Lulu shook her head. 'It was one of those things. Wrong time, wrong place.' She sighed. 'Before, I just accepted what the police said: it was a hit and run with no CCTV and that they would do what they could to find the driver.'

'No witnesses?'

'There was a couple who heard the bang but they didn't see it happen. And there was a pensioner walking his dog who saw the car drive away but he couldn't remember the colour, never mind the make.' She pointed down the road. 'The car came this way. No evidence that it braked before the collision. They found fragments of glass that suggested a headlight had been smashed and the forensics people were able to say that the glass had come from a Nissan but couldn't pinpoint the model.' She looked up and down the road. 'You know, seeing it like this, you realize that the driver would have to have been blind not to have seen Simon crossing the road.'

'Or distracted by a phone, as you said.'

Lulu shook her head. 'But Simon crossed at the intersection. The driver would have to turn here, either right or left, so he'd have to be looking. Even if he was on the phone, he'd have to have looked up to make the turn.'

'Then maybe he was drunk, like the cops said.'

Lulu looked left and right again. 'It wasn't an accident,' she said firmly.

'I think you're right.'

'I'm starting to think they killed Simon. For the inheritance. With Simon dead, they inherited everything.'

'If that's what's happened, they're evil,' said Phil. 'Truly evil.'

'Yes,' said Lulu. 'It all had to be planned. They had to kill Simon and they had to kill Emily.' She put a hand over her mouth. 'I feel sick.'

'Take deep breaths,' said Phil.

'I feel faint,' she said. 'I need to sit down.'

He flicked away what was left of his cigarette. 'Can you walk back to the pub?'

Lulu nodded. 'I think so.' She walked slowly back to the Hero of Maida. One of the tables was empty and Conrad jumped down off her shoulders and onto the pavement, then leaped up onto one of the chairs. Lulu sat down next to him as Phil went into the pub. He returned a few minutes later with two cups of coffee. 'Do you want something?' he asked Conrad.

Conrad looked up at him and meowed.

'He says he's fine,' said Lulu. She took her coffee and sipped it as Phil sat down at the table. There wasn't much of a view. The pub looked over two council blocks and off to the right was the Amadeus Centre, a former Welsh Presbyterian chapel that had been painted powder blue and rebranded as an events venue, mainly for wedding receptions. Lulu sighed. Her mind was in a whirl and she took long slow breaths to calm herself down.

'Are you okay?' asked Phil.

Lulu nodded. 'The police were sure that Simon's death was an accident. Maybe caused by a distracted or a drunk driver, but an accident nevertheless. I did ask them how confident they were of catching the driver and they said there was a good chance because there would have been some damage to the front of the car: the glass in the road from a broken headlight.' Coffee slopped over her cup and she smiled apologetically at Phil. 'I can't stop shaking,' she whispered.

She felt numb as she tried to come to terms with the thought that Richard and Maria had deliberately set out to kill Simon and Emily. Was it possible? She frowned and took another gulp of coffee. 'The first time I met Maria was at Simon's funeral and she was so sweet, hugging me and saying that she was there for me, no matter what I needed. I'm sure there were tears in her eyes several times during the service. They came to the reception afterwards, but left early. Richard apologized but said they had to get back to Malaga – something about a problem with the restaurant. At the time I was too grief-stricken to appreciate what was happening, but afterwards I thought their appearance was all very rushed. They arrived at the church in a taxi minutes before the service began and left midway through the reception. Richard did give a eulogy for Simon, and it was very touching, fond and funny memories of their childhood and how he regretted growing apart from Simon as they got older. Only now I can see that perhaps it was very much a performance. Richard was playing to the crowd and almost relishing the laughs and smiles that he was getting.'

'How did Richard and Maria meet?' asked Phil.

'In Spain, not long after Richard had divorced his second wife. Actually, she had divorced him. Fiona, her name was. Fiona was lovely. She was fifteen years younger than Richard, who had been running an English bar out in Fuengirola, the cheaper part of the Costa del Sol. Richard had swept her off her feet and into the cramped, sweaty kitchen where she turned out full English breakfasts, roast dinners and fish and chips for twelve hours a day. The marriage lasted almost as long as the bar. They had a child, though. A son. I don't think Richard has any contact with them. He does seem a lot closer to Maria; for most of the funeral he held her hand as if he was frightened of losing her.'

'So they were in love?'

'He loved Maria, I'm sure of that. He always thought with his heart, never his head. He had a knack for setting up a profitable business and then running it into the ground. He did it three times in the UK – a card shop, a small magazine publishing company and a spring water bottler – each time funded by loans from Emily and Frank, loans which more often than not ended up turning into gifts. He'd have a good idea but then he'd just get bored. After his third failure he'd borrowed from his parents and travelled for a year or two. He'd run a diving company in Bali and a trekking company in the Philippines, where he'd married and divorced his first wife, and tried his hand at yacht brokering in Singapore. He'd left Singapore with half a dozen creditors on his tail and had ended up in Spain. Frank had always been happy to fund his wayward son, and after his death Emily had also been relaxed with the chequebook.'

'The prodigal son?' said Phil.

'Very much so.' Lulu took another sip of coffee. 'Once

L T Shearer

the Alzheimer's kicked in with a vengeance, the handouts were less forthcoming. Simon had taken over most of Emily's finances and put all the utilities in his name. A year ago, Richard flew over to London and presented Simon with a business proposal to set up an estate agency in Malaga. Simon listened and then said no, but Richard wouldn't accept the refusal and went down to the basement to harangue Emily. We heard Emily crying so we went to see what was happening. It was clear that Richard didn't understand the issues his mother was dealing with, and when Simon tried to explain Richard cut him short and stormed out of the house. That was the last time I saw him, prior to Simon's funeral.' She swallowed. 'They could have planned this, right from the start.'

'You said the broken glass they found on the road belonged to a Nissan. Do we know what car Richard drives?'

'He probably wasn't in the country at the time. I suppose it's possible that he paid someone to kill Simon.' She put a hand up to her face. 'I can't believe I just said that.'

Phil nodded. 'After what happened on your boat, we're going to have to consider all the options.'

She took her phone from her pocket and showed him the photograph she had taken outside the solicitor's office. 'He and his wife turned up for the reading of the will in this.'

Phil peered at the screen. 'A Nissan Juke?'

'Yes. But I can't see that he'd still be driving it around if he'd used it to run Simon over. I didn't see any damage or signs that it had been repaired.'

'Well, if he did have it repaired, you probably wouldn't be able to tell. Not just by looking at it. He would be crazy to keep driving it if it was involved in a fatal hit and run.

248

Let me take a note of the registration number and I'll check it out.'

Lulu held the phone as Phil took out his notebook and scribbled down the number. Just as he finished, his mobile rang and he fished it out of his pocket. 'Yes. Great. Yes. Blomfield Road. I'll be waiting for you.' He put the phone away. 'Forensics are on the way.'

Lulu looked at her watch. 'I'll pop along to the home, see if I can catch Ildi on her way into work.'

'Ildi?'

'The nurse. I need to ask her something.'

'About Emily?'

Lulu nodded. 'About the box of chocolates that I think Richard gave Emily. The box disappeared after she died.'

Phil frowned. 'Disappeared?'

'I was given all of her belongings the day after she passed away. The chocolates weren't there.'

'These are the ones you think might have been spiked with sesame seeds?'

'Or sesame oil. Yes. I'm going to go back to the home to talk to Ildi. She was looking after Emily. I'll ask her if she knows what happened to the chocolates.'

'Let me know what she says.'

'Of course I will.'

30

Lulu saw Ildi hurrying along the road towards the home, her head down and her heels clicking on the pavement. 'Ildi!' she called. She was on the opposite side of the road and she waved to get the nurse's attention.

Ildi looked over, shaded her eyes with her hand and then smiled when she recognized Lulu. She stopped and Lulu hurried across the road. 'Good morning,' said Ildi. 'Are you coming to visit Shirley again?' Her eyes widened when she realized that Conrad was sitting on Lulu's shoulders. 'How does he do that?'

Conrad jumped down and landed on the pavement. 'Actually, I wanted a quick word with you,' said Lulu.

'Do you want to go inside?'

'It might be better if we spoke out here,' said Lulu.

Ildi frowned. 'Is something wrong?'

'I'm not sure,' said Lulu. 'Do you remember the box of chocolates that Emily had? The handmade ones?'

'Yes . . .' said Ildi cautiously.

'Well, the thing is, when I got Emily's belongings, the chocolates weren't there. Do you have any idea what happened to them?'

Ildi's face fell and Lulu could tell immediately that something was wrong. 'I didn't steal them, if that's what you think,' said the nurse.

'Of course not, that was the last thing on my mind. But

I would like to know if someone took them, or if they were thrown away. I'm really not accusing anybody of anything, least of all you.'

'I took them,' said Ildi quietly.

'Oh,' said Lulu. It wasn't at all what she had expected to hear.

'Well, I didn't really take them. Mrs Lewis gave them to me. She said she thought they were too sweet. She knew I loved them, so she said I could have them.'

'When was this?'

'Sunday evening. I was doing a last-minute check to make sure she'd taken her medication. She sometimes forgets. Anyway, she was just getting ready to take her tablets and she asked me if I wanted the chocolates and of course I said yes because they were delicious.'

'Yes, they certainly were,' said Lulu.

Ildi frowned. 'Am I in trouble?'

Lulu flashed Ildi her most reassuring smile. 'No, of course not. I just wanted to make sure they hadn't been left in the room.'

'No, I took them home on Sunday night. There were six left and I had three on Monday and three on Tuesday.'

'So Emily didn't have one on Sunday before she went to sleep?'

Ildi shook her head. 'No. As I said, she thought they were too sweet. I thought it was a bit strange, because she'd said she loved them before. I think maybe the last one she had was a ginger one and she didn't like ginger.'

'That's maybe it,' said Lulu. 'Emily never liked ginger.'

Ildi looked at her watch. 'I have to clock in,' she said. 'Mrs Fitzgerald doesn't like us being late.'

'Then I won't keep you,' said Lulu.

'I am so sorry about your loss,' said Ildi. 'Mrs Lewis was a lovely lady.'

'Thank you,' said Lulu. 'And I'm sorry to have bothered you. I know Emily really liked you and appreciated everything that you did for her. I'm sure that's why she wanted you to have the chocolates.' She knelt down and Conrad jumped up onto her shoulders.

Ildi laughed. 'It's amazing how he does that,' she said.

'He is an amazing cat,' said Lulu.

31

Two forensic investigators were getting off *The Lark* when Lulu arrived back at the mooring. They were wearing white paper suits, blue shoe coverings and blue latex gloves. They were both carrying black cases containing their equipment.

Phil was standing on the towpath, smoking. He waved his cigarette at her. 'Perfect timing,' he said. 'They're just about finished here.'

The two investigators nodded at the inspector and smiled at Lulu and Conrad. 'What a lovely cat,' said the older of the two, a woman with chestnut hair and black-rimmed spectacles. She had a Sony SLR camera hanging around her neck.

'Meow,' said Conrad.

'And talkative. Lovely.' The investigator nodded at Lulu's feet. 'We photographed your footwear on the boat. Can we just get a picture of the ones you're wearing?'

'Of course,' said Lulu.

'They've found a few shoe prints on the roof and the towpath,' explained Phil. 'We just need to rule yours out.' He smiled ruefully. 'Mine too.'

'We're just glad you remembered to wear gloves when you opened the carbon-monoxide detector,' said the investigator. She smiled at Lulu. 'Amanda Elliott,' she said. 'We actually met years ago, not long after I started on the job. But I had masks and goggles on at the time so I doubt you'd remember me.'

'The murder-suicide in Bayswater,' said Lulu. 'I remember. That was a pretty gruesome case, wasn't it?'

Amanda nodded. 'It was my second real violent crime scene and I'm always amazed that I didn't throw up.'

Lulu stepped onto the boat, sat down and removed her trainers. She handed them to Amanda, who placed them on the ground, soles up, and put a ruler next to them before taking several photographs. 'There you go,' she said, handing the trainers back to Lulu. 'We'll get out of your hair.'

She and her colleague headed off down the towpath. 'Fancy a coffee?' Lulu asked Phil.

'I'd love one,' said the inspector. He climbed on the boat and went down through the double doors as Lulu sat and slipped her trainers back on. She joined him in the cabin and put the kettle on to boil.

Phil sat down on the sofa. 'So, they found some decent shoe prints on the roof and matched them with prints on the towpath. Plenty of smudges on the mushroom vents and more smudge marks in the mud that was smeared on the door vents. There are more smudges on the chimney, so it's a good bet that your visitor was wearing gloves.'

Lulu took mugs out of one of the overhead cupboards along with a jar of Nescafe Gold Blend. 'They obviously came prepared.'

'Yes, but the leaves and rag looked as if they had been sourced locally.'

'Maybe they were thinking that it might just look like an accident.'

'I suppose so.'

'And the carbon-monoxide detector?'

'There are prints on it, outside and inside. But Amanda

was showing me marks that suggest the cover was pulled off with the insides of the fingers rather than the fingertips.'

'A palm print, then? That could be as good as fingerprints.'

'Nah, sadly not. Just the minimum contact needed to get enough of a grip to pull it off. And if you were careful you could pull out the batteries without leaving any prints inside. She's taken the cover and they'll look for DNA in the lab. It looks to me as if the removal of the batteries was opportunistic, so they didn't have gloves. Then they came back later, better prepared.'

'What do you think? The shoes are the best bet?'

'I think so. Size twelve, Amanda reckons, so not yours. The leaves and rag might be helpful; when they gathered it up they might have dropped some of their own DNA on it, skin flakes or hair, so they'll be having a more detailed look in the lab. It's not looking likely that we'll be able to ID who took the batteries out of the detector, but never say never.'

Lulu spooned coffee into the mugs. 'Still two sugars, right?'

Phil laughed. 'Yes, but black these days, boss. No milk.'

'I managed to speak to Ildi about the chocolates. Apparently my mother-in-law gave them to her on the Sunday night.'

'Did she, now?'

'And Ildi says that Emily didn't have a chocolate that night. She gave them all to Ildi.'

'So that means it wasn't the chocolates? I mean, if it was a reaction to sesame seeds, they weren't in the chocolates?'

Lulu nodded. 'Looks that way.'

'So if it wasn't in the chocolates, then your brother-in-law doesn't have anything to cover up, does he?'

Lulu frowned. 'What do you mean?'

'Motive,' said Phil. 'Your brother-in-law has a clear motive for killing Simon and Emily. Money. But there's no financial gain to be had by killing you. The attempt on your life must have been for another reason. Now if the chocolates had been spiked with sesame seeds, your brother would want you off the case. But now we know that the chocolates have nothing to do with her death, that motive goes out of the window.'

'I suppose you're right.' She frowned. 'But then we come down to motive again. I really can't think of anyone else who would want to cause me harm.'

'Boss, you put away thousands of crims during your career.'

'I've been retired more than a decade, Phil. Why wait so long?'

'Someone just out of prison? Someone you put away for a long stretch.'

'Murder, you mean?' She nodded thoughtfully. 'That's possible. Okay, I'll sit down with my notebooks and see if I can come up with any names.'

The kettle began to boil and she switched off the hob and poured hot water into the mugs. She put a splash of milk in one and added two spoons of sugar to the other and gave it to Phil, then sat down on the chair.

'I have to say that I think the deaths of Emily and Simon and the attack on me are connected,' she said.

'It's a possibility, but I think we should still be considering every option,' said Phil. 'You taught me that, boss. There's no such thing as open and shut. Remember that murder in Clerkenwell? The woman who was almost decapitated. I was sure that her husband had done it, I would have bet my pension on it. He had the motive – she was sleeping with his nephew. He had the opportunity – he'd left work early that day. And he had the means.'

'Open and shut,' said Lulu. She sipped her coffee.

Conrad jumped up onto the sofa and curled up next to Phil. The inspector reached down and began to stroke him along the back. 'And then it turned out to be a random nutter. Not that we can call them that these days, of course. But it was just a case of her being in the wrong place at the wrong time. If you hadn't spotted the cigarette butts and had them tested for DNA, the husband would still be behind bars.' He raised his mug to her. 'You taught me a hell of a lot, boss.'

'Nice of you to say so, Phil. But you always had it in you.'

'Thanks.'

'And you're right, of course. You have to let the evidence point the way. It's just that right from the start I had a gut feeling that Emily's death wasn't from natural causes. And that hasn't gone away.'

'But you know now that the chocolates weren't responsible,' he said.

'Yes, you're right.'

'So how about this? We look for whoever tried to kill you this morning. There's no doubt what happened here, so there'll be a full investigation. And I'll pull the file on your husband's hit and run and see if there are any links to your brother-in-law. Let's see what progress we make on those fronts before we decide how to proceed with your mother-in-law's death.'

'Okay, that sounds like a plan.'

They drank their coffee and reminisced about the days they had worked together. Phil kept asking her if she was okay and Lulu assured him that she was. Eventually he looked at his watch and said that he had to get back to work. Lulu and Conrad stood on the back deck and watched him go. She had the feeling that Phil was more worried about the attempt on her life than she was.

'He has a good aura,' said Conrad. 'Lots of purple and indigo.'

Lulu nodded. 'He was a good colleague, and a good friend, too.'

'He cares about you,' said Conrad. 'A lot.'

Phil stopped to light a cigarette, turned to give them a final wave, and then disappeared onto Blomfield Road.

'I know,' said Lulu. 'I'm lucky to have him as a friend.'

32

Lulu spent the rest of the morning cleaning *The Lark*. She started on the roof, scrubbing off the mess left by the forensic specialists, then wiping down the sides, the windows and the prow. She washed down the back deck and removed the mud that was blocking the vents on the double doors. After that she cleaned the engine and checked the oil levels, the drive belt tension, the bilge and coolant levels and made sure that all the hoses were in good condition.

Once she'd finished she went inside, made another coffee, and then started cleaning the cabin. She had spare AA batteries, which she put in the carbon-monoxide detector after wiping off the fingerprint powder the technicians had used. She was changing the sheets on her bed when her phone buzzed to let her know that she'd received a message. It was from Phil Jackson. 'PERMISSION TO COME ABOARD?' She smiled and walked up the steps to the back deck, where the inspector was standing on the towpath, halfway through a cigarette.

'Well, this is a nice surprise,' she said. 'I didn't expect to see you again this quickly.'

'I was in the area,' he said.

'I really don't believe that.'

He grinned. 'It's a fair cop.' He reached into his pocket and brought out a rose-gold Cartier watch. Lulu's eyes widened when she saw it. He gave it to her and she held it in her right hand, her mouth open in surprise.

'You were right, Gary Wilkinson stole it. I ran a PNC check on him and he has a history of petty theft. He managed to hide his past from the home. To be honest, they're so desperate for staff I don't think they even check references. Anyway, I went to see him and – long story short – he gave up the watch. And some other items that he'd stolen from other residents at the home. I'll go around and talk to Mrs Fitzgerald at some point.'

'So you'll be charging him?'

Phil sighed. 'Well, that's where it gets a bit awkward. When I confronted him, he flat-out denied that he'd taken the watch. And I didn't have a warrant to search his bedsit and I almost certainly didn't have enough probable cause to get one. So we were in a bit of a stand-off. Eventually I offered him a deal: if he came clean and gave me the watch, I'd make sure he wasn't charged.' He smiled. 'That was the carrot. The stick was that I'd beat him black and blue if he didn't hand it over.'

'Phil, that was reckless. You could lose your job for that.'

'He's a scrote, boss. His word against mine. But it worked out just fine, he chose the carrot.'

'So he gets away with it?'

'Well, to be honest he gets away with it all the time. He's been in court four times on theft charges and each time he got a slap on the wrist. He says he's sorry and he won't do it again and blames his deprived childhood. He's never been to prison and with thefts like this he probably won't. Even if I charged him and put a case together, and even if the CPS approved it, a magistrate would probably just give him proba-tion and a stern talking-to. Hurt feelings on social media is a big issue for the police these days; thefts from the recently deceased, not so much.'

Lulu smiled thinly. 'I guess so.'

'It's the way it is now, boss, there's no point in fighting it. Besides, it was so well hidden that even if I had got a warrant I doubt that I would have found it. He had this energy can drink in the fridge. It looked and felt like the real thing but you could unscrew the bottom and hide stuff there. The choice was to offer him a deal, or never see the watch again. On the plus side, he gave me the details of a jeweller's in Kilburn that he sells the stuff to. I'm assuming it's a major fencing operation, so I'll get that looked at and see what else we can recover.'

'Okay, Phil. I get it. And thank you.'

'Not a problem, boss. Happy to help.'

'And what about Gary? He gets off scot-free?'

'As I said, even if he goes to court he won't really be punished,' said Phil. 'All I can do is damage limitation. So I've told him to quit the home, today. And to leave our patch.'

'Make him somebody else's problem?'

'Sorry about that. But I've told him that wherever he goes I'll be watching him, and that if he puts a foot wrong again I'll come down on him like a ton of bricks. I'm not sure if he knows that's a bluff or not, but it's the best I can do.'

Lulu looked at the watch and smiled. She already had her Rolex on her left wrist so she put the Cartier on her right. 'Thank you so much.'

'It's a beautiful watch,' said Phil. 'Are you going to keep it?'

'I'd love to, Phil, but I don't see that I can. All Emily's

possessions now belong to Richard. And Maria. I'll have to give it to them.'

'Well, let's see what Jamie has to say first,' said Phil. 'I've arranged a FaceTime chat with him and I want you to sit in.' He held up his cigarette. 'I'll just finish this, if that's okay.'

'Go ahead,' she said.

'You've never been tempted to smoke again?'

Lulu shook her head. 'It's coming up for fifteen years since I stopped and I've never regretted it.'

'I wish I had your willpower.' He took a drag on his cigarette and blew smoke up at the clear blue sky. 'So, first things first. Neither Richard nor his wife, Maria, were in the UK when your husband was killed. We know that for a fact because they flew in two days before the funeral on an EasyJet flight. That was the first time they had left Spain in more than six months. They flew back to Malaga two days after the funeral and all the time they were in the UK they stayed at the Premier Inn County Hall, the one across the river from the Houses of Parliament. As far as we can see, they didn't hire a car while they were here.' Phil looked at his notebook. 'They returned to the UK about three weeks after the funeral and used AirBnB to rent a flat in Beckenham. They stayed there a week and then moved to a house in the same area, this time taking it for a month, which they then renewed. The car you saw them in is a rental, and they took out a lease on it a week after they moved to Beckenham.' He looked up from his notebook. 'With the best will in the world, they couldn't have been driving the car that hit your husband.'

'I see that. But . . .'

He held up his hand. 'I'm ahead of you,' he said. 'It wouldn't be difficult for them to have paid someone else to do their dirty work, especially as they were living on the Costa del Crime. But that's out of my area of expertise, obviously. Jamie texted me to say that we could have a chat at lunchtime. I thought it best if we talk to him together, and you being a civilian I figured best we don't do it in the office. I did think it might be nostalgic to call him from one of our old pub haunts, but these days all it takes is a punter with a phone and my career is dead in the water.'

'So you decided we should call him from here?'

'That's my plan.'

'Coffee?'

'That would hit the spot.' He finished his cigarette and looked at her. 'I suppose it would be wrong to flick this into the canal?'

'It would, yes.'

'Towpath?'

She shook her head.

'So what do I do with it?'

Lulu laughed. 'Bring it on board and you can put it in my rubbish bin.'

'Right, boss.' He joined her on the deck and followed her through the double doors and down the steps. She pointed at the rubbish bin and he stubbed out the cigarette on its metal lid and dropped it in, then sat down on the sofa. Lulu lit the hob and put the kettle on the flames.

Phil took out his phone and looked around for something to rest it against. Lulu spooned coffee into the mug, then screwed the lid back on and gave the coffee jar to him. 'Perfect,' he said. He leaned the phone against the jar and tapped on the screen. Lulu put the mug of steaming black coffee on the table and sat down next to him.

The phone rang out and after a few seconds Jamie answered. It had been at least fifteen years since Lulu had seen him, but he was as fresh-faced as ever, albeit a bit greyer. He grinned when he saw Lulu. 'Hello, boss. Great to see you.'

'You too, Jamie. You're looking good.' He was tanned and wearing a white open-necked linen shirt and had a thick gold chain around his neck. Gel glistened in his slicked-back hair.

'I put it down to the Mediterranean diet, and the fact that I'm off the booze.'

'Good to hear it. How's the Costa?'

'Well, the weather's better than London, and I like the lifestyle. I'm mainly into intelligence-gathering and liaising with the Spanish cops, keeping track of who's out here and what they're up to. Keeps me away from all the Met politics. The Met isn't the job it used to be, as I'm sure you know.'

'Yes, I hear that a lot, Jamie.'

'You got out at the right time and that's a fact.' Jamie peered at the screen. 'Where are you, boss? Looks like a boat.'

'It's a narrowboat,' said Lulu. 'On the canal. Little Venice.'

'Lovely,' said Jamie. 'A life on the ocean waves.'

'Hardly,' said Lulu.

'I spent a week on a narrowboat with the missus about ten years ago. She divorced me a couple of months later. I was never sure if it was the boat trip or me being a tosser.'

'Probably a bit of both,' said Phil.

Jamie laughed. 'Fair comment,' he said. 'Anyway, boss,

sorry to hear what happened to your husband. And to your mother-in-law. I just hope bad news doesn't come in threes. But from the sound of it, it nearly did.'

'Yeah, I had a lucky escape, that's for sure.' She looked over at Conrad and flashed him a smile.

'So, on that score, I've got the dates that Richard Lewis and his wife Maria entered the country, the first time to attend the funeral of Mr Lewis, and the second time a few weeks later when they appear to have moved to the UK,' said Phil. 'How did you get on, Jamie?'

'Well, yes, they're definitely man and wife,' said Jamie. 'I've got a copy of their marriage certificate. And a copy of his divorce from his previous wife, Fiona. I went down to Marbella and they've definitely gone. They lived above a restaurant in Marbella Old Town and the whole place is shuttered with For Sale signs up. Interesting thing, though, is that most of their stuff went into storage, which suggests they might be coming back.'

'What sort of reputation has he got around town?' asked Lulu.

'Bit of an idiot, to be honest. Keeps setting up businesses or buying them, and then runs them into the ground. He's a charmer, loads of friends, and he's always happy to pick up the bill. But that sort always attracts freeloaders and he didn't appear to be able to spot them.'

'It looks as if he was in Spain when Mr Lewis was killed, but we were wondering how easy it would have been for Richard to have hired someone to do it,' said Phil.

Jamie nodded. 'Yeah, it's the perfect part of the world when it comes to hiring a hitman,' he said. 'You've got Russian gangsters, Hungarian, Bulgarian, Serbian, Bosnian – you name it, they're out here, and most of them work cheap. If it's a hit in Spain you can get it done for a few thousand euros. Organizing a hit in London would be a bit more complicated if they were flying back and forth, but it's very doable.'

'And would Richard have the connections?' asked Lulu.

Jamie smiled grimly. 'They don't call it the Costa del Crime for nothing, boss. You can't throw a spanner down the beach road without hitting a London face or an Essex wide boy. And being in the bar business, he'd be crossing paths with all the crims.'

'Anyone in particular, Jamie?' asked Lulu.

'I could ask around,' said Jamie. 'And I could run checks on the airlines to see if any known villains flew to London and back around the time of the hit and run.'

'Has Richard been behaving himself in Spain?' asked Lulu.

'I'm trying to run a criminal records check on him but my Policía Nacional contact has been away; he's not back at his desk until this afternoon. Sadly it's still very much *mañana, mañana* over here. But it's in hand. I'll check out Richard's record here, and his wife's.'

'Can you do another check for me, too, Jamie? Maria has a brother. Juan. He's over here with them.'

'Will do, yes.'

'And what do you know about Maria?'

'She's from Granada, originally. That was where she was born, anyway, according to the marriage certificate. Maria Garcia Lopez. This is her first marriage. No children.'

'And just as a matter of interest, Jamie, do you know what car Richard drove over there?'

'That's easy. He had a yellow Porsche. Still has – that got put into storage as well.'

'How easy would it be to get hold of their phone records for three to four months ago?' asked Lulu.

'Not as easy as it used to be before Brexit,' said Jamie. 'And I'd need a case number, which at present we don't have.'

Lulu looked across at Phil. 'It would be handy if we could get a look at his calls and messages and his GPS data.'

Phil looked pained. 'Yeah, but Jamie's right. We'd need a case number and there's a long waiting period. Partly because of *mañana*, but there's also a fair bit of teaching us a lesson for leaving the EU. The Spanish aren't being as vindictive as the Germans and the French, but they're definitely not making life easy for us.' He nodded at Jamie. 'Okay, mate, we'll leave it with you. But soon as you can, yeah?'

'Sure, yes, no problem. And great to see you again, boss.'

'You too, Jamie. Stay safe.'

The call ended and Phil put his phone away. 'So, according to the forensic team, there's no useful DNA and the only prints are yours. The footprints on the roof are a different matter. They're size twelve and fairly distinctive. They also found similar prints on the towpath going to and from Blomfield Road. It's unlikely that Maria would have feet that big, so we'd be looking at Richard or Maria's brother. We could go in and get all their footwear but I'm reluctant to show our cards so early.'

'I hear you, Phil.'

He finished his coffee and stood up. 'Let's see what Jamie comes up with and then we'll see where we go from there. I'm getting the area checked for CCTV cameras; there might be one on the Waterway or elsewhere on Formosa Street that will show whoever it was arriving, but that's a long shot.'

'I appreciate all the work you're doing, Phil. Thank you.'

'Nothing to thank me for, boss.'

'You're an angel, Phil,' said Lulu. 'I don't know what I'd do without you.'

Phil winked at her, gave Conrad a thumbs-up and went up the stairs. Lulu and Conrad followed him. The boat rocked as he climbed out onto the towpath. She waved at him as he walked away and he threw her a mock salute.

'He's such a nice man,' said Conrad.

'He is,' said Lulu. 'One of the best.'

'Drink? To celebrate finishing your spring clean?'

'I haven't quite finished yet, but I was thinking of maybe a glass of mint tea.'

Conrad shook his head and smiled. 'No you weren't.'

33

Once Lulu had finished cleaning the boat inside and outside, she showered and changed into a flower-print dress. She had bought it the previous week, on sale at H&M. She had made a conscious decision to have only new clothes on the boat so that she didn't have to wear anything that she had worn with Simon. Her old clothes brought back too many memories, so she had left them in the house. She walked to Raoul's Deli in Clifton Road and bought a selection of salads, some cheese, and a couple of freshly baked croissants. Conrad rode on her shoulders, but he had to jump down and wait outside while she was inside.

'What can I get you?' she asked when she came out of Raoul's. 'I didn't really see anything there you'd like.'

Conrad twitched his whiskers. 'Trout would be a treat. I'm partial to a piece of trout.'

'Tesco has trout.'

'Perfect.'

She picked him up and carried him across the road and then put him down outside the supermarket. She went in and bought fresh trout for him, cleaning products and a few other essentials.

She came back out and bent down so that he could jump onto her shoulders. 'Do you know why it's called Tesco?' he asked once he was comfortably seated.

'I don't, actually,' she said. 'I assume the CO comes from company?'

'No, the C and the O are the first two letters of the founder's surname. Jack Cohen. And the TES comes from the initials of one of his suppliers – T. E. Stockwell. They started selling Tesco tea and kept the name when they started opening stores.'

'I did not know that.'

'He's buried only four miles away. In the Willesden Jewish Cemetery.'

Lulu frowned. 'How would you know that?'

'You pick up a lot just by listening,' he said. 'I'm a good listener.'

Lulu took a short detour so that she could walk by Emily's house. There was no sign of anyone inside and she didn't see a red Nissan Juke in the street. Perhaps Maria had finished her inventory?

'*Inventario*,' said Conrad, in a Spanish accent.

Lulu stopped in her tracks. 'How did you know what I was thinking?'

Conrad chuckled. 'You were staring at the house, then you looked up and down the road, obviously checking for a car. I assumed you were thinking about Maria.'

'You are one smart cat,' said Lulu as she began walking again.

'I see things,' said Conrad.

'Yes, you do,' said Lulu.

They got back to the boat. Lulu prepared her late lunch, then put Conrad's trout on a pretty Wedgwood plate and carried it out to the deck. The sky was clear and there was a soft wind blowing down the canal. She put Conrad's plate on the seat so that he could sit next to her as they ate.

'I like it here,' he said, between mouthfuls.

'It's lovely,' said Lulu. 'We're in London, but it's so peaceful. It's like being in a small village.' She smiled down at him. 'I hope you'll stay.'

'I think I will.'

'I'd miss you if you left me.'

Conrad nodded. 'I'd miss you, too.'

Lulu was finishing off her last chunk of croissant when her phone rang. It was a landline. She took the call. It was Phil. 'Hi boss,' he said. 'Can you talk?'

'Sure, Phil. What's up?'

'The investigation into your brother-in-law has taken an interesting turn.'

'I'm all ears.'

'You're not going to believe this, but Jamie was digging around Maria's family, and she doesn't have a brother.'

'What? Impossible. I've met him.'

'Whoever you met, he isn't Maria's brother. She's an only child. The Spanish births, deaths and marriages data is all computerized on a state-of-the-art system. Jamie's contact has full access and there's no doubt.'

'I'm shocked. I am truly shocked.'

'Well, Jamie is still on the case, so let's see what else he can come up with. Do you have a photograph of this Juan?'

'No, sorry.'

'A description then?'

'Tall. Over six foot. Six one, maybe. Late thirties. Black hair with a curl to it. Blue eyes. Olive skin. He had a seven o'clock shadow thing going on. Looks like he spends a lot of time in the gym.'

'That's great. Jamie can run the description past Maria's parents.'

'No, Phil, they're dead. They died when she was a teen-ager.'

'No, boss. Antonio and Dolores are very much alive and well and living in Granada. Jamie's driving up there as we speak.'

Lulu frowned. 'Well that's interesting. And something of a surprise.'

'She's claiming to be an orphan?'

'That's what Richard told me.'

'Then there's something very strange going on, boss.'

'Looks that way.'

'Anyway, I'll pass your description of Juan over to Jamie and we'll see what Maria's parents have to say.'

'Get back to me as soon as you have anything, Phil.'

'You can count on it, boss. Where are you sleeping tonight, by the way?'

'On the boat, of course.'

'Do you think that's a good idea?'

'I won't have the stove on. And I'll sleep with one eye open.'

'I'd offer to put a man outside but I know we don't have the resources.'

'That's okay, Phil. I've got Conrad to look after me.'

'Conrad?' He chuckled. 'Oh, your cat.'

'My guard cat. He'll protect me.'

Phil ended the call and Lulu put the phone down. 'Everything okay?' asked Conrad.

'Not really,' said Lulu. She explained what the inspector had told her.

'So Richard has been lying?' said Conrad.

'Or more likely Maria lied to Richard and he just repeats what she tells him.'

'But if Juan isn't her brother, then who is he?'

'That, Conrad, is a very good question that needs some considerable thought. And you know what always helps me think?'

Conrad smiled up at her. 'A nice crisp Chardonnay?'

Lulu laughed. 'I was actually thinking about mint tea,' she said. She put on the kettle, picked some fresh mint and made herself a glass of tea. 'Let's sit outside,' she said. Conrad followed her up the steps and sat next to her on the back deck. Lulu sipped her tea as a gentle breeze ruffled her hair. 'Maybe I've misjudged Richard,' she said.

'His aura does suggest that he's easily led,' said Conrad.

'So, Maria lies to him and he believes it. She pretends to be a poor orphan who has always had to fight for everything she needs but finally meets a white knight who will take care of her. She becomes his loving wife, but what if it's all a lie?' She cupped her hands round the glass thoughtfully. 'And if this Juan isn't her brother, is he something else?'

'Her lover?'

'That's what I'm thinking,' said Lulu. She smiled. 'But you knew that.' She looked up at the clear blue sky. 'Richard said that Maria loved Emily, didn't he? Presumably because that's what she told him.'

'He said she'd visited her on her own, several times.'

'Yes, he did, didn't he?' She put her glass down on the seat and took out her phone. She scrolled through the photographs on it until she reached the ones she'd taken of the nursing home's visitors' book. 'Well, she was there with

Richard last Friday,' she said. 'At noon.' She flicked through the photographs, reading the names and dates in the book. 'And she was there on her own on Monday. Early afternoon. That's when Emily used to nap.' She frowned as she continued to scrutinize the photographs. 'She was there on her own on the previous Friday. Again in the early afternoon. And she was there that week on Tuesday morning. On her own.' She nodded. 'Okay, so she did visit Emily. But why? It was very clear from Maria's performance at the will reading that they weren't close.' Her frown deepened. 'Tuesday morning, Friday afternoon, Monday afternoon.' She frowned and flicked through to the last of the photographs. 'But only one visit prior to that, and that was with Richard. So on three visits she was alone. But Richard said she didn't like to drive. So did she use public transport to get all the way from Beckenham to the home? That seems unlikely, doesn't it?'

'Maybe Juan drove her?'

'Exactly. But if Juan drove her, why didn't he go in with her? She only signed herself in, which means he must have waited outside in the car.' She put down the phone and picked up her tea.

'You don't think she was just visiting, do you?' asked Conrad.

'She didn't like Emily, that's as clear as day. And if it was a genuine visit, she'd have taken her brother in with her.'

'Except we know that Juan isn't her brother.'

'Indeed. So what was she up to?'

'Well, we know it was nothing to do with the chocolates, because Emily gave them to Ildi on Sunday, which means that Emily didn't eat one on Sunday night.'

'True,' said Lulu. She sipped her mint tea thoughtfully. 'So what else? What else might Emily have eaten or drunk that could have contained sesame seeds?' Her eyes widened. 'Her medication. Emily took tablets every night before she went to sleep.'

'So someone could have interfered with her tablets?'

'It would have to have been someone who worked at the home. Or a visitor.' She put down her glass. 'Do you feel like a walk? Or a ride?'

'Lead on, Macduff.'

Lulu smiled. 'Now that's a good name for a cat. Macduff.'

Conrad's eyes narrowed. 'Don't even think about it.'

34

Lulu let herself into the basement flat and walked down the hallway to the kitchen. Conrad followed her. His paws made no sound on the tiled floor. 'How do you walk so quietly?' asked Lulu.

'I'm light on my feet,' he said.

'I guess it helps you creep up on birds and mice and things.'

'That's what cats do.' He broke into a run and got to the kitchen before her. The cardboard box was on the pine table where she'd left it. The framed photographs were piled up next to it. She peered into the box and smiled with relief when she saw the silver trinket box was there. She picked it up and opened it. It was still full of Emily's bracelets, earrings, rings and necklaces.

'You thought Maria had taken the jewellery, didn't you?' asked Conrad.

Lulu chuckled. 'I did, yes.'

'She probably doesn't have a key to the basement flat.'

'You're right. I suppose the solicitor only gave them the keys to the main building.' She smiled tightly. 'What a shame.' She put the trinket box down and reached for the ziplock plastic bag containing Emily's medication. She had second thoughts and went over to the kitchen sink. She opened a drawer and took out a brand new pack of bright yellow Marigold rubber gloves. She put them on and went back to the table.

'Fingerprints?' said Conrad.

'Exactly.' She opened the bag and took out the pill dispenser. All fourteen compartments were empty. That made sense because the last two compartments were labelled SUNDAY AM and SUNDAY PM, so Emily would have taken the last tablets on Sunday night. She took out the bottles of medication and put them on the table, then opened them one by one and examined the contents. When she had finished she put the bottles and the dispenser back into the plastic bag, sealed it, and put it into her handbag.

She took off her gloves and took out her phone. She knew that Phil wouldn't want to talk to her on his mobile so she sent him a text message: 'PLEASE CALL ME'. After five minutes she received a call from a landline. 'It's me, boss.'

'Yes, Phil, I'm sorry to bother you but I wanted to go and have a chat with Dr Khan. Or whatever his real name is.'

'He calls himself Sammy. I'm not sure that'd be a good idea, boss.'

'If nothing else, I feel I should apologize to him. And there are a few questions I want to ask him.'

'You retired, boss. Remember?'

She chuckled. 'Once a copper, always a copper, Phil.'

'That's true,' said Phil.

'Somewhere in Kilburn, you said.'

Phil sighed. 'Okay.' He gave her the address and she scribbled it down. 'Be careful, boss.'

'I will.'

She ended the call and put the address into Google Maps. It was a twenty-minute walk. 'Let's go,' she said to Conrad. He jumped onto a chair and then onto her shoulders and wrapped himself around her neck.

Lulu went out and locked the door, then headed up Warrington Crescent. Her route took her along the A5, towards Kilburn High Street station. The traffic was heavy so she kept to the left of the pavement, well away from the road. It was always a strange experience, moving from Maida Vale to Kilburn. Maida Vale was looked after by Westminster City Council and the streets were clean, graffiti was removed promptly, rubbish was collected regularly and there were healthy trees everywhere. As soon as you crossed the border into Kilburn you were in Camden territory on the right and Brent on the left. Neither council was a patch on Westminster. There was litter and graffiti everywhere and the few trees that were there seemed to be struggling to survive.

The people were different, too. As she walked through Maida Vale, she and Conrad were smiled at, nodded to, and generally welcomed. Once they were in Kilburn the only glances they got bordered on the hostile. Most people ignored them completely but those that did make eye contact seemed annoyed to see the cat on her shoulders. Conrad could obviously sense the tension because he felt less comfortable around her neck and there was no purring.

Dr Khan lived in a house around the corner from the Tube station. It was a three-storey terraced house that had once been white but was now a dingy grey with greenish stains running from the windowsills. The roof was dotted with moss and several slates had slid out of place. An old television aerial had broken away from the brickwork and was hanging down next to a chimney dotted with pigeon droppings. There was an old bicycle chained to the railings in front of the house. The seat had been removed, either by thieves or by a cautious owner who didn't want it stolen.

There were eight doorbells, but no intercom. Lulu pressed the button for Dr Khan's flat. After thirty seconds or so she heard a heavy footfall and then the door opened. He was wearing a green pullover and cargo pants and his hair was unkempt. There were dark patches under his eyes as if he hadn't slept well.

'Dr Khan, I'm sorry to bother you at home.'

He squinted at her, then sighed. 'Oh, it's you. What do you want? Haven't you done enough already?'

'I'm so sorry about what happened, Dr Khan. It really wasn't my intention to cause you any problems.'

He sighed. 'My name is Sammy,' he said.

'I really am very, very sorry, Sammy.'

He opened the door wider. 'I suppose you might as well come in.' He headed slowly up stairs that were covered with a threadbare, stained carpet. Lulu followed him. The stairs led to a small landing with three doors and Sammy pushed open the middle one.

Lulu followed him inside. It was a compact studio flat, with a single bed, a built-in wardrobe, a tiny sofa and a cooking area with a small sink, a two-ring electric hob and an ancient fridge that was vibrating noisily. There was a bicycle seat and a cycle helmet on top of the fridge. An open door led to a shower room that reeked of mould. In the middle of the room was an open suitcase, half-filled with clothes and medical books. 'You're leaving?' asked Lulu. Conrad jumped off her shoulders and stood behind her, rubbing himself against her legs.

'They've said that if I buy my own ticket and leave within forty-eight hours then I won't be blacklisted and I can come back if I get the proper visa.' He looked over at two framed photographs on a bedside table. One was a wedding photo-graph, Sammy with a pretty Indian girl, both in traditional dress. The other was Sammy and his wife with two small children, all smiling at the camera. 'At least I will be able to hold my family instead of just seeing them on FaceTime.'

'I really am sorry, Sammy.'

'Is that why you came, to apologize?'

'Partly,' she said. 'But I need your help. Or your advice.'

He sighed. 'Are you still going on about your mother-in-law? You know that a police surgeon signed a second death certificate? She also put the cause of death down as dementia.'

'Yes, I know.' She opened her handbag and took out the bag of medicine. 'I wanted to talk to you about this.'

He took it from her and frowned. 'This is Mrs Lewis's medication.'

'Yes, it was returned to me with her personal effects.'

He nodded and gave the bag back to her. 'So now you think there was something wrong with her medication?'

'I just want to know what the procedure was. All her tablets went into the pill dispenser, correct?'

'Yes. When a patient has memory issues like Emily did, it helps us keep track of what she has taken.'

'And when would you load the dispenser?'

'First thing Monday morning. I wouldn't do it personally, that would be one of the nurses. But at some point every Monday I would check that it had been done correctly.'

'And there were tablets for the morning, and the evening?'

Sammy nodded. 'Yes, with separate compartments for both.'

'Okay, and which tablets would have gone in the section for Sunday night?'

'Let me have another look,' he said. Lulu gave him back the bag. He picked up a pair of glasses, put them on and scrutinized the contents. 'Okay, so we were trying her on various cholinesterase inhibitors to see if they improved her Alzheimer's. The latest was Donepezil. There are two pain-killers, to deal with her joint pain. Paracetamol was generally all she needed unless the pain was especially bad. One statin, we had tried others but latterly she was on Lipitor. And five milligrams of Ramipril for her blood pressure. A calcium supplement. And magnesium. And vitamin B. The supplements were taken in the morning, after breakfast, along with one of the painkillers and the Lipitor. The rest were in the evening, after dinner.'

Lulu took the bag from him. 'And of those, only Ramipril is a capsule? All the rest are tablets?'

'Yes.' He frowned. 'Do you think there was something wrong with Mrs Lewis's medication?'

'No, I think you did a very good job prescribing her what she needed. But tell me this, Sammy. Could someone inter-fere with the capsule? Could they open it up, remove the powder inside and replace it with – for example – sesame seeds?'

His eyes widened. 'Is that what you think happened?' He took off his glasses.

'I'm afraid I do, Sammy. Is it possible? Could somebody interfere with the capsules?'

He nodded. 'Yes,' he said. 'They could. It wouldn't be difficult at all.'

Lulu's phone began to ring. She put the bag of medication in her handbag and took out her phone. It was a landline calling. 'I'm going to have to take this, I'm sorry.'

'Go ahead,' said Sammy, and he went back to packing clothes into his suitcase.

'Boss, it's me,' said Phil as soon as Lulu answered. 'Jamie has spoken to Maria's parents. Can you pop around to the station and we'll do the call from here.'

'Can't you tell me what they said over the phone?'

Phil laughed. 'Jamie's playing his cards very close to his chest,' he said. 'Truth be told, I think he's worried that I'll steal the credit.'

'I'm on my way,' said Lulu.

35

Kensington Police Station was in Earls Court Road. It was one of the few police stations left in Westminster where people could go in and talk face to face with a police officer. When Lulu had been in the force – in the days before it became a service – there were stations dotted all over the borough. Maida Vale used to have its own station, as did St John's Wood and Kilburn. Almost all had been shut down. It was as if the powers that be wanted the public to contact the police only by phone, and that any response would be from a mobile unit rather than having bobbies on the beat turning up. Lulu couldn't help but smile at the thought of real-life police officers walking a beat. She almost never saw an officer on foot in Maida Vale – the only exception had been during the Covid pandemic, when they had turned up in force at Paddington Recreation Ground to hassle dog walkers and sunbathers who weren't wearing masks.

The station was a featureless six-storey brick building with an entrance to the left, complete with a blue lamp, probably the only thing that remained of old-style policing. Lulu went inside with Conrad on her shoulder. A bored uniformed sergeant who looked as if he had more important things to do than dealing with the public glanced at her coldly and asked if he could help her, though his tone suggested that he would rather she had used the phone. She smiled brightly and said that she was there to see Inspector Philip Jackson.

'Is he expecting you?' the man growled.

Lulu had to fight the urge to say that yes of course he was expecting her, why else would she be there, but she just smiled and said yes, he was. If she had still been a superintendent she would have given him a talking-to about his attitude, but these days she was simply a member of the public and had to accept the way the world was. He pointed with his pen at a line of plastic chairs and told her to take a seat. It was a command rather than a request and again Lulu had to bite her tongue. She sat down but only had to wait a few minutes before Phil appeared, opening a door at the side of the counter. He held the door open and waved her over. 'Good to see you've brought Conrad with you,' he said.

'He goes pretty much everywhere with me these days,' she said.

'We can use one of the interview rooms,' he said. He took her along a corridor and opened the door to a small room with a single window at head height. There was a table with four chairs, two either side. There were CCTV cameras at either end of the room and on the table was a tape recorder with slots for two tapes. A thin plastic alarm line ran around the walls. If pressed it would sound an alarm to summon help.

Lulu sat down and Conrad jumped down off her shoulders to sit on the chair next to her. Phil took a seat opposite. He looked up at the clock on the wall. 'Okay, here we go.' He put his phone on the table and leaned it against the wall, then opened WhatsApp and called Jamie.

Jamie answered almost immediately. He was bare-chested and his hair was wet. There were splashing sounds in the background. He grinned and waved. 'Hi boss, hi Phil.'

'We've not called at a bad time, have we?' asked Lulu.

'I'm on surveillance, boss,' said Jamie. He moved his phone and gave them a view of a large swimming pool with more than a dozen girls in bikinis drinking and clearly enjoying themselves. A group of short stocky men in polo shirts and shorts were standing at a poolside bar, drinking beer from bottles. Jamie came back into view. 'It's a shit job, but somebody's got to do it,' he said.

'You've obviously got your nose to the grindstone, so we won't keep you,' said Phil. 'Why not just tell the boss what you wouldn't tell me.'

Jamie laughed. 'Okay, will do,' he said. 'First things first. I checked with the airlines and I can't find any crims who flew to London in the days before your husband died, and none returning to Spain in the days after. But the guy you said was Maria's brother, this Juan fellow, he did fly to London the week before the accident. Juan Carro Martínez is his name. Definitely not Maria's brother.'

'It wasn't an accident, Jamie,' said Lulu.

'Sorry, boss, you know what I mean. He flew in the week before and didn't fly back. So far as I can tell, he stayed in the London area. Now, this is where it gets very interesting. I went to talk to Maria's parents – they're a lovely couple, by the way – and asked them about Juan. They know him all right. They know the whole story. And, boss, you're not going to believe me when I tell you what they had to say . . .'

36

A shadow passed over the sofa and Lulu looked up from her copy of *One Day in the Life of Ivan Denisovich* just in time to see a second figure walk by along the towpath. The boat began to move as someone climbed on board. 'I wonder who that can be?' said Lulu. She looked at her watch. It was almost nine o'clock at night.

Conrad, who was sitting on the sofa, lifted his head. 'I thought it was impolite to board a vessel without permission.'

'It is,' said Lulu. 'Very.'

She put down her book. A pair of Timberland boots and blue jeans appeared through the double doors. It was Juan. He was wearing a black leather bomber jacket and a red Manchester United baseball cap. He came down the steps and stood by the sofa, his hands on his hips. 'What have you done, you stupid bitch?' he sneered.

'What do you mean?' asked Lulu. Conrad jumped down off the sofa and padded over to Lulu's chair.

'You've had Richard arrested,' said Maria, coming down the steps to join Juan. 'The police came to take him away. They say he killed Emily and that he tried to kill you.'

'Well, I'm sure that the police know what they're doing.'

'They said they were acting on information you gave them,' said Juan. 'What information?'

'I really don't know what you're talking about,' said Lulu. 'Now, will you please get off my boat?'

'You're just upset because of the will,' said Maria. 'I understand that.' She sat down on the sofa. 'Look, I'm sorry that the house came to me, but that's what Emily wanted.'

'She didn't leave the house to you, she left it to Richard.'

'And Richard is my husband. What's mine is his.'

'What's his is yours, that's what you mean to say. But no, my dear, you don't have anything.'

'Is that your plan?' said Juan. 'You get Richard arrested for murdering the old woman so that he can't inherit her money, which means it all goes to you? Is that what this is about?'

Lulu gestured at Juan. 'Why did you bring him?' she asked Maria.

Maria took Juan's hand and pulled him down onto the sofa. 'What do you want?' Juan snarled at Lulu. 'You want a pay-off, is that what you want?'

'It's not about money.'

Conrad walked back towards the sofa and began rubbing himself against Maria's legs. She reached down to rub his back and he began to purr.

'So what is it about, Lulu?' asked Maria. 'Emily made it clear what she wanted. And it's not as if you're poor, is it? You and Simon sold your house when you went to live with Emily, so you must have a small fortune. Maybe a big one.' She looked around the boat and frowned. 'And yet you choose to live on this tiny boat. Why is that? With all your money you could live anywhere.'

'Money doesn't make you happy, my dear,' said Lulu.

'Only someone rich would say that,' growled Juan.

Conrad jumped onto the sofa and curled up next to Maria. Maria stroked him and he purred softly.

'Was it worth it?' asked Lulu softly. 'To kill two people, just for money? How can you live with yourself?'

'Who said we killed anybody?' asked Juan.

Lulu chuckled. 'Seriously, Juan? You're going to deny it?'

'Deny what?'

'You are such a bad liar,' said Lulu, shaking her head.

'The police have arrested Richard,' said Maria. 'It's nothing to do with us.'

Lulu's eyes narrowed. 'We all know it wasn't Richard.'

'What is it you think we did?' asked Juan.

'For a start, you lied to everyone about who you are. You are most definitely not Maria's brother.'

'You're *loca*,' he said. 'Crazy.'

'Am I? You see, I had you checked out, Juan. Through a former colleague who now works with Interpol out in Marbella. The Costa del Crime, we call it. The first thing he did was check out Maria's birth certificate. No problem at all finding it. But not so much luck when it came to your birth certificate. You see, Maria is an only child. Oh, and unlike what she told us all, her parents are very much alive and well.'

'You spoke to my parents?' asked Maria.

'I didn't, but my former colleague did. Seems as though you haven't been in touch for a few years now. Not since you emptied your father's bank account and stole your mother's jewellery.'

'You had no right to talk to my parents.'

'They were very hurt to hear that you had been describing yourself as an orphan,' said Lulu. 'And even more hurt to discover that you were still involved with Juan.' She looked at him, her eyes cold. 'They have a very low opinion of you,

Juan. How long were you in prison? Five years in total, they said. Three years for fraud and two years for assault. It seems that Juan Carro Martínez is very well known to the cops there.'

'He was protecting me!' said Maria.

'He was your pimp,' said Lulu. 'And he made a habit of beating up and robbing your clients.'

'That's not true!' said Maria. 'He was protecting me.'

'By bursting into the hotel rooms where you entertained your clients and stealing from them? I've seen copies of the police reports, Maria.'

'The Spanish police lie,' said Juan. 'They are corrupt and evil.'

'Two words that could equally apply to the two of you,' said Lulu. 'Along with murderer.'

'You are deluded,' said Maria. 'We haven't killed anyone.'

'You poisoned Emily,' said Lulu.

'You're not still going on about those chocolates, are you?' said Maria. 'Richard said you wouldn't shut up about them. There was nothing wrong with the chocolates.'

'Yes, I know that now. It was never about the chocolates.'

Lulu stood up and walked to one of the overhead cupboards. She opened it, took out the ziplock plastic bag that contained Emily's medications and sat down again. Maria and Juan stared at the bag in her lap. Lulu smiled at their obvious discomfort.

'I was so busy worrying about the chocolates that I missed the obvious,' said Lulu. 'Emily was taking medication in the morning and last thing at night. For her arthritis pain, to help her sleep, to deal with her cholesterol and antacid and of course her blood pressure medicines. Her Alzheimer's meant that she had trouble remembering whether or not she'd taken her tablets, so the home's doctor used a pill organizer.' She pointed at it in the plastic bag. 'Such a simple but clever idea. Separate compartments, each with its own lid, and labelled with the day of the week, and AM or PM. Each Monday morning a nurse would put in her tablets for the week. Then Emily could see at a glance what needed to be taken, and the staff could check that she was up to date.' Lulu smiled over at Maria. 'You'd have seen the organizer when you visited the first time, with Richard. And because of the clear plastic lids, you could see which tablets she was taking and when. Most of them were hard tablets but one was a capsule. Five milligrams of Ramipril in a pretty red and white capsule. Emily used to joke that they were perfect for an Arsenal fan. Anyway, I think you spotted the capsule and decided it would be the perfect way of ending Emily's life. You knew about the family's problems with sesame seeds and how life-threatening it was. Richard was always the least careful and had to use an epinephrine pen a couple of times a year, so you had seen up close and personal just how dangerous it was. Now, for your plan to work, you needed one of those capsules, which meant you had to visit on your own. There was no way that Richard would allow you to carry out your plan so you visited Emily by yourself, early in the afternoon when she usually took a nap. I checked the visitors' book and you were there on Friday. That was when you took a capsule from her bottle. Maybe a few, so that you could practise. You took the capsules home and filled one of them with sesame seeds. All you had to do was to return to the home and replace one of the capsules in the organizer with the doctored one.' She smiled, 'Doctored?

No pun intended. Anyway, the visitors' book shows that you were there again on Monday afternoon. Alone. You went at the time you knew that Emily would be having her nap. And that was when you put the tainted capsule in the SUNDAY PM slot. Then all you had to do was to wait. On Sunday evening, Emily would swallow the capsule last thing at night, lie down, and die. And if by any chance she forgot to take her medicines, a staff member would remind her.'

Maria sneered at her. 'It's a fascinating story, but it would be impossible to prove.'

'Oh, I disagree,' said Lulu. 'You see, I very much doubt that you wore gloves when you put the capsule into the pill organizer. I'm sure that your prints and DNA will be all over it.' She held up the bag full of medicines. 'And all over the Ramipril bottle.'

The look of panic on Maria's face told Lulu that she was right. She turned towards Juan. 'I know that you killed my husband,' she said. 'That was always your plan, right from the start. To kill Simon and then kill Emily, so that all her estate would go to Richard. And I bet you bought or rented a Nissan when you arrived in London. And it was a Nissan that killed Simon.'

'Why do you say that?' said Juan. 'You can't possibly say that.'

'A headlight was smashed in the crash and they analysed the glass. It was a particular sort of glass only used by Nissan.'

'There are plenty of Nissans in England,' said Juan.

'Yes, that's true. But not so many showing the sort of damage that suggests the car was involved in a fatal hit and run. Because that's what you did, Juan. You waited for my husband to leave the pub and then you ran him over. You wouldn't have been able to take the car to be repaired, it would be too obvious that you had hit someone. That means you've had to keep the car hidden and once I've told the police they'll look for it and they will find it.' She looked down at his shoes. 'What size shoes do you wear, Juan?'

'What?'

'Your shoes. Are they size twelve? Because they look like an exact match to the prints on my roof worn by whoever tried to kill me.'

Juan frowned and Lulu realized he didn't understand British sizes. 'You left your size forty-six footprints all over the roof,' she said.

Juan's jaw tightened and his fists clenched. 'You interfering bitch,' he hissed. He looked over at Maria, who was still stroking Conrad. 'I told you, I should have killed her with her husband. I could have done the two of them together, done it as if it was a robbery. But no, you said I should use the car and make it look like an accident. Now if they find it, we're fucked.'

'They won't find it. They don't know where you live. And they won't know about the lock-up.' She glared at Lulu. 'You shouldn't have stuck your nose into this.'

'Let sleeping dogs lie?' said Lulu. 'No, that was never going to happen.'

'There are just the three of us here, Lulu,' said Juan. 'No witnesses. And no one to help you.' He stood up, linked his fingers and cracked his knuckles. 'You've brought this upon yourself. What happens now is all down to you. It's your own fault.'

'You killed my husband,' said Lulu quietly.

Juan shrugged. 'Everybody dies.'

'You ran him over and left him to die in the road.'

'If it makes you feel any better, I'm sure he died almost instantly. I hit him really hard and then ran over him.' He sneered at her as if daring her to criticize him.

'And you felt no guilt?'

Juan shrugged again. 'It's a lot of money. Millions.'

Lulu shook her head in disgust. 'Shame on you.' She glared at Maria. 'And shame on you.'

'She was an old woman,' said Maria. 'And she was senile. For her it was a mercy.'

'And you feel no guilt for what you did?'

'Like Juan says, it's a lot of money.'

'And what about Richard?'

Maria frowned. 'What about him?'

'You planned to use him right from the start, didn't you? Once you found out about his family situation, you married him purely to get at the family fortune. You killed my husband so that Richard would inherit everything. But what now? What will you do now that Richard has the money? You'll divorce him and take half?'

Juan laughed. 'Why would we settle for half when we can have it all? We'll give it a few months and she can give him a sandwich loaded with sesame seeds and make sure his epinephrine pens are out of reach.'

'You are evil,' said Lulu. 'Truly, truly evil.'

'Enough chit-chat,' snapped Juan. 'Let's get this over with. No playing around with the stove this time. I'll take her to the bedroom and put a pillow over her head. You get ready to burn the boat.' He took a step towards Lulu and held out his hand. 'Give me the bag.'

Lulu shook her head. 'No.'

Juan sneered at her. 'Listen to me, you stupid woman. This is going to happen whether you resist or not. You're all alone and you are weak and defenceless. Do as I say and I'll make this as painless as possible. Fight me and you'll die in a lot of pain.'

Lulu clasped the plastic bag to her chest. 'You're quite wrong,' she said quietly.

'About what?'

'About my being alone. I'm not.'

'Not what?' said Juan, frowning.

'Not alone,' said Lulu.

Juan looked over at Maria. 'She's as senile as the old woman,' he said.

'You see, Conrad is here,' said Lulu.

'Conrad?' repeated Juan.

'The cat,' said Maria, pointing at Conrad. 'She's talking about her cat.'

Juan clicked his fingers at Lulu. 'Give me the bag.'

'Conrad has seen and heard everything,' said Lulu. 'He's a witness.'

'Then I'll kill the cat, too,' said Juan.

Lulu smiled. 'I think we're ready now, Conrad. What do you think?'

'Meow,' said Conrad.

Juan stared down at the cat and for the first time noticed the collar and the small black disc by the buckle. 'What is that?' he hissed. 'On his collar?'

'You can come in now, Inspector Jackson,' said Lulu, raising her voice. 'No weapons so far as I can see.'

'What are you talking about?' said Maria.

Juan bent down and tried to grab the disc on Conrad's

collar but Conrad was too quick; he sat back on his haunches and raked his claws across Juan's hand. Blood spurted and Juan screamed and jumped back. Juan lashed out with his foot but Conrad was too fast for him, jumping onto the floor and then up onto the sink.

'Fucking cat!' screamed Juan. He licked his wounds as he stared resentfully at Conrad. Conrad hissed at him, his tail twitching from side to side.

They all heard the sound of boots thudding along the towpath and Lulu caught a glimpse of men dressed in black cradling assault rifles. The one at the rear stopped at the galley window and pointed his weapon at Juan. 'Armed police, hands in the air!' he shouted.

The second officer stopped by the window above the sofa. Maria got to her feet, her mouth wide open in shock. 'Hands in the air!' shouted the second officer. She was a woman, with short, curly black hair.

'*No dispares!*' shouted Maria, raising her hands. 'Don't shoot!'

Conrad jumped down off the sink, landed with a thud on the floor next to Lulu's chair, then leaped up onto her lap.

The boat lurched as the final armed policeman stepped aboard and moved down the steps, his carbine at the ready. 'Armed police, nobody move and keep your hands in the air!' he shouted. He was in his forties with steel-grey hair cut short and a Scottish accent.

'Does that mean me, young man?' asked Lulu.

'No, ma'am, you're good,' said the officer. He told Juan to turn around and put his hands behind his back, then he deftly handcuffed him.

The female officer had climbed onto the boat and she

came down the steps and cuffed Maria. The two officers took their prisoners up the steps and onto the back deck, then helped them onto the towpath, where two more uniformed constables were waiting.

The constables took Maria and Juan along the towpath to a white police van waiting on Blomfield Road. Phil appeared on the back deck of *Moor Often Than Knot*. He stepped onto the towpath and walked over to Lulu. 'Are you okay?' he asked.

'Yes, I'm fine. I'm just so glad that the transmitter worked as planned.'

'Meow!' said Conrad from the rear of *The Lark*.

'And there's the hero of the hour,' said Phil. 'We should make Conrad an honorary detective.'

'Well, you have police dogs,' said Lulu. 'Why not police cats?'

Conrad sat down, his ears twitching. The inspector walked over and gently undid the collar and removed it. He examined the small black disk and nodded his approval. 'It worked a treat,' he said.

'You heard everything?' asked Lulu.

'Heard and recorded,' said the inspector. 'Plus Conrad's purring, for atmosphere.' He reached out and rubbed Conrad's head. Conrad purred and pushed against the hand.

'What happens now?' asked Lulu.

The inspector walked over and took the plastic bag from her. 'We'll get these tested for Maria's prints, for a start. We've confirmed that Juan arrived in the country a week before your husband was killed and he bought a second-hand Nissan Qashqai in Bromley. Now that we know that he has stored the car in a lock-up, we'll start looking for it. It's probably in Beckenham, near where they have been staying, but even if it isn't we'll find it eventually. We'll be able to use the GPS on their phones to track their movements so it shouldn't be difficult. Hopefully it'll show us which of them climbed onto *The Lark* and blocked the vents. We might even be lucky and be able to place Juan in the street where your husband was killed.' He held up the collar. 'But this is gold, boss. This alone will put them away. You always were a bloody good interrogator, and you obviously haven't lost it.'

Lulu grinned. 'They thought they had the advantage and they wanted me to know how clever they were. Serves them right.'

'You were brilliant, boss.' He looked over at Conrad. 'You too, Conrad.'

Conrad meowed.

'I love the way he answers back,' said the inspector. 'Anyway, I'll head back to Kensington and get the questioning started. I'll keep you in the loop, but this is open and shut.'

'Thanks, Phil.'

Richard appeared on the front deck of *Moor Often Than Knot*. He had been waiting inside with Phil and the armed police. He stepped off the boat and stood with his arms folded as if he wasn't sure what to do or say.

'I'll leave you to it,' said Phil. 'I'll be in touch about a statement, probably first thing tomorrow.' He lit a cigarette as he headed along the towpath after his team.

Richard walked over to Lulu. 'I'm so sorry,' he said.

'You've nothing to be sorry for, Richard. You were a victim as much as anyone else.'

'No, I'm the reason this all happened,' he said. He sniffed

and she could see that he was close to tears. She reached her arms around him and hugged him. 'I've been such a bloody idiot,' he said.

'It was well planned, they're professional grifters. You mustn't blame yourself.'

He forced a smile and hugged her back. 'If I hadn't brought them into our lives, Simon and Emily would still be alive.'

Lulu didn't know what to say to that, because it was the truth. Maria had latched onto Richard in Spain and brought her boyfriend into the mix and between them they had concocted their evil scheme, not caring what they did or who they killed to get their hands on the money. They had killed Simon and they had killed Emily and they were planning to kill Lulu and Richard. But there was no way she could say that to him. Blaming him wouldn't take back what had happened. It was done, it was in the past; all they could do was to move forward. 'We'll get through this,' she whispered.

'I'm not sure if I will, Lulu,' he said. 'I don't think I can live with what I've done.'

'You have to, Richard. If you do anything silly, then they'll have won. You need to stay strong.'

He nodded and sniffed again. 'I'll try,' he said.

She released her grip on him. 'What are you going to do?'

He sighed. 'I'll need to get Emily's estate sorted. I'll give you half, obviously.'

'You don't have to do that.'

He shook his head fiercely. 'I do. If it hadn't been for Maria, you and Simon would have inherited half, and that's the way it's going to be.' His eyes widened. 'Do you want the house? I can sign the house over to you.'

Lulu looked over at *The Lark*. Conrad was still on the

back deck, watching them. 'Actually, Richard, I really don't want the house.'

'Then we'll sell it and split the money.'

'I don't need . . .' she began, but he stopped her with a wave of his hand.

'It's not up for discussion, Lulu.'

'Okay,' she said. 'Thank you.'

'And you need to take anything you want of a sentimental nature. Anything. I'll do the same. The things we don't want, we can sell. And the house in Cornwall that she and my dad bought years ago. I think I'd like that.'

'Of course.' It was a two-bedroomed cottage in Mousehole, overlooking the sea. Frank and Emily had bought it more than sixty years earlier, long before the seaside town had become a tourist trap and a Mecca for wealthy Londoners wanting a second, or third, home. Lulu and Simon had used it many times, and they had even talked about one day retiring there.

'I'm through with the Costa del Sol and Ibiza and all that nonsense,' said Richard. 'I thought I might spend some time in Cornwall, try to get my head together.'

'That sounds like a very good idea.'

'Maybe start a windsurfing school or a jet-ski rental place. Maybe a bar. A surf bar. With jazz.'

'Well, I'd give the getting your head together thing a go first,' she said, patting him on the arm.

Richard laughed. 'Yes, probably best.' He hugged her again, kissing her on the cheek. 'I'm going back to Beckenham to get things straightened up.'

'You'll probably find a police forensic team already there,' said Lulu. 'Inspector Jackson said he'd have them in the moment they arrested Maria.'

'It's only a rental,' said Richard. 'I'll probably just grab a few things and check into a hotel. I guess I can afford it now.'

'Yes,' said Lulu. 'I guess you can.'

She watched him walk away along the towpath before joining Conrad on the back deck. She sat down next to him and stroked the back of his head. He purred loudly. 'Alone at last,' she said, looking up at the full moon in the night sky. 'I have to say, you did a great job down there, getting so close that the police could hear every word. Job well done.'

Conrad purred again, then looked up at her and smiled. 'Teamwork,' he said.

'So is that it? Your job is done? You're the cat who solved a murder and caught a killer. Well, two murders, actually. And two killers.'

'I did, didn't I?'

'So what happens next?'

Conrad sat up and looked at her. 'That's up to you, I suppose.'

'Why do you say that?'

'Well, *The Lark* is your boat. I can't stay here if you don't want me to.'

'Of course I want you to. I was just worried you might have other things to do, that's all.'

'I'm very happy here, with you. I made a good choice.'

Lulu rubbed his head, between the ears. 'So did I.'

'Well, to be fair now, Lulu, I was the one who made the choice. Let's not forget that.'

Lulu chuckled. 'That's very true,' she said. 'And I'm grateful. I still don't understand why you came into my life, but I'm so glad that you did.'

'Are you tired? Do you want to sleep?'

'I don't think I could sleep right now,' said Lulu. 'Too much adrenalin in my system. That was so . . . exciting. I mean, it was scary, but my goodness it was exciting.'

'Yes, it was,' said Conrad.

'So let's just sit here for a while and watch the moon. What about you? Are you tired? What am I saying? Of course you're not. Cats are nocturnal.'

'Actually, we're not. Cats are crepuscular.'

'Crepuscular?' Lulu repeated.

'It means we are most active at dawn and dusk.' Conrad sighed. 'You've got so much to learn.' He butted his head softly against her hip. 'But I'll be happy to teach you.'

37

Emily's funeral was held in Kensal Green Cemetery, which lay between Harrow Road and the Paddington arm of the Grand Union Canal. It was London's oldest public cemetery, having opened in 1833, and in the early days earth from the graves had been taken away on canal boats. Lots of famous people were buried in the seventy-two-acre cemetery, including the engineer Isambard Kingdom Brunel and the playwright Harold Pinter.

Emily's husband had bought two plots years earlier, one for him and one for Emily, side by side. These days, Lulu knew, plots could only be bought when someone had died – and they sold for twenty-five thousand pounds apiece. Frank Lewis had always had a good eye for property investment and his grave was in a beautiful part of the grounds, close to the Dissenters' Chapel, where Emily's service was held. Of the three chapels in the graveyard, Lulu felt the Portland stone and rendered brick Dissenters' Chapel was the most impressive, with its massive Ionic portico and columns and two large curved flanking colonnades. Its grandeur was tarnished somewhat by streaks of soot and dirt and it faced a motley collection of old gravestones and memorials, many tilted disjointedly. 'It always reminds me of an old horror movie set,' Conrad had whispered from Lulu's shoulder as she had walked towards it. It was a grey, cloudy day and she was wearing a long, black overcoat with the collar up.

'Me too,' she had whispered back.

Inside were modern pews facing a pulpit and a reading desk. The east wall was lined with ornamental pilasters and the chapel had a sealed catacomb.

Lulu sat in the front pew with Richard on her right and Conrad on her left. It had been a lovely service. Richard's eulogy had been quite wonderful. He had stood at the desk and spoken about his love for his mother, and her love for Frank, and how they would now be together for eternity. There were funny stories from his childhood, some that Lulu had heard before and others that were new to her. He had them all giggling at his tale of how Emily had decided to teach him to cycle. Emily had mounted the bike herself and promptly crashed into a tree, breaking her wrist and ending up in the Accident and Emergency department of St Mary's Hospital. But the next day she was back teaching him to ride, her wrist encased in plaster. He spoke movingly about Emily's illness and thanked the home for taking care of her. Mrs Fitzgerald had attended, as had her assistant, Mrs Reynolds, and Kayla, the home's chef, and Richard made a point of thanking them all.

John Eastman stood with his back ramrod straight as if he was on parade all the time he was at the desk. He said he would miss Emily's friendship, and their games of bridge, and that his life would be the poorer without her in it, but that he would always be grateful for the memories he had, and so long as he had the memories she would always be with him. By the time he finished, there were tears running down his cheeks and most of the mourners were dabbing at their eyes. Maggie hugged him tightly when he returned to his pew and she sat with her arm around him for the rest of the service.

Celia Christopherson went up to the desk next, and Lulu's heart was thumping in her chest when she opened her mouth to speak. Conrad bumped his head against Lulu's hip as if trying to reassure her, and he was right: Celia made no mention of Emily's affair. Instead she spoke movingly about friendship and love, and how she regretted the distance that had come between them. Lulu had smiled at that – physically there had been almost no distance, it was all emotional. And yes, it had been a pity that two such good friends had spent so much time apart. But Lulu understood how Celia felt. Emily had betrayed her, and Frank. But that wasn't something to be dwelt on, not now that Emily had passed away, so Lulu pushed the thoughts to the back of her mind and concentrated on what Celia had to stay. Unlike John Eastman, Celia didn't cry as she spoke, but her voice trembled at times and her hands were shaking. Lulu wasn't sure if it was because she was uncomfortable speaking in front of so many people, or if it was because she was sick herself, but it was clear that Celia wasn't well. Lulu had her hands clasped into tight fists as she willed Celia to stay strong, and she did, finishing her eulogy with a 'God bless Emily, and each and every one of us.'

As Celia made her way back to the pews, Richard looked at Lulu and nodded at the desk. 'No, no, I couldn't,' Lulu whispered. Conrad meowed and Lulu looked down at him. He stared at her with his vibrant green eyes. 'Fine,' she said. She stood up and slowly walked towards the desk, her mind in a whirl. She hadn't planned to speak at the funeral and definitely hadn't given any thought to what she should say. She hadn't spoken at Simon's funeral; in fact, as she took her place behind the desk, she realized that she had never given a eulogy before. Ever.

Her mouth had gone dry and she licked her lips as she looked out over the packed pews. Conrad was sitting up now, his ears pointed towards her, his eyes fixed on her face. Lulu forced a smile and took a deep breath. 'I am going to miss Emily so much,' she said. She shook her head. 'What am I saying? I miss her already. I miss her so much that sometimes I just want to curl up and cry. But then I remember all the good things she brought into my life, and I concentrate on that. She gave me her son, Simon, the love of my life. And I take some consolation that they are now together. And that she is with Frank, who was the love of her life.'

As she looked out over the congregation, she locked eyes with Celia. Celia smiled and mouthed, 'It's okay.' Lulu flashed her a smile.

'Emily taught me so much. About art, about music, about the theatre. She opened my eyes to so many things. The one thing she never taught me was her recipe for fisherman's pie, which was Simon's favourite dish. She said she would take that with her to the grave, and unfortunately she kept her word.' There were several chuckles from around the chapel. Richard was grinning and nodding. Like Simon, he had been a big fan of Emily's fisherman's pie.

'So much of what I do now, so much of what I enjoy, so much of what makes me happy, comes from her. If I see a painting, I imagine her talking to me about it. If I hear a beautiful piece of music, she's with me, telling me how it makes her feel. She took me to my first ever cricket match. We went to Lord's. Frank was away so we made a girls' day of it, and yes, we did share a bottle of wine. Actually, it was champagne. She said my first ever game had to be celebrated, and we did. I seem to remember celebrating so much that we had trouble walking home.' There were more chuckles. Lulu looked over at Conrad, who was smiling and nodding. 'To this day, I can remember how, over our second or third glass of champagne, she explained the rules to me.' She smiled as she looked around the chapel. 'This is what she told me. Bear in mind, champagne had been drunk. So you have two sides, one out in the field and one in the pavilion. Each man that's in the side that's in goes out and when he's out he comes in and the next man goes in until he's out. When they are all out, the side that's out comes in and the side that's been in goes out and tries to get those coming in out. When both sides have been in and everybody is out then the game is finished.'

There were more chuckles from around the chapel.

'So you can understand why whenever I see a game of cricket, I think of Emily and I smile. And that's the sign of a good life, a life well lived. My heart is filled with good memories, of good times, and I will always have those memories.'

A sudden thought hit Lulu, and a chill ran down her spine. Memories didn't always stay for ever. Sometimes diseases like Alzheimer's and dementia took them away. Towards the end, Emily often hadn't even remembered the names of her visitors. She looked over at Conrad. He was staring at her, his ears pointed in her direction. Then he smiled, and nodded, and the dark thoughts vanished. Lulu went on, 'I will miss Emily, but I will always be grateful that she was a part of my life. And if there is an afterlife, if there is something beyond this life . . .' She looked up at the chapel ceiling. 'Please, Emily, let me know your recipe for fisherman's pie.'

People were still laughing and smiling as Lulu went back

to sit between Conrad and Richard. Richard reached over, took her hand, and gave it a soft squeeze. Conrad headbutted her gently on the hip. 'Was that okay?' Lulu whispered.

'It was perfect,' said Richard.

'Meow,' said Conrad.

'Good,' whispered Lulu.

38

The interment of Emily's coffin was a much more sombre affair. The mourners stood and watched as the coffin was slowly lowered into the ground, alone with their thoughts. Lulu had never liked the idea of burial. She understood that Emily had wanted to be in the ground with Frank, but Lulu had always preferred the idea of cremation. Death was usually sudden and always final, and putting a body into the ground to rot and decay just seemed to extend the process unnecessarily. There was something cleansing about a body being reduced to ashes. Simon had felt the same way, and pretty much every time he had visited his father's grave he had reiterated that he wanted to be cremated and his ashes scattered underneath trees. Any trees – he didn't care which – he just wanted his ashes to become part of something that was living and growing. His death had come so unexpectedly that there hadn't been time to discuss it in any more detail, so Lulu had settled on Hyde Park, which Simon had always been fond of. She assumed that applying for permission to scatter ashes in a royal park would require a plethora of forms to be filled in, so she did it late one evening, hiding the urn in her large Louis Vuitton bag and scattering the ashes beneath a clump of plane trees. She had marked the location of the trees on a printout from Google Earth and had lodged it with her will, along with instructions that her ashes be scattered there. She found it so much more comforting knowing that she and Simon would be together in a living tree, rather than rotting under six feet of soil.

'Meow,' said Conrad. She looked down. He was sitting by her feet, watching the coffin disappear.

'I know,' said Lulu.

'Know what?' said Richard, who was standing next to her, his hands clasped together.

'Nothing, sorry, just thinking out loud,' said Lulu.

As the coffin reached the bottom of the grave the clouds parted and the sun shone through, warming Lulu's face. She smiled, taking it as a good sign.

'She'll be happy now,' said Richard. 'It's what she wanted.'

'Yes, together for ever.' Lulu shivered despite the sun.

'Are you okay?'

'It's a funeral. I never enjoy funerals.'

Richard smiled thinly. 'I don't think anyone does.' He put a hand on her arm, his face suddenly serious. 'I'm really sorry about all the cremation stuff before. It wasn't my idea.'

'I assumed as much.'

'With hindsight, she obviously wanted a cremation to get rid of any evidence.'

Lulu forced a smile. 'Anyway, we need to thank everyone for coming.'

They walked together from the grave to the footpath and spent the next twenty minutes saying goodbye to all the mourners, sometimes with a hug or a handshake, sometimes with just a smile and a few sympathetic words. A lot of people had come to say goodbye to Emily, and several of Lulu's friends had come to support her. There was a line of cars ready to take people to a reception at the Colonnade Hotel and eventually there was just one car left and only Lulu and Richard on the path, with Conrad.

'I'm going to give the reception a miss,' said Richard. 'I still feel responsible. And a lot of people must know what happened by now. Maida Vale has always been a village. News spreads fast.'

'You're not the bad guy here, Richard.'

He sighed. 'We'll have to agree to disagree on that.' He forced a smile. 'And what about you, Lulu? Do you plan to stay on the boat?'

'I think so. I like it. It's got everything I need, and everything has its purpose. And there's something so relaxing about living on the water. I was thinking about taking her on a trip.'

'Her?'

'*The Lark*. Boats are always she.'

'Where would you go?'

Lulu sighed. 'Oh, anywhere. There are more than two thousand miles of canals and another two thousand or so miles of navigable rivers. At an average of twenty miles a day it would take more than six months to travel them all.'

'So you'll be gone for some time?'

Lulu laughed. 'No, I'd just go for a few weeks. Up to Oxford, maybe. Or to Bath.'

'And you can sail it yourself?'

'You drive rather than sail. But yes. The locks can be difficult but it's doable.'

Conrad meowed and Lulu laughed. 'Conrad says he'll help me. Richard, why don't you keep the house, for a while at least? You never know, you might find yourself a decent wife one of these days.'

Richard chuckled ruefully. 'I'll have to divorce the present Mrs Lewis first.'

Lulu raised an eyebrow. 'Under the circumstances, I don't see that would be a problem.'

'That's true.'

'Inspector Jackson tells me that they're blaming each other, so they'll both go down. But as Juan was the only one in London when Simon was run over, he'll be charged with Simon's murder. They found the car in a lock-up with Juan's prints on the steering wheel and Simon's blood on the grille. Open and shut, as they say.'

'I'm so sorry, Lulu.'

'At least he'll be punished. Maria, too. Juan's saying that it was her idea to add the sesame seeds to the capsules, and the police found her fingerprints on the pill case.' She smiled. 'Seriously, you should give up travelling. Come back home.'

'London isn't my home any more, Lulu. It hasn't been for a long time. I'll sell the house. And the contents. And we'll split the money between us. Just let me know what you want to keep. I meant what I said about trying Mousehole for a while, if you don't mind me hanging on to it.'

'Go for it,' said Lulu. 'I think you might enjoy Cornwall.'

Something soft rubbed against the back of Lulu's legs and she looked down to see Conrad, his tail up. The cat meowed and butted his head against her left leg. She bent down and scooped him up. 'It's been a pleasure meeting you, Conrad,' said Richard. He reached out and gently patted Conrad on the head. Conrad meowed and purred. 'I wish you the best of luck, Lulu,' he said. He leaned forward and kissed her on the cheek. 'You stay safe. You too, Conrad.'

Richard turned away and walked towards the cemetery gate.

'Do you think he'll be okay?' asked Lulu.

'His aura is looking better already,' said Conrad. 'He's stronger and more confident. I think Maria was dragging him down. Now she's out of his life, I think he'll do just fine.'

'I do hope you're right.'

Conrad rubbed his head against her chin. 'You can trust me,' he said. 'I'm a cat.'

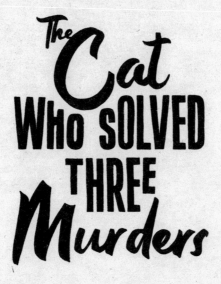

The Cat Who Solved Three Murders

Retired police detective Lulu Lewis's life changed forever
when she met a street cat named Conrad. There's
something very special about Conrad, but it's a secret
she has to keep to herself.

When Lulu takes her narrowboat to Oxford, she is
planning nothing more stressful than attending a friend's
birthday party. And drinking a few glasses of Chardonnay.

But a brutal murder and a daring art theft means her plans
are shattered – instead she and Conrad find themselves
on the trail of a killer.

A killer who may well strike again.

*Read on for a teaser extract from the next book
in the series . . .*

1

The Prius slowed at the front gate and the driver twisted around in his seat. His name was Mo, which Lulu assumed was short for Mohammed. He was in his mid-forties and had been the perfect Uber driver, offering her hand sanitizer, breath mints and bottled water before setting off from Oxford city centre and asking her what music she would like played during their journey. He had looked surprised when she had walked up with Conrad sitting on her shoulders, but if he had any objections at all to riding with a calico cat, he had kept them to himself. Conrad was standing on the seat next to Lulu, his paws up against the glass as he peered at the house in the distance. Lulu could see his reflection in the glass – the right side of his head was mainly black with a white patch around the nose and mouth, and the left side was brown and white.

'Is this it?' Mo asked. 'It looks like a hotel.'

'It does, doesn't it?'

'You said it was a house. But this is where the GPS is bringing me.'

'Then this must be it,' said Lulu.

'Sometimes the GPS is wrong.'

There were two black wrought-iron gates, each almost twelve feet high, and they were open. There were weathered stone turrets either side of the gates set into an eight-foot-high stone wall. A tarmac driveway cut through several acres of manicured lawns, leading to a Georgian mansion with four massive chimney stacks. There were several cars and vans parked outside and Mo was right – it definitely had the look of a hotel.

Conrad twisted around and looked at Lulu. 'Meow!' he said and pointedly looked back at the turret on the right. There was a brass sign set into the stonework: HEPWORTH HOUSE.

'This is definitely it,' said Lulu.

'So this is a house?' Mo took both his hands off the steering wheel and opened his palms wide. 'For one family?'

'My friends don't have children,' said Lulu.

'So just two people live here?' He shook his head. 'Unbelievable. They must be very rich.'

'I think they are, now,' said Lulu.

Mo put his hands back on the steering wheel, turned the Prius into the driveway and drove slowly towards the house, muttering under his breath. Lulu could understand his astonishment. The house was breathtakingly beautiful, and so big that it really didn't make sense that only two people lived there. It was a far cry from the last home that Julia and Bernard Grenville had lived in, a small terraced house in what could only be described as a deprived area of Oxford. The house was nice enough but the area had one of the highest crime rates in the city and during dinner at least half a dozen car alarms had gone off. But that was six years ago, back when Bernard was a struggling antique shop owner and Julia was working as a lab researcher. Things had taken a turn for the better since those days, clearly.

Lulu and Julia had been firm friends for more than thirty years. Their paths had first crossed when Julia had been a forensic investigator while Lulu had been walking a beat in Stoke Newington. The friendship had lasted even though Julia and her husband had left London for Oxford. The invitation to Bernard's sixtieth birthday party had come out of the blue, but Lulu had eagerly accepted – she had nothing pressing to do and was keen to catch up with them. Julia had mentioned that they had come into some money now that her company was about to go public, but clearly 'some money' was a gross understatement.

Mo brought the Prius to a stop next to a gleaming white Bentley. 'Have a nice day,' he said. He looked at the Bentley and sighed. 'Now that is a wicked car.'

'It is, isn't it?' said Lulu. The last time she had seen Bernard and Julia, they were driving a three-year-old Ford Fiesta. She opened the door and Conrad jumped off the seat and onto the ground. Lulu climbed out, picked him up, and closed the door. Mo flashed the Bentley another jealous glance and drove off.

Lulu held Conrad up so that he could climb onto her shoulders and settle around her neck. 'This house is amazing,' he said. Conrad hadn't said a word during the twenty-minute drive from the city centre. Lulu was the only person he ever spoke to; he never said anything other than 'meow' when there was anyone else around. Lulu had come to accept that Conrad could talk, but there were times when she still thought that perhaps she was dreaming and that one day she would wake up. Cats didn't talk, obviously. That was a fact of life. Except that Conrad did. He was an exceptional cat, perhaps one of a kind. He was a calico cat. Often referred to as a tortoiseshell but Lulu never liked that name as Conrad looked nothing like a tortoise. Most calico cats were female, but Conrad was indeed exceptional. In so many ways.

L T Shearer

'It's not what I expected,' said Lulu. She looked over at the vehicles parked in a line to their left. One was a Mercedes Sprinter van in the livery of Thames Valley Police, another was a nondescript blue Ford Mondeo which she instinctively recognized as a police vehicle. There was also a white BMW, a grey Volvo and a blue Range Rover, both less than a year old.

'They're scientists, you said.'

'Julia was; she studied forensic science at university but then did a PhD in virology. Her husband is an art dealer. Well, antiques really. But these days he mainly helps her run the company.'

'What does it do, again? This company?'

'Julia did explain but I couldn't really follow it. It's something to do with vaccines but the techniques they use have wider implications for all sorts of illnesses.' She reached up and rubbed him under the chin and he purred. 'I'll tell you what, I'll ask her to explain it to me again and you can hear it from the horse's mouth.'

'See now, I have never understood that phrase. Horses don't talk. Have you ever heard a horse talk? No. So why don't they say "from the cat's mouth" instead?'

'Well, strictly speaking, cats don't usually talk, either.'

'That's true. I am special.' He wrinkled his nose.

'Oh, I would say unique.'

Lulu walked up to the front door. There was a large brass knocker in the shape of a lion's head in the centre, but on the wall to the right was a brass bell push. She pressed it but didn't hear anything from inside the house. 'Do you think it's working?' she said.

'Hard to tell,' said Conrad. 'Maybe the maid has to find the under butler and the under butler has to find the butler

318

and then the butler will have to make his way to the front door.'

Lulu laughed. 'It is a very big house, isn't it?'

'It's enormous,' said Conrad. 'It's a mansion.'

They heard footsteps and then the handle turned and the door opened. Lulu had half expected to be greeted by a liveried butler so she was pleasantly surprised to see that it was Julia. She was wearing a pretty blue cotton dress and had her blonde hair tied back in a ponytail. If anything her hair colour was even brighter than last time Lulu had seen her. Lulu had stopped dyeing her hair years ago and had embraced her greyness, which her hairdresser always kindly referred to as platinum.

Julia's face broke into a beaming smile. 'Lulu, my goodness, you're here.'

'Well, yes. You invited me, remember?'

Julia frowned. 'And there's a cat on your shoulders.'

'Yes, there is.'

'No, there's a cat on your shoulders. Why is there a cat on your shoulders?'

'This is Conrad,' said Lulu.

Julia laughed. 'Your date?'

'Very much so.'

'Meow,' said Conrad.

'Oh my goodness, he talks.'

'Yes,' said Lulu. 'He does.'

Conrad jumped down off her shoulders and landed with a dull plop on the doorstep.

Julia looked over Lulu's shoulder. 'Where's your car?'

'We took an Uber.'

'From London?'

'From Oxford. We came on *The Lark*.'

'*The Lark*?'

'My narrowboat.'

'You sailed from Maida Vale?'

'You drive a narrowboat rather than sail her, but yes.'

'But don't they travel at five miles an hour or something?'

'Between three or four. Pretty much walking pace.'

Julia frowned. 'So how long did it take?'

'Well, we weren't rushing, so eight days.' She gestured at the Sprinter van. 'Julia, why are the police here?'

'I'm so glad you came, Lulu,' said Julia, stepping forward and hugging her. She air-kissed her on both cheeks and then hugged her again. 'It's just that something rather awful happened yesterday.'

'What? What happened?'

Julia put her arm around Lulu and guided her through the doorway. 'I'll make you a cup of tea and tell you all about it,' she said.

They walked into a double-height hall with a sweeping double marble staircase that curved around a chandelier that must have been fifteen feet tall and composed of thousands of pieces of glass. It had the look of a crystal waterfall and it shimmered as Lulu looked up at it.

'This way,' said Julia, taking Lulu down a hallway to the left. The hallway was lined with modern paintings, large canvases with splashes of colour. There were doors leading off both sides. The kitchen was at the end of the hallway; it was ultra-modern, with gleaming white marble and stainless-steel appliances and a huge white oak island surrounded by half a dozen chrome-and-leather stools, above which hung a set of copper pans.

'Oh, this is lovely,' said Lulu.

'Really? I think it looks like a hotel kitchen, ready to serve up two dozen English breakfasts at a moment's notice. Bernard is the chef in the family, I can barely boil an egg.'

'Where is Bernard?'

'Well, that's the thing, Lulu. Look, I really don't want to drink tea – how would you feel about champagne?'

'Champagne?'

Julia opened one side of a large fridge to reveal half a dozen bottles of champagne. 'I really could do with a drink and seeing you after so long would seem to be the perfect excuse. And I have fresh orange juice too if you wanted a Buck's Fizz.'

'I'm always happy to have an excuse for a drink,' said Lulu.

'Excellent.' Julia put the champagne on the island, then took a pitcher of orange juice from the fridge and gave it to Lulu. 'You hold this and we'll go through to the conservatory. And what about Conrad? What does he drink?'

'Water would be great,' said Lulu.

'Tap water?'

'Meow!' said Conrad, looking up at Julia with his bright green eyes.

'I'll take that as a definite no,' said Julia.

'He likes Evian.'

'Well, of course he does,' said Julia. She took a bottle of Evian from the fridge and gave it to Lulu. 'Through there,' she said, nodding at two sliding doors that led to a large conservatory. She picked up two flutes and a glass bowl, retrieved the champagne and followed Lulu through the doors.

The conservatory overlooked the expansive grounds, which included a small lake, a wooden gazebo and several greenhouses and outbuildings. There was a wood in the distance. 'This is just lovely, Julia,' said Lulu, admiring the view. 'It's like a stately home.'

'It's not a home yet,' said Julia. 'But we're getting there.' Two large wooden-bladed fans were turning overhead. There were three rattan sofas with overstuffed floral cushions around a circular glass-topped rattan table. Julia put the glasses, bowl and champagne onto the table and sat down with a sigh.

Lulu put the orange juice and the Evian bottle down and then she sat next to Julia. There was clearly something wrong with Bernard, but she figured it was best to let Julia talk about it in her own time. Lulu had been a police officer in a previous life and had carried out more than her fair share of interrogations. Sometimes it was best to simply say nothing and to wait for the other person to fill the silence.

Julia uncorked the champagne with an ease that suggested she had done it many times before. She poured some into the two flutes and then added orange juice, while Lulu opened the bottle of Evian and sloshed some into the bowl. Lulu put the bowl down in front of Conrad and he lapped at it.

Julia handed a glass of Buck's Fizz to Lulu. 'I'm so happy to see you again,' said Julia. They clinked glasses and drank. Conrad curled up at Lulu's feet and rested his chin on his paws. 'How long has it been?'

Lulu forced a smile. 'Since Simon's funeral, I suppose.' Lulu's husband had died, and not long afterwards she had moved onto *The Lark*. A new start.

'Oh my gosh, yes. It was. I'm so sorry I let things slide,

we were just so busy with the company. We literally haven't had a day off in the last year.' She sipped her drink, then looked out over the gardens. She was clearly getting ready to say something, so Lulu stayed quiet. Julia sighed. 'Something terrible happened yesterday, Lulu. I'm still in shock. There was a robbery here, some paintings were stolen, and a man was killed. Bernard was hurt; he's in bed at the moment.'

'Julia! Why didn't you say something?'

Julia smiled ruefully. 'I'm saying something now. It wouldn't have been right to hit you with it before you'd crossed the threshold, would it?'

'Is Bernard okay?'

'The doctor says he'll be fine. They gave him a scan yesterday and they told him to take it easy, but there's no lasting damage.'

Lulu covered her mouth with her hand. 'Oh, Julia, that's terrible. Why didn't you cancel tomorrow's party? Everyone would have understood.'

'We talked about it, but it was such a terrible thing to happen that we didn't want it to overshadow Bernard's birthday. If we allow it to affect us, it'll affect us for ever. His birthday will always be a reminder that someone was killed in our house – it would be blighted. This way, we just keep that room closed, we have the party, we bring fresh life into the house and we move on.'

'Yes, I suppose so.'

'There is no suppose so, Lulu. It was a terrible thing to happen but we can't allow it to control the way we behave. Plus a lot of VIPs have been invited, people that are involved with our company. We don't want to mess them around by cancelling at such short notice.'

'And the police are okay with that? All those people trampling over a crime scene?'

Julia grinned. 'They weren't happy at all. But Bernard is in the local Rotary Club with the assistant chief constable and he rang him up and explained everything. Bernard's friend fast-tracked the forensic investigation and they should be finished by this evening.'

Lulu nodded, then sipped her drink. 'Could I see the room where it happened?'

Julia laughed. 'You really can never forget that you were a police officer, can you?'

Lulu smiled. 'Guilty as charged. Is the room still being treated as a crime scene?'

'I'm afraid so. The very nice detective who came along said she thought we might have the room back this afternoon, but if you really want a peep, I can show you through the window.'

'No, it's okay.'

'You are so funny, Lulu. I know you really want to have a snoop around, it's your nature. And you can't fight your nature.'

Lulu laughed. 'I'm sorry, you know me too well.'

Julia put down her glass and stood up. 'Come on.' She looked at the glass and smiled. 'On second thoughts, I'll take this with me.' She picked up the glass again.

Lulu looked down at Conrad. 'Come on,' she said. 'Let's go for a walk.'

Conrad got to his feet, stretched, and jumped up onto the sofa. He meowed and then jumped up onto her shoulders. Lulu stood up carefully and Conrad adjusted his position before settling down.

'That is amazing,' said Julia. 'Did it take a lot of training?'

'I got the hang of it pretty quickly,' said Lulu.

'No, I meant . . .' She laughed as she realized that Lulu was joking. 'Right. I walked into that one, didn't I?'

Julia opened a sliding door and stepped out onto a flagged walkway. She turned right and Lulu followed her. 'How many acres do you have here?' Lulu asked as she looked out over the garden.

'There's about five acres that make up the grounds, which is marked by the stone wall. But we own several of the adjoining fields. They're rented out to local farmers.'

'How do you take care of it all?'

'Oh, there's a gardening firm does all the hard work, though Bernard is threatening to get one of those ride-on lawnmowers.'

Ahead of them was a stone barn that had been renovated, with a new slate roof. 'This will be Bernard's studio, when he eventually starts painting again.'

'He was such a good artist, I remember.'

'Past tense is right,' said Julia. 'It's been twenty-five years since he picked up a brush. He could never make any money from it. But if everything goes as planned he'll have time to paint again, and that's where he'll be doing it.'

She turned around the corner and led the way towards a large raised terrace with massive stone urns at each corner. There were steps on three sides leading up to the terrace. In the distance were woods and Lulu saw movement. She shaded her eyes with her hand and realized that there were half a dozen uniformed police officers moving among the trees. 'Julia, what's happening over there?' she asked, pointing at the woods.

Julia turned to look. 'Ah, they're doing a search. That's where the thieves went. I suppose they're looking for clues.'

Julia walked up the steps and Lulu went up after her. There were several trees in large ornate ceramic pots that had been trimmed into the shapes of animals. There was a sitting dog, a dolphin, a lion and some sort of bird. There were strips of blue and white police crime scene tape running between the two urns closest to the building, clearly to stop anyone going through the French windows.

'That is the study,' said Julia. 'Bernard and I both work there, it's one of our favourite rooms in the house. Though whether it remains that way after what happened – well, we'll see.' She smiled grimly.

Lulu walked up to the police tape. One of the panels of glass was broken. She peered through the hole into the room. It was very large and when she saw two doors leading off to the corridor she realized that it was actually two rooms knocked into one. There were desks at either end of the room. The one on the right was glass and chrome with two large Apple monitors, the other was an old oak desk that looked as if it might have belonged in a Napoleonic general's war room.

Conrad jumped down off Lulu's shoulders and landed on the flagstones with a dull thud.

'So this is how they got in?' asked Lulu.

'Apparently, yes. And they left the same way.' Julia waved her champagne flute at the woods. 'They must have run across the lawn to the trees.'

'What's over there, behind the wood?'

'A field. Potatoes. And beyond that is Featherdown Farm. Old Mr Reynolds runs it. He rents the field from us. I forget what he pays but it includes all the potatoes we can eat.'

Lulu looked through the windows again. 'There doesn't seem to be much damage?'

'No, there isn't. Just some blood on the floor.'

'And the man who died – who was he?'

'An insurance broker who was talking about policies with Bernard. They smashed their way in and attacked Bernard and the broker and then escaped with some paintings.'

'Were you in the house?'

Julia shook her head. 'I was at the florist's, discussing the flower arrangements for tomorrow and checking that the cake was OK. In a way it was lucky I wasn't here, but then if I had been here I might have . . .' She shrugged. 'I don't know, I feel guilty about not being here.'

'How many robbers were there?'

'I don't really know.'

'Well, I'm sure Bernard is just grateful that you weren't in harm's way.'

Conrad was pushing his nose against the glass to get a better look into the study.

'He is so cute,' said Julia. 'Does he go everywhere with you?'

'Pretty much.'

'You said his name is Conrad? That's an unusual name for a cat. Why did you call him that?'

'I didn't.'

'Oh, is he a rescue cat?'

'I think actually he rescued me,' said Lulu. She bent down and Conrad jumped up onto her shoulders. 'This terrace is amazing,' said Lulu, trying to change the subject because she didn't want to tell Julia that Conrad had named himself. Lulu had long since become used to the fact that

Conrad could talk, but as he had made it clear he wasn't prepared to talk to anyone else, it was probably information best kept to herself.

'The plan was to have the party out here if the weather was good,' said Julia. 'We were going to have tables out and a marquee on the lawn. But after what happened in the study . . .' She grimaced and left the sentence unfinished.

'I don't know. If you did have a lot of people moving through the room to the terrace, you might erase the bad memories.'

'A man died in there, Lulu.'

'Well, yes. But this is a very old house, isn't it? And in the old days people generally used to die at home. A lot of people have probably died here over the centuries.'

'A fact which the estate agent neglected to mention,' said Julia. She chuckled. 'You're right, of course. We need to wash the bad memories away, and what better way to do that than with a party? Let's see what Bernard thinks.'